# ZEKE

HEROES AT HEART

MARYANN JORDAN

Zeke (Heroes at Heart) Copyright 2019

ISBN ebook: 978-1-947214-46-0

ISBN print: 978-1-947214-47-7

❀ Created with Vellum

## Author's Note

Please remember that this is a work of fiction. I have lived in numerous states as well as overseas, but for the last twenty years have called Virginia my home. I often choose to use fictional city names with some geographical accuracies.

These fictionally named cities allow me to use my creativity and not feel constricted by attempting to accurately portray the areas.

It is my hope that my readers will allow me this creative license and understand my fictional world.

I also do quite a bit of research on my books and try to write on subjects with accuracy. There will always be points where creative license will be used in order to create scenes or plots.

Zeke Kemp stood just inside the front door of the house that he was going to be living in. He had stared up at the two-story house as he approached, its manicured lawn, picket fence, and flowerbeds not impressing him. He knew what could hide behind the exterior of a house.

He eyed the social worker chatting with a thin, older lady, and he fought to keep from turning and storming back down the front steps. *Jesus, this is fucked. Hell, my whole life right now is fucked.*

Anger raged inside, an emotion that had ripped through him so often in the past. Anger at his mom for having left years ago. Anger at his dad who had no self-control. And now anger at a life that had landed him on the steps of an old lady in a big house in a fuckin' neighborhood that looked like it ought to be in some movie. *Fuckin' perfect little yard within a fuckin' perfect little fence that'll try to hold me in.*

It was a habit to listen to what people were saying about him, but he noticed the social worker did not mention any particulars. The old lady had probably gotten a file on him already and had made up her mind what type of person he was. He was used to that, too. Forcing his body to stand still, he clutched his suitcase in one hand, and his other hand stayed jammed into his jeans pocket to hide his fist.

He could not help but notice the woman introduced as Miss Ethel. At thirteen, he was already as tall as she and definitely heavier. *Why the hell would she take on a foster boy?* He knew the answer...probably for the money. He was sure she must have a bunch of little kids running around and wondered if she would expect him to watch after them for her.

He heard the sound of voices approaching from the front walk and twisted his head around to see who it was. He jolted in surprise at the sight of six boys walking toward the house, backpacks slung over their shoulders, smiles on their faces. Most looked to be older than him and just as big, if not bigger.

The screen door was pulled open, and the six boys trooped into the house, their voices immediately softening. Zeke watched narrow-eyed in stunned silence as they nodded politely to the social worker before greeting Miss Ethel affectionately.

"Oh, I hope everyone had a good day at school," Miss Ethel said. Her smile was wide, and her blue eyes fairly twinkled as she gazed at the group of boys, all towering over her. "I've got someone for you to meet. This is Zeke Kemp."

His stomach clenched as all the eyes in the room now turned toward him. He felt his body tense as he tried to adopt a *don't fuck with me* expression. He need not have bothered because the other boys just smiled as they offered chin lifts in greeting.

"This is Zander, my oldest," Miss Ethel said. "He's a junior at the high school you will go to. Next, are Rafe and Cael, both sophomores. My twins, Jaxon and Jayden are freshmen. And Asher, like you, is in eighth grade."

He blinked as Zander stepped forward, his hand out. Not able to come up with an alternate plan, he set his suitcase on the floor and reached out, feeling his hand engulfed in a firm—but not aggressive—shake.

"I know it can be hard to remember all our names, so don't be afraid to ask," Zander said. "Good to have you with us, Zeke." Zander chuckled, and Zeke stiffened. He was used to others laughing at his name. It was usually when his fist hit their face that they stopped the taunts and ran away. Wondering if he could take the older, bigger boy, he startled when Zander added, "It's kind of cool to have someone else whose name starts with Z." Blinking, the air left his lungs in a whoosh.

As Zander stepped aside, the same action occurred with each of the others, shaking his hand and greeting him warmly. Feeling unsettled, he was uncertain where to look so he cast his gaze back to the social worker.

"Boys, why don't you take Zeke into the kitchen? I'm sure everyone is hungry after school. I'll be in just as soon as I finish speaking with Ms. Barker."

Not knowing why the words bubbled forth, he said, "Ms. Barker wants to get you alone so she can tell you about my dad killing a man."

If he expected shock, fright, or anger from Miss

Ethel, he did not receive it. Instead, her blue eyes settled on him and she said gently, "I'm not concerned about your father, Zeke. I only care about you. Remember, you are not your father."

Stunned silent for the millionth time since he had stepped into her home, he barely noticed when Rafe picked up his suitcase and Zander threw an arm around his shoulder and led him down the back hall past the dining room toward the kitchen. Tears threatened to spill, knowing what he said was an asshole remark. But it seemed lately those were the only words coming out of his mouth.

Wondering about the reactions of the other boys, he managed to get hold of his inner shaking as they bustled around the kitchen pulling out snacks and milk, ignoring his previous comment. Somehow, they managed to do that without ignoring him, for which he was grateful.

A few minutes later, Miss Ethel came into the kitchen, her smile still firmly on her face. He surreptitiously watched her, wondering how she would act now that the social worker was gone. She continued to chat with the boys as she filled a tray with cookies. He followed as they made their way into the dining room, a large room with a massive table in the middle.

The others took seats, and he hesitated. He was invited to grab any chair and make himself at home. The cookies smelled delicious, and since he had not eaten since breakfast, he took several as soon as the others had filled their plates. A tall glass of milk was placed next to him, and Miss Ethel's gentle hand touched his shoulder.

She moved around to the head of the table, and with a nod, Zeke watched as she gave silent permission for everyone to begin eating. He could not remember the last time he had had homemade cookies, and the treat, along with a glass of milk, went a long way to settle his nerves.

Zeke remained quiet but watchful as the easy conversation flowed between the others. Miss Ethel listened as they talked about their school day and offered advice when asked. He had blurted out his father's transgressions, but no one seemed shocked or upset. That was a first. It was something he was so ashamed of, and yet, when he wanted to throw up his defense walls, he would let people know about his father. But Miss Ethel and the others did not seem to mind.

Before he had a chance to ponder that further, she said, "Boys, go ahead and start your homework, and I'm going to take Zeke upstairs to show him his room."

"I put his suitcase in the room," Rafe said, gaining Miss Ethel's nod.

She rose from the chair, and the boys stood as well. Zeke scooted his chair back and quickly took to his feet, finding himself no longer wanting to stand out in a bad way.

At her bidding, he followed her down the hall and up the stairs. She really was quite thin, a simple dress that buttoned in the front and belted at the waist covering her tall frame. She had rubber-soled shoes that did not make a noise as she climbed the wooden steps. Even at thirteen years old he knew they were not fashionable, but they looked comfortable. He had no idea how long her hair was since it was pulled back into a bun at the back of her head. She had wire-rimmed glasses, and the blue eyes that peered from behind them seemed to stare into the depths of him. It was a little frightening, but so far, she had done nothing except be friendly.

At the top of the stairs, she led him down the hall and explained, "My bedroom is downstairs. Up here, I have three bedrooms. Two of them contain bunk beds and a single so that six boys can comfortably stay. The bathroom is for everyone and is at the end of the hall. I have another smaller room with its own private bathroom."

As she faced him, she lifted her arm and placed her hand gently on his shoulder. Continuing, she said, "I firmly believe that my boys bond like brothers when they can spend time together. Zander was the first to come to me, and he, Rafe, and Cael share a room. Jaxon, Jayden, and Asher share another."

Zeke quickly assessed that she was going to put him in the single room by himself. *That's fine, I don't need anyone anyway.* And yet, as that thought moved through his mind, he thought of the six boys downstairs and their camaraderie.

"Zander, as the oldest and a junior in high school, has reached a time where he can have more privacy. He's going to be taking the single room, and I'll have you share a room with Rafe and Cael."

She had managed to shock him once again, but

before he had a chance to say anything, she quickly added, "I know they're older than you, but all of my boys will be a good influence and good friends. I'm sure you'll get along wonderfully."

She turned and walked through an open door into a large bedroom, bunk beds against one wall and a single bed on the opposite wall. His suitcase was already on the single bed, and she said, "We'll put your clothes in this chest, and you'll have room in the closet.

"Since today is Friday, you'll have the weekend to get acclimated before we go to school on Monday. I don't have the boys finish their homework on Friday, but I'd like them to get some of it done so that Sunday evening is not so hectic. I'll let you have a few minutes to unpack, and then I'd like you to come downstairs and join us."

She turned to leave, but Zeke halted her with his words, once more blurting out. "I'm sorry, Miss Ethel. About what I said...um...about my dad." He had not meant to apologize but seemed unable to control himself around her. Her countenance was so calm that he hated he had lashed out.

She turned and walked back, her blue eyes holding his captive, and her lips curved into a slow smile. She reached out and placed her hand on his shoulder again, this time her fingers gently massaging into the tense muscles. "The Goblins of Eros is a book by Warren Eyster and deals with a mythical revolution. An interesting author and I have read several of his works."

He stared at her, having no idea what she was

talking about, but forced himself to be respectfully quiet.

"He wrote, 'We are born with our father's names. We are not responsible for their actions.'" She peered deeply into his eyes, and he squirmed under her perusal. "Ezekiel Kemp. Do you know what your name means?"

Eyes wide, he jerked his head back and forth, not understanding her question.

"Ezekiel. It means strength. You're going to be a big man, Zeke. A strong man. How you use that strength is completely up to you. And Kemp. An old English word, I believe. It means warrior or champion. I believe you will live up to your name, my dear. A strong champion." With a final squeeze of her fingers, she turned and walked back out of the bedroom, leaving him staring in her wake, numb silence filling him.

No one had ever said that to him before. No one had ever treated him like he would be any different than his dad. Oh, his dad was strong enough, all right. Some might even consider him to be a warrior. But a champion? That gave a completely different connotation to the idea of strength. A champion.

Dragging in a ragged breath, he pushed those thoughts to the side and turned to the bed, opening his suitcase. Taking out his belongings, he placed them into the dresser and closet. He spent as much time as he could upstairs, dreading going downstairs.

Hearing a noise at the door, he turned around in haste and observed Zander leaning with his shoulder propped against the doorframe, his hands jammed into his pockets. Uncertain what to say, Zeke mumbled, "She said I'm in your old room. If that's a problem, I can—"

"Nah, it's no problem," Zander said, pushing himself off the doorframe and stepping into the room. "I've been here since I was a little kid. In this room, actually. Loved it, but I don't mind having a room to myself now." Shrugging, he chuckled and added, "Not that I'll spend a lot of time in there by myself anyway. We tend to do most things together here."

Zeke was not sure how to respond, so he remained quiet, hoping that Zander would continue to talk.

"When we were kids, we'd all gather in one of the bedrooms and I'd read to everybody—Miss Ethel encouraged reading—and then we'd discuss the stories. Most of us had not had that before coming here, so it was good for learning as well as bonding."

Shrugging, Zeke admitted, "I never really spent a lot of time reading. It's okay but not my favorite subject in school."

"No worries," Zander said with a grin. "You'll get used to the way things are around here." Glancing at Zeke's now-empty suitcase, he said, "You ready to come downstairs?"

Not having an excuse to dawdle anymore, he nodded. As he started to follow Zander out to the hall, he asked, "She for real?"

Zander turned around, his brows lowered and his head tilted to the side. "For real?"

Now embarrassed that he had spoken at all, he mumbled again, "Yeah, Miss Ethel. She seems... uh...nice."

Nodding slowly, Zander said, "Oh, and you're wondering if it's all for show." Zander stepped right in front of Zeke, a few inches taller than him, and looked down. "I can tell you all about her, but you're going to find out on your own. But, yeah, she's the real deal. Anybody will tell you she's the best foster mom out there. You might not realize it now, but you're lucky to have ended up in her house. It doesn't matter what brought you here...we all have our stories. But you'll discover you've just landed with a mom and brothers that'll have your back."

With that, Zander turned and headed down the stairs, and he followed. Uncertainty still coursed through him, but his anger had abated.

At the bottom of the stairs, he turned to the right and entered the large living room. A dark green sofa sat against the wall near the windows that looked over the front yard. It was flanked with two wooden tables, covered in lace cloths with lamps perched in the middle. The floors were wood, but the living room was covered with a thick rug, green and dark red swirls making a pattern. Two cushioned chairs sat facing the sofa, Miss Ethel in one, and Zander plopped into the other.

The back wall contained a fireplace, shelves on either side filled with books. Jayden and Jaxon were sitting on the floor, their notebooks on the coffee table. Cael and Rafe were on either end of the sofa, one with a calculator perched in his lap and the other typing on a laptop. Asher was also sitting on the floor, his back leaning against the sofa. He looked up and smiled, patting the rug next to him.

Zeke walked over and sat down, but with no schoolwork to work on, he felt restless. He glanced up at Miss Ethel, watching as her fingers held quickly-moving knitting needles, fascinated with the intricate pattern that was falling into her lap.

"You are never going to believe what Mr. Paulson is having us do in sophomore literature," Cael said. Grinning widely, he stated, "Fairytales."

Everyone laughed, and he remembered what Zander had just told him about the stories they'd read. Miss Ethel settled her warm gaze on him and said, "I've had the boys read stories since they all first came to me. We often discuss them, so I have a feeling Cael is quite glad that he has an advantage in his English class."

"What kind of books you like to read?" Asher asked, looking at Zeke.

Shrugging, he said, "Don't much like to read." Embarrassed, he hoped his comment would go unnoticed by most.

"Then you're definitely in the right house," Zander said softly. "There's a lot you can learn here."

Having nothing to say to that comment, he remained quiet but glanced back up to Miss Ethel, expecting to see the censure when instead he thought he spied understanding in her eyes.

She smiled and said, "And I think there's a lot that Zeke can teach us, as well."

He had no idea what she was talking about. The only thing he had learned from his dad was using his body to intimidate and threaten. He was certain that was a lesson no one else needed to learn.

But looking around the room, seeing the other six boys working diligently, their conversation easy, sharing laughs and help, a kernel of peace settled deep inside. Maybe, just maybe, this was not a bad place to have landed.

## 2

TWO YEARS LATER

The rest of the class groaned, several with frowns on their faces. Zeke looked around his sophomore English class, and no one had their hand up. Mr. Paulson, one of Zeke's favorite teachers, was also looking around, waiting to see if anyone had an answer.

Lifting his hand, he caught Mr. Paulson's gaze. At his teacher's nod, he said, "The Charles Perrault version of Cinderella was based on folktales from a number of cultures. There was even a story from the Greek, sometime around 10 A.D., and is considered to be one of the earliest known Cinderella stories. There were French versions, an Asian version, and even one from the Arabian Nights. The Perrault version made the story popular because he added things like a pumpkin, a fairy godmother, and a glass slipper. The brothers Grimm wrote one in the nineteenth century, but it was more intense...actually kind of gross."

As Zeke spoke, Mr. Paulson smiled, continuing to

nod. He heard grumbling from around, and one of the other boys in the class asked, "You know this stuff? This is lame, Mr. Paulson. This is the kind of stuff we watched with Disney cartoons."

Irritation flamed through Zeke, but he breathed slow and easy to contain his frustration with his classmates. *It wasn't so long ago that I was like them.*

Zeke was close to all of his brothers, but Zander had been the one who took him under his wing. Spending a lot of time together, Zander had been a patient teacher and helped Zeke with his reading. They had not been exaggerating when they said that literature was discussed at great lengths in Miss Ethel's house. He had learned more in the two years he had been with her than he could ever remember learning before. He often wished that he had gone to her when he was younger and had been able to sit around at night and listen to the stories that Zander read.

But even as teenagers, Miss Ethel made sure their world was open to the ideas and thoughts of others through literature. She encouraged the memorization of passages that meant something to them and often quoted them at appropriate times herself.

Zander had been a senior in high school last year when Zeke and Asher were freshmen. The boys were all large, but Zeke had learned to temper his strength watching each of them mature. Miss Ethel encouraged athletics, and she never minded that her backyard often resembled a ball field. They made sure not to trample her rose bushes, but other than that, her large yard experienced many late-night homeruns over the back fence.

Miss Ethel sometimes accepted a boy on a temporary emergency basis, but with a full house, she did that rarely. Since he had joined the family, there was only one more who had come to live with them as brothers. Castiel moved in several months after Zeke did. They added a bunk to the single bed in the younger boys' room, and Cas moved in with Jaxon, Jayden, and Asher.

He had learned a lot about his brothers in the past two years. Zander's mom had been a drug addict, and he often lived on his own as a child, fending for himself. When he came to Miss Ethel at the age of eight, he had not attended school. Rafe's parents were killed in a car accident, and he had no other relatives. Cael's father was killed in the military, and his mother was unable to handle her grief, giving him up to the care of others. Jaxon and Jayden's mom died when they were babies. They lived with relatives for several years until landing on Miss Ethel's doorstep. And Asher's mom gave up her parental rights so that she could stay with an abusive boyfriend. Cas' parents had been killed in an act of violence…something that always struck Zeke in the gut when he thought about it, considering the sins of his own father.

At fifteen, Zeke was already aware of how lucky he was to be with Miss Ethel. She gave him the family he craved, the acceptance he needed, and the love that she insisted he deserved.

His mom had always wanted him to learn manners,

but his dad had little use for them. In contrast, Miss Ethel's meals included table manners as well as lively conversation. Now, of course, there was an empty chair at the table.

Zander had only been gone for a few months, having joined the Army after he graduated from high school, but Zeke felt the loss intensely. He was close to all his brothers, but Zander was the one who, by quiet instruction, helped him become a better reader.

"Stop complaining," one of the girls in the class said, startling Zeke out of his thoughts. "At least all we'll have to do is watch the Disney movies and can get an 'A' in this class."

Mr. Paulson heard her comment and grinned. "Zeke, would you agree with Annie's assessment?"

Shaking his head, he said, "No. Fairytales are an important part of literature, and the Disney versions bear little resemblance to the actual stories."

"Can you give us an example with Cinderella?" Mr. Paulson asked.

"In the Grimm's version, the father did not die and the stepsisters mutilated their feet to try to get them into a golden slipper—"

Gasping, several of his classmates cried out, "That's disgusting!"

Continuing, he said, "In some versions, the father plays an active role in humiliating his daughter. Disney would not have wanted that as part of their children's movie, so they had him die instead. The glass slipper is only found in the Perrault version."

Throwing her hand up, Annie cried, "Mr. Paulson, what's the point? Why do we have to study fairytales at this age? Wouldn't that be better for elementary school?"

"What I hope you learn from this class is that there are lessons to be taken away from all kinds of literature."

One of the boys in the back of the room smirked and said, "Let's have Zeke tell us what we can learn from a story about a stupid girl who stays out too late and drops her shoe."

Shifting in his seat, Zeke pierced the boy with a glance that made the smirk fall off his face. Miss Ethel encouraged the boys to find their own style, and he had been growing his hair out for a while. It now brushed just below his shoulders, the dark waves streaked with blond giving him an air of wild. Even as a sophomore he had to shave, and when he did not, he had a thick shadow over his jaw. His eyes were light-colored, a combination of gray and green that he had heard some girls liked, but with no smile on his face, he knew it could be unnerving.

"It's a folktale. They started out as stories told around campfires and in villages. Usually with a theme or taught as a lesson. Cinderella? Unjust oppression and then reward. No matter who the girl was in the various stories, she was unfairly oppressed. Enslaved. Living in a far corner of the house. Maybe even beaten or abused. And then," he shrugged, looking over at his classmates, "she overcomes and is rewarded."

Mr. Paulson nodded enthusiastically and said, "Zeke has set the stage perfectly for our study. In chapter seven of your English Lit book, you will read three different versions of Cinderella during this week, and we will discuss them, looking for similarities and differences." Looking at the clock, he said, "The bell is almost ready to ring. Make sure you get the first story read by tomorrow."

As the class filed out of the room, Mr. Paulson moved toward Zeke. "I want to thank you for adding to the discussion today. You, so much more than me, are able to let the students know that what we're studying is not just for kids."

Shrugging, he said, "No problem. It's something I understand."

"I know of Miss Ethel," Mr. Paulson said, immediately drawing Zeke's attention. "I taught your older brothers, and, of course, have Asher and Cas in one of my other periods. I don't know what happened to lead you to her door, and so to say that you were lucky would be very presumptuous on my part. But let me just say that I'm glad you have her."

Unable to keep the smile from slipping across his lips, he ducked his head. "Me too." Walking out of his sophomore English class, he grinned.

---

That evening, he stood at the stove in the kitchen, sautéing minced garlic, chopped onion and zucchini, Italian sausage, and marinara sauce. Throwing in some

Italian seasoning, he continued to stir while Miss Ethel checked the garlic bread in the oven.

Just like she did almost every evening, she clucked over the food he was preparing. In the two years he had been in her house, he had discovered that he not only loved the kitchen for the time it gave him with her, but he also had an affinity for cooking. She insisted that cooking for the family came after homework or the sports he and his brothers were doing but admitted that she loved his company in the kitchen as well.

He had been regaling her with tales of his English Lit class while Asher and Cas gathered the plates, throwing in their comments also. As the twins moved through the kitchen, they remembered the Fairytale lessons from the previous year, and, of course, Rafe and Cael had loved Mr. Paulson.

Once they were gathered around the table and dug into the delicious food, Rafe said, "I bet Zander is missing this right now. No way he's getting food this good in the Army."

"He should have gone in as a cook," Cael said. "Then he could have always fixed something good."

Looking up, Zeke asked, "You can be a cook in the Army?"

"Absolutely," Miss Ethel said. "All of the different services have cooks." She tilted her head to the side and looked at him, but said nothing.

"I'm going to be a Medic," Rafe said. "I've talked to the recruiter at school."

"I talked to them also," Cael piped up. "I'm looking into construction. Maybe Corps of Engineers."

His thoughts tumbled as he thought that at the end of this school year, two more of his brothers would graduate, having already decided to join the military, following in Zander's footsteps. He had not given a lot of thought to what he wanted to do after high school, and even though he was only a sophomore, he knew the time would come quickly. *A cook? A cook in the Army?* A slow smile spread across his face as the idea took hold. Continuing to eat, he glanced up at Miss Ethel, seeing the smile on her face as well. He had no idea how she knew, but he was certain she had ascertained his thoughts...and she approved.

That evening, after his brothers headed to bed, Zeke stayed in the living room continuing to read. With his laptop, he had read online a version of Rhodopis, the oldest known oral version of the Cinderella story from ancient Greece. He had skimmed literary comments about a few of the Asian versions and Cenerentola by Basile. Then he reread the English translation of the French version by Perrault, planning on reading the Grimm version the next evening.

He was so engrossed in the stories he did not notice Miss Ethel walking back into the living room until she spoke.

"Are you still reading the versions of Cinderella?"

Jerking his head up, he grinned sheepishly. "Yeah, I know our assignments aren't due, but once I started reading, it was hard to stop." He glanced around and asked, "Has everyone else gone to bed?"

Nodding, she said, "Everyone is upstairs. I think most are reading."

Still grinning, he asked, "And you said goodnight?" He remembered the first night he spent in Miss Ethel's house. She had made her way to each of the boys, offering a quiet word, a bit of advice, or just a good night. He had learned from the others that when they were younger, she would tuck each one in. At first, the habit seemed strange to him, but he quickly learned to crave her soft voice at the end of the day. As though no matter what the day had held, good or bad, the evening would end in peace.

She met his smile and nodded. "Of course. And in my own way, I'll whisper my goodnight to Zander before I go to bed, hoping my words can travel around the world and he can feel them in his heart."

Sobering, he said, "I'm sure he can, Miss Ethel." She settled in her chair and picked up her knitting. After a moment, he said, "I miss him. I know I haven't been here as long as the others, but I miss him."

A flash of something undefinable passed over her face, and he sucked in his breath, wondering if he should have admitted his feelings.

Her face settled into a gentle smile, and she said, "Thomas Carlyle once wrote, 'A mystic bond of brotherhood makes all men one.' I wanted my boys to understand brotherhood. And so, for all the wonderful things that brotherhood brings, it also brings heartache when you're separated."

He nodded, understanding her sentiment. Looking back down at his book, he had only read for another moment when she asked, "What does Cinderella say to you personally? Not just the general morals that it can teach, but to you as an individual."

He gave thought to her question, his eyes moving from the page back to her. "No matter which version I read, the story is all about the unjust oppression of someone but how she refused to succumb to what was being forced upon her. Some scholars talk about the morals of kindness toward others, forgiving others for doing wrong to them, not letting bad things ruin your dreams." He hesitated and said, "I felt like everything fell apart when my mom left and my dad was sent to prison. I hadn't done anything wrong, and yet I was shuttled from one place to the other and made to feel as though somehow everything that was happening to me was my fault. It made me angry, and as big as I was, I didn't want my anger to come out in the same ways that it had with my dad."

Miss Ethel tucked her knitting back into her basket and sat with her hands clasped in her lap, facing him. "You are such a gentle soul and nothing like your father."

Sucking in his lips, he said, "When I get angry, I still have to remind myself not to react the same way that he did. In Cinderella's case, she could have become as mean and nasty as her oppressors. But instead, she stayed true to herself. So I guess that's the lesson I take from the story. I have to stay true to myself."

Miss Ethel smiled and said, "I could not agree more."

Standing, Zeke said, "I'll head to bed now." She stood and wrapped her arms around him, and even at the age of fifteen, he towered over her. Embracing her, he felt the strength in her thin frame, her arms just as sure as ever.

"Goodnight, my strong, sweet champion," she said.

As he climbed the stairs, Zeke smiled. She had given him a mom with staying power. She had given him brothers. And she had given him the desire to live up to his name.

## 3

TWELVE YEARS LATER

Zeke finished the prep for the food and left his cooks in charge as he walked through the connecting door between Grimm's restaurant and bar. When Zander was discharged from the Army, he came back to Richmond and bought an old bar in a rundown neighborhood. Zeke was still stationed overseas at the time but loved hearing about Zander's new enterprise, appropriately named after the Brothers Grimm from the many stories he had read in his younger years.

A lot of hard work had to be accomplished to turn what Zander called 'a wreck' into his place of business. "At least the bones of the building are solid," Zander had told him on one of their few calls between the States and Afghanistan. With the help of some of their other brothers who were also out of the military by then, Zander had built a great neighborhood bar.

Two years later, when Zeke left the Army, he came back home, uncertain what to do with his life. Zander once again took him under his wing. Zeke began as a bouncer at Grimm's, a job that became more complicated as the bar became more popular.

At first, Grimm's only lured a small group of regulars. Faces they knew and people they could talk to. It was easy to keep an eye on who was drinking too much and who might need assistance getting home. But as the neighborhood underwent a resurgence of development, more white-collar workers discovered the bar, and word got around that it was a good place to gather after work.

So Grimm's became packed with bodies, all vying for the bartender's attention. With the addition of a jukebox and an area for dancing, the customers stayed happy. Zeke was good as a bouncer. He had the height, the muscles, and could throw an intimidating look when necessary. He did not put up with anyone hitting on the waitresses, making a customer uncomfortable, or just being an asshole. He had no problem getting angry, but he always kept himself in check. He learned how to handle an inebriated man looking for a fight, immobilizing him until they called for a taxi.

He watched out for the women customers who were alone, making sure they got to their cars or taxis as well. The latter was a lesson learned the hard way when Zander first met the woman he eventually married. Rosalie was attacked outside their bar. Zeke was grateful for the job, proud that Zander trusted him, but he dreamed of more.

With all the changes in the bar, Zander had grumbled at the growth, but Zeke loved the expanding business. It took a year of slowly convincing Zander that

Grimm's needed to offer food before Zander finally agreed. Zeke knew that people who were eating as well as drinking would stay longer. The food helped counter the alcohol, making them more compliant customers. Also, the longer they stayed, the more alcohol they would order. It was a win-win all around.

When the storefront next door became available, Zeke and Zander went together to buy the space and opened up the kitchen area for the bar. Zeke was in his element, cooking wings, nachos, burgers, and loaded fries to serve alongside the drinks the bartenders were slinging. Best of all...Zander made him a partner.

As Zeke walked through the room, his eyes skimmed through the familiar area. The bar ran along the left side of the long room, ending at a hall that led to the bathrooms, office, and stockrooms. Round wooden tables filled most of the space, sturdy wooden chairs circling each one. The walls held little adornment, and Zeke smiled. Zander said people came to eat and drink and did not care what the decor looked like. With the money he and Zander were making, he could not argue with that logic.

Continuing past the bar, he made his way down the hall and entered the office, seeing Zander sitting behind the desk. Piles of paper were scattered about, and no matter how much Rosalie popped in to organize, it did not take long for it to end up in chaos once again. But since it had been that way since Zeke first joined the business, he was as used to it as Zander obviously was.

His brother looked up as he walked in and Zeke watched Zander slide off his reading glasses, tossing them to the desk. They often introduced themselves to others as brothers, and Zeke always laughed at the expressions they received. Zander was not as tall as he but was bulkier. Zander had short, sandy brown hair, and deep-set, Nordic blue eyes. Zeke's hair was now down below his shoulders, the ends tinted slightly blonde. His beard was scraggly, not caring to shave often.

But with names like Zeke and Zander, people still believed they were blood brothers.

Cutting to the chase, Zander asked, "You ready for this?"

Lifting his eyebrows, he asked, "Are you asking me if I'm sure?"

Zander leaned back in his chair and said, "I know you're up for the challenge, bro. We've been partners for several years, and I know you can do this. But there's no way we can do it all on our own, so it's gonna take hiring good people. You won't always get to be the man at the stove."

Nodding, he replied, "I thought about that. But what we've got here works, Zander. It works fuckin' good. And I think if we keep doing what we've been doing, it'll be a success."

Zander grinned, placed his hands flat on the desk, and pushed himself up. "Okay, then let's do this."

An hour later, Zeke sat next to Zander in the realtor's office, filling out paperwork. He waited to see if buyer's remorse settled in, but it did not. Miss Ethel had always taught him to listen to his heart, and while they were filling out reams of paperwork, he never had a doubt about what they were doing. When they walked out of the office, they shook hands and pulled each other in for a backslapping hug.

"Going to be there this afternoon?" Zeke asked, although he knew it was an unnecessary question.

"We'll all be there," came the expected reply.

Climbing back into his truck, he heaved a sigh of relief. It seemed like dreams really were coming true.

---

Hours later, Zeke parked in front of Miss Ethel's house. He was always pleased to see that the neighborhood had changed little over the years except for some minor improvements made with neighboring houses. He and his brothers shared chores, making sure that her grass was cut, the bushes trimmed, and the household repairs always kept up to date.

As he walked up the sidewalk toward the front porch, he looked to either side at her rosebushes and grinned. Those were her domain.

He entered the house, the joyous sounds of family emanating from the back. He always loved Miss Ethel's kitchen, recognizing it as the hub of her home. Walking down the hall, he came to a sharp halt as a beautiful toddler waddled his way, her eyes bright with excitement. He bent and scooped up Charity, Zander and Rosalie's little girl, blowing raspberries against her neck. Peals of giggles came forth from her tiny body, and he reveled in the sound.

Turning the corner, he almost ran into Zander who

was looking for his daughter. Huffing a sigh of relief, Zander said, "I can't believe how fast she is. I looked away for a second, and she had already left the dining room!"

Handing Charity back to her dad, he watched as Rafe came up from behind, his arms filled with a baby. Rafe had left the Army for a modeling career, then met the enigmatic Eleanor, a veteran nurse who had suffered burns when in the service. Rafe and Eleanor now ran a burn clinic for veterans and had just given birth to a baby boy named Rory.

Zeke pulled back the blanket and stared into the perfect face of Rafe's son. Looking up into his brother's eyes, he said, "Beautiful, man. Just beautiful." Eleanor walked in, and he leaned over to kiss her cheek, congratulating her as well.

Continuing into the kitchen, he saw Regina, a statuesque redhead who had captured the heart of Cael and now carried his child. Morgan, a world-renowned swimmer now sidelined by an injury, who was happily married to Jaxon and also pregnant, was standing next to Regina.

Ruby was setting the table, the soft-spoken beauty now married to Jayden. Last, but not least, he greeted Penny, who had recently married Asher. It was not lost on him that most of his brothers were no longer single. Except for Cas, his brothers had found someone special, and he loved his sisters-in-law dearly.

Cas was more of a recluse, living outside the city where he had his woodworking shop. But for Zeke, it was not for lack of interest or even lack of available women, but definitely for lack of meeting *the one*. He wanted marriage. He wanted a family. But he was willing to wait for the right person.

Finally, amidst the loving crush of people, he saw Miss Ethel pulling out more food from the refrigerator. He walked over, wrapped his arms around her, and gave her a squeeze.

"Oh, my goodness! I was beginning to wonder if you were going to show up," she teased.

"I've never missed a party yet," he said, kissing her cheek.

Reaching up, she patted his shoulder, and he stared into her eyes that were now more grey than blue. She smiled and said, "I knew you'd be here."

Miss Ethel had long since given up taking in foster boys, but the family she created had remained closer than ever. Between birthdays and anniversaries, special occasions, and no occasions, they got together often.

Soon they gathered in the dining room, more chairs brought in to accommodate their ever-growing family.

Looking over at Asher and Zeke, Miss Ethel asked, "How are things at the homeless shelter?"

Zeke glanced toward Asher, offering a slight nod, allowing him to answer first. Asher, having lived part of his early years in a homeless shelter, had donated a substantial amount of money, along with working to obtain grants to establish one of the homeless shelters in the city. It recently opened the women's wing, accommodating women and those who had children. Zeke worked there almost every morning before going to Grimm's, helping with food and serving. It was

31

something he started doing when Asher became involved, and then he discovered it fulfilled a need inside of him...a need to help others because he had been given so much.

Asher smiled and said, "It's going great. I wish we could say there was no need for a homeless shelter, but of course, there is."

Her eyes moved to Zeke, and he shrugged, "I still get out there almost every morning for the breakfast service."

Miss Ethel shook her head and clucked, saying, "I don't see how you do it. You're there almost every morning, then head over to Grimm's where you work until late at night."

Deflecting, he said, "I like to stay busy."

As the words left his mouth, he and Zander passed a look between them, something that Miss Ethel did not miss.

Cocking her head to the side, she said, "I always knew when my boys were up to something, and that hasn't changed in the subsequent years."

Rosalie giggled and said, "You two might as well confess. It's going to come out soon enough anyway."

Zeke realized everyone at the table had grown quiet and was now looking at them. Sucking in a deep breath before letting it out slowly, he said, "Grimm's is doing so well that Zander and I have decided to take our partnership further. We're going to open a second Grimm's, appropriately named Grimm's Two."

The congratulations from everyone was immediate, and pride surged through him.

"Oh, my goodness! Tell us about it!" Regina said.

"It's going to be just like Grimm's, only in the High Park area of town. It's kind of run-down, but they're also having a lot of renewal in that area. New businesses are going in, and it should be a good place to establish a bar."

Zander piped up and said, "Our idea is to do exactly like the original Grimm's. A basic bar with the kitchen in the back that'll serve food."

Zeke added, "It'll mean expanding, hiring more people, but I think it's the right next step for us."

Miss Ethel beamed, and the others called out their congratulations. The rest of the dinner fell into easy conversation and camaraderie. After the meal, some of their crew helped with the cleanup while others walked outside to see if there was anything Miss Ethel needed. The men came up with a list of a few things, such as cleaning out the gutters and giving the porch a fresh coat of paint. They quickly divvied up the tasks and decided to continue the same rotation of lawn care.

Rafe and Eleanor left soon after, everyone kissing Rory's head. They were followed by the other couples, and the crowd slowly dispersed.

Cas clasped Zeke's hand and said, "If you need any help or special pieces made for Grimm's Two let me know."

Thanking him, Zeke watched as his last brother headed to his vehicle. He held back as Miss Ethel took him by the hand, and they walked over to two of the rockers on the front porch. Making sure she was settled first, he moved to the rocker next to her, finding the movement to be soothing.

"I could tell you wanted to talk to me," he said, his lips curving into a smile.

She took a moment as though gathering her thoughts, her gaze drifting out over her yard before moving back to his face. "I'm very proud of you Zeke," she said.

Her words soothed through him as they always had, and he knew that pleasing her would always bring that kind of satisfaction.

"I'm proud of all my boys," she continued. "The men you are. The success you have."

He held her gaze and said, "You do know that we owe it all to you, Miss Ethel?"

She waved her hand dismissively in front of her and said, "Oh, posh. I don't deny that I've had a hand in helping each of you, but the brotherhood you formed has given each of you individual as well as collective strength."

Agreeing, he said, "Yes, and you're the one that gave us that brotherhood. You created a family out of a bunch of boys who didn't know anything about family."

They were quiet for a moment, and he added, "I wasn't sure it would work for me."

Her face scrunched slightly, the wrinkles settling deeper. "I don't understand what you mean."

"You got the others when they were much younger. Me? I was already thirteen years old. An angry thirteen-year-old. I could have already been beyond help."

She continued rocking and did not immediately refute his statement. Finally, she said, "There was already something in you, learned from your parents. You know, we sometimes learn how to act from our parents, but we also learn how we don't want to act. By the time you came to me, yes, you were angry. Angry at life, and angry at your mom for leaving, and your dad for not controlling his temper. But unlike your dad, you didn't turn that anger outward on others. You had already learned to control it, and I just simply gave you a good family to focus on."

They continued rocking for a moment, and then she finally spoke again. "I worry that you're taking on too much work."

This time he grinned, those words being what he expected to hear from her. "We all work hard," he said. "You always worked hard."

"Yes, but your brothers have found that there's more to life than work. They found love as well."

Ruefully shaking his head back and forth, he said, "I'm not opposed to that, Miss Ethel. I figure I'll know it when it hits me."

With that, her laughter burst forth, and she said, "It's true. Sometimes we don't always know when love comes our way. I just hope you'll be open to it when the opportunity presents itself."

"I'm no prince," he said. "I'm just a hard-working man, and it'll take a special woman to see that."

"Your brothers found it. You'll find it, too." She smiled then said, "Remember Robert Browning? 'I was made and meant to look for you and wait for you—"

"And become yours forever," they finished together, his smile matching hers.

She spoke with such conviction, and considering she always seemed to know things, he could not dismiss her words. They continued to rock in companionable silence for a few more minutes before he finally said, "I'm going to head on out, Miss Ethel. I want to go by the homeless shelter this evening to see if there's anything special I needed to get for the breakfast service tomorrow."

He assisted her to stand, then wrapped his arms around her and felt hers wrap around his waist in return. She was not quite as tall as she used to be, her frame slightly thinner. But her hug contained the same fierceness of love and protection as it had many years ago.

4

Zeke hustled into the homeless shelter through the back door that led into the kitchen, shaking off the raindrops that had pelted him as he ran from his truck. The shelter was large enough to fill an entire city block and was three stories tall. Located in an old brick building, one wing had been designated for women, either single or with children. The other wing was for men. A small section on the second floor was set aside for families.

The first floor housed offices, meeting rooms, the reception area, and a large dining room with an attached kitchen. The kitchen ran largely on grants and donations, but the shelter's residents were expected to serve at meals, and often community or church groups would cook food, especially at night. Zeke liked to help out in the mornings before he went to work at Grimm's.

It only took a few minutes for him to ascertain what he would need for the next morning's breakfast. The meal was often simple, such as scrambled eggs, toast, and bacon. But occasionally he liked to liven things up with ham and cheese omelets, French toast, or fluffy biscuits and sausage gravy.

Needing to see who might be assisting in the kitchen during the week, he walked out of the dining hall hoping to catch Lori Fox, the director of the shelter.

As he rounded the corner, he saw a bedraggled young woman entering the building. Drops of water were falling off her pink rain slicker onto the floor. Standing on the entry rug, she set her suitcase and backpack onto the floor and pulled off the raincoat, giving it a little shake.

Her long, golden hair was braided, but loose tendrils were now wet and plastered about her face. She was not tall, and he wondered if she would even come to his chin or would stand more at his shoulder. Her age was indeterminate, but her curves gave evidence that she was definitely a woman, not a girl. Her jeans were wet at the bottom, and so were her sneakers. As she looked up, he observed her face, only slightly adorned with a little makeup, but it was flawless.

Bedraggled, she appeared to have the weight of the world on her tiny shoulders. She sighed heavily and pushed some of her wet hair back from her face. After a moment, she sucked in a huge breath, let it out slowly, and squared her shoulders as she stood up straight. It was as though she found her inner strength, and he was awed to have the opportunity to watch her inner fortitude snap into place.

Swiping the water from her face that dripped from her hair, she bent to pick up her suitcase and backpack again. He rushed forward to assist her, and she startled, her eyes flying open wide as she looked up, taking him in. Skidding to a halt, afraid of appearing imposing, he threw his hands up and said, "I'm sorry, Miss. I didn't mean to scare you. I was just going to help you with your bags."

She sucked in her lips, her wide, blue eyes moving over him. She must have decided that he was not a threat as a small smile curved her lips. "Thank you. But I've got it. Um...do you know who I need to talk to? Um...about getting a bed?"

Her face was flaming red, and he assumed she had never stayed in a homeless shelter before. Wanting to put her at ease, he said, "Sure, it's right through there." He pointed toward the director's office, her gaze followed the direction of his finger, and she nodded.

With hesitation, her voice shaking with a small quiver, she said, "Thank you. This is all, well, new to me."

"It's okay," he said, wanting to make her feel less self-conscious about needing a bed at the shelter. He found himself wanting to know what her story was. Why was she here? What had happened to her?

Knowing it was none of his business, he watched as she attempted a smile that did not reach her eyes and said, "I'm sure you understand," before she lugged her suitcase and backpack toward the director's office.

He blinked at her words, then it hit him that she

thought he was a resident at the shelter. He almost corrected her but did not want to make her feel even more self-conscious. He turned and walked back through the dining room, his mind more on her than the next day's breakfast. Now he had even more of a reason to come back. He wanted to see her again.

---

The next morning dawned with a grey drizzle, so much like the night before. Cynthia Ellison woke, and it took her a moment to figure out where she was. Glancing around, she could see the three other beds in the room were still filled with sleeping women. She sat up and observed the room that she had barely had a chance to see the night before. Dorm style, there were four twin beds and four lockers, each secured with a padlock that had been issued by the director.

When she went into the room the previous evening, she took the only available bed and hated to think that she would stay long enough to need to put her clothes into the locker. Even though the other women had smiled their greetings toward her, she did not want to leave her belongings in her suitcase. She hated to be suspicious but had no idea what to expect.

Her work uniforms were too valuable for her to have them stolen, as were her extra pair of shoes. She had slipped her hand onto the small pouch containing a pair of small diamond stud earrings, the only thing of value she had left from her mother besides her memories, which no one could take from her.

The other three women did not talk much as they were busy getting ready for bed about the time she arrived. Like her, they were down on their luck but pleasant.

*Jesus, how did it come to this?* She knew the answer. A stepfamily that turned their back on her. A minimum wage job. An illness with no health insurance. *Who knew how close any of us are to living in a homeless shelter?*

Her mind drifted back to the previous evening and the man she saw in the reception area of the shelter. Tall, handsome, with kind eyes. She was embarrassed at having no other place to go than the shelter, but she figured he must have understood that feeling, being here himself. *That was probably why he seemed so kind. At least it's better than his pity.*

It was not unusual for her to notice handsome men. After all, she was a healthy, red-blooded female. But it did seem unusual for him to notice her. At work, she was just one of the many people who were overlooked. The kind of person who was expected to do their job and do it well but stay mostly out of sight. And having no extra money for things like restaurants or bars, there was little place to meet men. Not that she had time in her life anyway.

Sighing, she wondered if she would see him again and found herself hoping that he might be at breakfast. If nothing else, just to see his smile and kind eyes turned her way before she headed back out into the world.

The director had told her last night when she checked in that she was welcome to stay there, and the fact that she had a full-time job would be in her favor. They encouraged the residents to work as much as possible. She was also expected to help out with the meals when available. Since she did not have to report to work until eight o'clock in the morning, that gave her the opportunity to serve the shelter's breakfast.

While the other women were still sleeping, she climbed from the bed, gathered clean clothes, and slipped down the hall to the women's communal bathroom. Taking care of business, she also hopped in for a quick shower. Without a dryer, she simply braided her long hair and wound it into a bun at the back of her head.

Not willing to get her work uniform messy while serving breakfast, she slipped back into her jeans and a clean T-shirt, jamming her feet into her still-damp sneakers before going back into her room. Only one of the women had awakened, and she smiled politely in her direction.

Thinking of Emily Dickenson, she whispered to herself, "Hope is the thing with feathers - That perches in the soul - And sings the tune without the words - And never stops - at all."

Smiling as she thought of her mother, she opened the small makeup kit in her purse and dabbed on a little powder, using her pink lipstick on both her lips and cheeks before swiping mascara on her lashes. She tried to tell herself that she was doing no more than what she normally did, but she knew she hoped she would see the man from last night.

He was tall, and she remembered having to lean her

head back as he approached. His hair was long, still wet from the rain, and hanging about his shoulders. With his unkempt beard, tats crawling down his arm, large and muscular, he did not look like the type of man that she encountered at her workplace, and yet his eyes were mesmerizing, holding her gaze with such kindness.

Tiptoeing out of the room, she went down the stairs from the women's wing, walked across the main reception hall where she had been last night, and into the dining facility. Only a few people were around that early, and she saw the serving line near the front. A door that led into the kitchen opened, and her heart leaped as she saw him walking toward the tables, carrying a large metal tray filled with scrambled eggs. Her mouth watered, and she wondered if it was from the scent of the delicious breakfast food or the sight of him.

Suddenly uncertain, she was not sure what to do when he looked up and caught her eyes. To her relief, a wide smile spread across his face, and she felt the air leave her lungs in a rush.

"Good morning!" he called out.

She walked closer, her head leaning back as she approached, keeping her eyes on his. "Hello," she greeted. She glanced toward the serving line and said, "I understand we're supposed to help if we can."

"You don't have to," he said. "It's not required."

She lifted her shoulders in a delicate shrug and said, "I've got no reason not to. I don't have to be at work until a little bit later."

He opened his mouth as though to say something

else but several more people walked into the dining hall, and she hurried around the back of the table. Watching what he did, she stood behind some of the platters and dished out scrambled eggs and breakfast potatoes.

Women came through the lines, sometimes in singles and sometimes with children in tow. A few families came through together, and the single men followed. Not everyone was friendly, but for the most part, everyone was polite. She could not help but think about the reasons why each of them was there as well.

Glancing surreptitiously to the side, she noticed that the man next to her served the food with a smile and took charge of carrying the empty platters back to the kitchen and returning with ones filled with fresh, hot food.

When the line slowed, he turned to her and said, "Grab a plate and fill it up."

She glanced at the large clock on the wall and said, "I don't have a lot of time before I need to leave."

Instead of blowing her off the way she assumed he would, his brows lowered, and he ordered, "Then get something quickly. You need to eat before you leave."

Another woman came up beside her and said, "Listen to him. You go on and eat. I've got this now."

Doing what she was told, she grabbed a plate and scooped a small amount of scrambled eggs, hash browns, and two strips of bacon. Glancing around, she found a table that held a mother and her two children and sat down. The woman smiled at her as she tried to balance her toddler in her lap and keep an eye on her preschooler. Eating quickly, she smiled at the preschooler, hoping to give the mother a quick respite.

A shadow passed by, and she twisted her head around, seeing the man place his plate next to hers. He plucked the preschooler up into his lap and entertained the child with one hand while eating with the other. He looked so natural, she could not help but smile through her disappointment. It was foolish for her to assume that he was single. She should have known a man as handsome as he would be taken.

Now that she was finished eating, Cynthia stood up but startled when he whipped his head around and said, "Are you leaving already?"

Nodding, she said, "Yes, I've got to get to work."

His face softened as he smiled and leaned closer. "I hope to see you again."

Her gaze shot to the woman dealing with the toddler, embarrassed that the man was flirting with her. The woman did not seem to mind her husband's roving eye, but Cynthia's lips tightened, and she picked up her plate and walked away, ignoring the look of confusion on his face.

She barely had enough time to run back to the room, change into her light blue uniform with the Prince Hotel logo over her breast pocket, and run out to catch a bus. Several stops later, she left the bus and crossed the street near the front of the beautiful, exclusive, privately-owned hotel. Walking past the front, she headed around to the back alley where the employees entered. From there, she hurried into the employee locker room, greeting her fellow housekeepers.

"You're always early, girl!" Lucy called out. "What happened today?"

Throwing her purse into the locker, she groaned. "I know, I know. I got held up at the..um…place where I'm staying right now."

"You still living with that friend over on fifth?" Susan asked, patting her much-sprayed hair.

Shaking her head, she said, "No, she and her boyfriend split up, and she needed to move to a smaller place."

Belinda came hustling in, grumbling about the weather. For a few minutes, the women chattered as they got their carts ready. Checking her detergent, spray cleaners, clean sheets, and folded towels along with all of the items that went into the coffee trays and bathroom products, Cynthia determined she was ready to go.

Carlos walked into the room and handed out slips of paper with room assignments. He had only been the Head of Housekeeping for the Prince Hotel for several months, and she was glad he looked after the women working for him.

"I made a few changes, Cynthia. You have the top two floors since Donna left."

Looking over her new room assignments, she was surprised. The top two floors were the executive suites. In fact, the owner of the Prince Hotel had his executive offices on the top floor also, but in a different wing from the rooms, and a night cleaning crew was responsible for them.

Depending on who stayed in the rooms on the executive floors, they might not be too horrible to clean, and there was the possibility of decent tips. But since they were not always filled, Carlos also gave her another floor. Sighing, she knew that schedule would keep her busy, probably through lunch.

He patted her on the shoulder and said, "Don't worry. If you can't get through, Belinda can come up and help." Leaning closer, he said, "But you're the best person on my staff, and I know I can trust you with the executive suites."

They left in groups, pushing their carts toward the service elevator. Cynthia stepped in with the others, pushing her cart to the very back. As the elevator rose, floor to floor, she said goodbye to each of her friends. At the sixth floor, she got off, glad that the hallway was clear and quiet.

Following the room order that was listed on her daily assignment, she started with one of the larger suites. She had a routine and stuck with it, finding that it kept her organized. She began in the bathroom, carrying the dirty linens out and replacing them with clean, thick, white towels. The bathtub was scrubbed, followed by the toilet, sink, and counter. She emptied the trash can, refilled the toilet paper and toiletries, and then mopped the bathroom as she backed out.

Next came the bed, stripped of the old linens and replaced with fresh ones. Again, she emptied the trash cans and then began dusting, going over all the furniture. She walked through the entire suite, giving a last look to make sure she had not missed anything. Finally, she vacuumed, starting from the far corner and ending at the door. When the room met her satisfaction, she walked out and locked the door behind her.

The next two rooms followed the same routine. The only time-consuming portion was that they were so large it took longer than a regular hotel room. Pleased that she was ahead of schedule, she realized that would all change when she opened the door to the fourth room. While an expensive suite, it was incredibly messy.

She had only taken a few steps into the room before realizing the numerous empty wine bottles had resulted in somebody throwing up. Heart sinking at the thought of cleaning puke off the carpet, she was actually relieved to find that the person had at least made it to the bathroom. Gross, but better than the carpet.

The housekeepers at the Prince Hotel always wore gloves, but she snapped on a second pair after tossing back the bed covers, finding used condoms lying about. Shuddering, she grabbed paper towels to pick them up, even with the double gloves. Tossing the condoms and the wrappers into the trashcan, she followed by collecting the empty wine bottles, tossing them as well. She set the cups and dishes onto the room service tray, called down for someone to come pick it up, then set it outside in the hall. The bathroom took a lot longer to scrub, and she battled the desire to gag as she cleaned up the puke.

By the time she finished with the room, it was spotless and smelled wonderful. And yet, looking at the clock, she realized she had worked through lunch. Glad that she had water bottles and some cheese crackers on her cart, she quickly ate before going down to the next floor.

She thought of her parents and tears threatened to form. Battling them back, she breathed deeply through her nose, clearing her eyes. Cynthia did not mind her job, although working as a hotel cleaner for low wages had never been her great career aspiration. But then, nothing in her life was quite going according to plan.

5

---

Zeke stood in the kitchen of Grimm's, pulling up another basket of chicken wings from the fryer and placing them in the warming tray. Without a full menu, they did not have much of a crowd at lunch, but some regulars still popped in to grab a bite. He liked to come in and get things ready for the service when it was calmer. He would then spend the afternoon prepping for the evening crowd but had other cooks available then.

He moved through the rote tasks of the food prep, his mind firmly on the girl from the shelter. She had seemed so friendly. Her voice soft and her smile easy. She caught on quickly to the breakfast service, having a polite word with those who came through the line. It appeared she was going to skip eating herself until he insisted, and even then she helped to entertain the little girl.

When he came over to join her, she appeared

surprised, then pleased. But then something changed, and her lips grew tight and her mannerism short.

Huffing, he could not imagine what he had done to flip the switch on her emotions but wished he could undo it.

Zander popped his head into the kitchen and said, "Let me know when you can leave. We've got some papers to sign."

Eyes wide, he asked, "Our bid was accepted?"

Zander grinned, his blue eyes twinkling as he said, "Looks like we're one step closer to Grimm's Two."

He fought the urge to throw his hands into the air, considering they were both covered in flour batter for the chicken wings. Looking over at his assistant, Lee, he said, "I'll let you take it from here."

Lee offered a chin lift and moved to the prep area while Zeke pulled off his gloves and then scrubbed his hands in the large industrial sink. Jerking off the hair net holding his long locks away from his face, he tossed it into the trash. Following Zander out the door, they rode together since they would both be coming back to Grimm's.

Arriving at the realtor's office, they went over the contracts and signed more papers. The realtor congratulated them and added, "As you can see, the seller is anxious to get rid of the building. He inherited it from his father and has no desire to be saddled with it. He would like to have a closing as soon as your finances are ready."

Zeke shared a look with Zander and then said,

"We've got everything lined up. Let us know when the closing can be, and we'll be there."

They had already made all the arrangements with the bank for a new business loan, and as they drove back to the bar, they discussed the timeline for getting Grimm's Two up and running.

"Cael and Asher are ready to go as soon as we need them," Zeke said. Both Cael and Asher worked in construction, owning their own businesses. Cael refurbished old houses, restoring them to their original beauty, and Asher flipped houses, some for resale and some to own for rentals.

"Last time, when I had to gut and start over with Grimm's, I know you were still in the Army," Zander said. "To be honest, I didn't know exactly what I was doing so it probably took longer than necessary. Since we want to replicate what we have in Grimm's and we all know more about what we're doing, it shouldn't take too long."

Zeke settled back into the seat for the rest of the ride, his thoughts on all that had happened since he left the Army. For a man who had never lived by a plan, he was very happy with the way life was going.

Asher and Cael came into the bar that afternoon for a congratulatory drink and began sketching out plans and materials. Zeke had no problem letting Zander take over the vision for the bar, but he had very definite ideas about the kitchen. When he had designed the space for the kitchen in Grimm's, he had been so excited about making sure it had all the necessities that he forgot about placing certain appliances and equipment in the most efficient design.

During the time that he and Zander began discussing expanding, he had begun studying commercial kitchen designs and had a much clearer idea of how he wanted it to look. His brothers were impressed with his knowledge, and both Asher and Cael declared there would be no problem to create his vision.

After a while, Zander said his goodbyes, heading home to Rosalie and Charity. He and Zander had hired someone to assist with managing so that Zander had a couple of evenings per week that he could spend with his family and not at Grimm's. Cael left with Zander, leaving him and Asher relaxed in Grimm's office.

Asher gave him a hard stare and asked, "Is there something on your mind? Something besides the new bar?"

Giving his head a shake, he said, "Nothing of real consequence." One of the things he loved about his brothers was they tended to wait until someone was ready to speak without peppering them with questions. He and Asher sat in companionable silence for a few minutes before he finally admitted, "I met a lady at the homeless shelter last night and saw her again this morning. There was something about her that captured my attention, but I don't even know her name."

Asher smiled, saying, "Sometimes it happens like that. I was falling for Penny before I even knew her name."

Startling, he said, "I'm not talking about falling for her. I don't even know her. It's just there was something about her that had a real pull. She seemed nice, although when she left this morning, I got the feeling I had done or said something wrong."

Lifting an eyebrow, Asher kept smiling. "Considering I haven't heard you mention a woman in a long time, that pull she had must've been something."

Shaking his head slowly, his brows lowered, he said, "I don't know. It was a weird sense of strength and vulnerability all at the same time. Anyway, I kind of hope I see her again tomorrow morning. If nothing else, to find out why she seemed unhappy with me when she left."

The two men stood and clasped hands. "Well, even if it's nothing, I'll be anxious to hear more about the woman that captured your attention so quickly."

"Don't hold your breath. The look she gave me as she left this morning, she may not talk to me again."

"Yeah, well, you know it's difficult for the people that seek the shelter. Some walk in with an attitude like they're owed something, and others are hesitant, embarrassed about their situation in life. If she's never been forced into a shelter before, she may have just felt very overwhelmed."

Nodding, Zeke said, "I thought about that. I'm hoping I get a chance to talk to her more. I'll definitely be back for the breakfast service. She seemed to indicate that was the one she can help with since she had to be at work."

"She has a job?" Asher asked.

"Yes, but she didn't say what she did."

"Well, Ms. Fox, the director, will help her. If she lost

her housing, then what she saves on rent for the little bit of time she stays at the shelter, she can make more with her paycheck." Grinning as he walked out, he said, "Make sure you tell me what goes on with this woman. You need another focus besides work."

Rolling his eyes, Zeke followed him out of the office and into the bar. Watching his brother leave, he sighed heavily and headed toward the kitchen. *Time to get the wings cooked.*

---

Cynthia was glad that Belinda came to her last floor to assist. They were almost finished, but as people were checking in, there was always a flurry of requests. Most people were polite when they sought her out in the hall, asking for an extra towel or coffee pod for the coffee makers in each room. But then there were the entitled ones...the guests who snapped their fingers, yelled down the hall for a maid, or berated them for a supposed slight. *"My sheets aren't soft enough." "The bathroom mirror has a streak through it." "I can't get onto the Wi-Fi." "There's a stain in the corner of the carpet."*

Everything was handled with a smile, and if Cynthia could not make it right, she radioed down to reception to have someone follow up with the guest.

Hurrying through the last three rooms, the two women managed to get them clean by the time their shift was over. Riding the service elevator down, she leaned her back against the wall and closed her eyes.

She had been on her feet since breakfast, and her water and cheese crackers no longer sustained her.

"Girl, you look worn out."

As they pushed their carts into the supply area along with the others and began filling them for the next day, she replied, "I didn't get a lot of sleep last night."

Belinda finished resupplying her cart and walked over to help Cynthia. "You mentioned that your friend had to get a smaller place. Are you sleeping on a couch?"

Sucking in her lips, she stared at the bottle of cleanser she was refilling, purposely keeping her eyes away from her friends.

"What are you not telling us?" Susan asked.

She looked into the eyes of the women that had become her friends as well as her coworkers and heaved a great sigh. "I spent last night at the downtown homeless shelter."

She expected protestations, but their wide-eyed, open-mouthed, silent stares greeted her. Then the protests began.

"Are you kidding?" Lucy sputtered.

"Honey, you can sleep on my couch!" Belinda offered, planting her hands on her hips.

Susan shook her head and said, "Cynthia, we can find you a place!"

She sighed once again and said gently, "Belinda, your brother is at your house sponging off of you so often, that couch practically has his name on it. Susan, right now I've got to save some money. I'm looking, Lucy, I promise. The most I can afford is to just rent a room from someone. I just haven't had a chance yet."

"What happened to the place you were staying?" Lucy asked.

"I was renting a room from a girl I'd met a couple of years ago, but she and her boyfriend had a huge fight, and he kicked her out. I didn't realize that the apartment was in his name, so when he kicked her out, I was out too. I thought maybe she and I could get a place, but then she moved in with someone else, so suddenly, I found myself without a place to live."

Belinda's hands that were still firmly on her generous hips curled into fists. "Your fuckin' family! I'll bet your stepsisters have a nice place to sleep!"

Shrugging, she said, "I try not to give them too much thought."

Lucy stepped closer and placed her hand on Cynthia's shoulder. Holding her gaze, she said, "I hate that you're living at the shelter. What can we do?"

Giving her head a shake, she smiled at her friends. "It's not bad. I'm in a room with three other women. I have a bed that's more comfortable than a couch. I have a locker with a padlock so I can keep my items there. I'm going to go talk to the director when I get off here and find out about some of the programs they offer. For the shelter residents who are working, they help to find low-income housing. And that'll give me a chance to find someone I can trust that I might rent a room from." Seeing the hesitant, concerned expressions on their faces, she added, "I'm fine. Honestly. I'm really fine."

She waved goodbye as they left the building and ran across the street to catch the bus back to the shelter. The skies had cleared, and the rain had passed. As she stepped off the bus and looked toward the front of the shelter, she realized how much from the outside it simply resembled an apartment building. Sucking in a deep, fortifying breath, she thought, *I can make this work. After all I've gone through in the past, I can make this work.*

Stepping inside the building, she saw the director leaving her office, and she threw her hand up to wave. Hustling over, she said, "Ms. Fox, I was wondering if we would have a chance to talk for a few minutes. Whenever is convenient for you."

Lori Fox smiled and said, "I've got the time right now. Come on back." She led the way back into her office, and Cynthia followed, settling into the chair as Lori sat down behind her desk.

"First of all, I want to thank you so much for allowing me to stay here," she began.

Lori waved her hand dismissively and said, "That's what we're here for, Cynthia. You met the criteria, and we wanted to make sure you had a safe place to stay."

"We didn't have a lot of time to talk last night, but I wanted to find out about the class you offer in money management. I know you probably think that I don't know how to save money or how to budget, but I assure you that I do. It's just that this past year I got sick, and without health insurance, well…everything fell apart. I lost my apartment but was living with a friend, and as you know, that situation changed. Now, my confidence in how I manage my money has been shaken."

Lori smiled as she nodded in understanding. "You're very rare, and yet your story is very common. Probably much more common than you realize. Our goal is to provide a safe, *temporary* place for someone to be able to stay. Unfortunately, we have some that are not employed and do not intend to look for employment, therefore it makes it much more difficult. You can be involved in our budgeting classes even when you're no longer staying here."

"I want to look for a room that I can rent from someone. Do you have a list here?"

"I'm afraid not because we can't be seen as recommending a place. You can certainly look online or in a newspaper, but I urge you to approach with caution. If you don't know the person ahead of time you want to make sure of the terms of the agreement, the safety of the house or apartment, and the ability to have a lock on your door."

Standing, she nodded and said, "I'll start looking tonight online."

"I think you should be able to find something," Lori said. "Certainly much easier than those who have children with them."

"Yes, I had breakfast with one of the families this morning. The woman and man with the toddler and little preschool girl who was so cute."

Lori's brow crinkled, and she asked, "I know the woman you're talking about, but there's no man here with her. She's divorced and was left with nothing right now."

Blinking in surprise, Cynthia said, "Oh, I thought the man was with her. The really big man with the beard and long hair who was serving at breakfast."

Lori's confused expression eased into a big smile.

"No, that's Zeke. He's always helping out with breakfast and is great with kids."

Cynthia stood and offered her goodbyes, walking back out into the lobby of the shelter. As she jogged up the stairs toward the women's wing, she could not deny that she was glad to find out that the man who had captured her attention was single. As she entered her room, she gave herself a little shake, thinking that the last thing on her mind should be a man. Right now... first up...finding a place to live.

6

The next morning dawned sunny and bright, and Zeke felt an extra bounce in his step at the idea that he might see the young woman again at breakfast. He hated that things ended on an awkward note between them the day before and hoped that today might be different.

He had decided on French toast, then realized his error since he would constantly be in the kitchen manning the griddle. He was just kicking himself when he heard a soft voice behind him.

"Good morning. Is there anything I can do to help?"

Jerking his head around, his gaze landed on the woman he had just been thinking about. Her blonde hair was pulled back into a neat bun at the back of her head. Wearing jeans and a t-shirt, she appeared youthful, but her blue eyes staring up at him held wisdom. He blinked for a second, thinking of Miss Ethel's eyes—the similarity was surprising.

As she smiled at him, he grinned like a teenager meeting the homecoming queen and rushed to greet,

"Good morning to you, too. I'd love some help." Now excited at the thought that he would be able to talk with her while they worked side-by-side, he was suddenly tongue-tied at what to say.

"My name is Cynthia, by the way," she said as she tied an apron around her waist.

The one-size-fits-all apron dwarfed her, but he thought she looked adorable. Her beauty was simple but astounding. She managed to be cute as hell and drop-dead gorgeous all at the same time.

He just stared, struck dumb, until she cocked her head to the side and asked, "And you are?"

Blinking, he jerked and said, "Zeke. Sorry...my name is Zeke."

"Zeke," she repeated. "I don't think I've ever known anyone named Zeke."

He turned back toward the griddle, flipping the French toast, and mumbled, "It's short for Ezekiel." He felt her presence as she stepped closer, her hand gently on his arm.

"I like it. It's different," she said.

Twisting his head to look down at her, he grinned. It was the first time he could remember someone saying that they liked his name since he landed at Miss Ethel's. She seemed to be much happier today, and he hoped that whatever had bothered her yesterday had passed. "I'm glad you came to help out today," he said.

She glanced around at the kitchen and said, "You can put me to work. I'm sure you're very busy. Just tell me what I need to do."

"Oh, that's not what I meant," he said in haste. "I just meant that I was hoping I got a chance to see you again."

She smiled up at him, her eyes warm as they held his. "I was hoping to also." A delicate blush crossed her face, and she said, "I know that yesterday you were very friendly toward me, and I rushed out without really saying goodbye. I'm afraid I made the mistake of thinking that you were with the woman who had the children…that they were your children."

His eyebrows lifted in surprise, and he said, "Oh, I see. You thought I was ignoring my wife to flirt with you?"

Blushing deeper, she shook her head and said, "Please forgive me. I shouldn't have made any assumptions."

Chuckling, he assured, "No worries. You don't owe me an apology. But," cocking his head to the side, "if you do feel like you slighted me, you can make it up by having breakfast with me this morning."

"I'd love to," she said, "as long as I can catch the seven-thirty bus that stops in front of the shelter."

"We can easily do that. Tell you what, if you keep flipping the French toast, I'll take the trays of eggs out."

She reached over, took the spatula from his hand, and gave them a quick flip. Laughing, she said, "That I can do."

For the next thirty minutes, they talked little as they worked side-by-side. Once the crowd had slowed, he grabbed two plates. Filling them both with French toast, butter, and syrup, then tossing on a couple of pieces of bacon and scrambled egg, he turned toward her.

Her eyes widened, and she stared at the two plates. "Are you going to eat all of that?"

"No. One is for you."

Shaking her head back and forth, she said, "I can't eat that much!"

Jerking his head toward the table, he said, "Come on. Let's go have a seat, and what you don't eat, I'm sure I can put away."

With the plates in his hands, he led her over to one of the empty tables, wanting to have her company all to himself. Setting both plates down, he then turned and grabbed the back of the chair, holding it for her.

"I don't remember the last time a man held a chair for me," she said.

Shrugging, he said, "My mom drilled manners into my brothers and me. I try to be careful because I know some people seem to be offended by them, but they're just second nature to me. I hope you're not offended."

She looked up at him once settled in her seat and smiled. "I don't think that good manners ever go out of style."

Sitting in the chair next to her, he grinned. "I agree, Cynthia," he said, liking the sound of her name.

For the next several minutes, they were silent as they ate their breakfast. After only eating half of what was on her plate, she leaned back, pushing the plate away. "I can't eat another bite," she exclaimed.

He gave her a stern look and said, "You're a little thing. You need to eat more."

"I like to eat, I just can't seem to eat a lot at one time." She reached out her hand and moved her plate closer to him. "You certainly don't have to eat anything, but you're more than welcome to it if you'd like."

By then, he had finished his breakfast and slid her plate over, finishing the extra piece of French toast she had been unable to eat.

"The food is really good," she said.

"Thanks. I like to cook. Another thing my mom taught me."

She looked at the clock on the wall and sighed. "I'm afraid I'm going to have to go to work now. Thank you for eating with me."

"Where do you work?" he managed to get out between bites, hating that she had to leave.

Looking down, she said, "I'm afraid it's nothing very glamorous. I'm a housekeeper at the Prince Hotel."

She stood, and he jumped to his feet as well. He looked down as she stuck out her hand, her gaze looking up at him expectantly. He hesitated for only a few seconds before wrapping his hand around hers.

"It's been nice getting to meet you, Zeke. I really enjoyed our breakfast."

He wanted to hold onto her, loving the feel of her hand in his. He wanted to tell her to skip work and spend the day with him. He wanted to ask questions about her life and find out how she ended up at the homeless shelter. But he knew she needed to go, and he could not think of how to ask the questions bouncing around his mind without sounding intrusive. Instead, he simply held her hand and smiled. "The pleasure has been all mine. I hope I see you again tomorrow."

Her shoulders slumped as she admitted, "I'm sure I'll

be here. I'm trying to find a room to rent, but I also want to be cautious."

Concern slashed through him, and he said, "You can't just take any room. That's not safe for a woman. Actually, it's not safe for anyone."

She nodded her agreement. "I know. But a room is all I can afford right now. There are a lot listed in the want ads and online, but I've just started sifting through them."

He opened his mouth to protest once more, but she slid her hand from his and said, "I really do have to go. I can't afford to be late to work."

With that, she turned and walked out of the dining hall, leaving him staring after her. He picked up their plates and walked to the kitchen, handing them to the crew of volunteers who were cleaning up after breakfast. His mind swirled with thoughts of her, and he wondered if he could come back that evening, perhaps to see her again. After all, waiting until tomorrow morning seemed too long.

---

Once again, Carlos gave Cynthia the executive suites to clean, but she was glad to see that Lucy would be sharing the floor of regular rooms. Looking over at Lucy as they rode up in the elevator, she said, "Hopefully, I didn't have anybody too nasty spend the night there so we can get through on time today."

As Lucy pushed her cart off the elevator on to her

floor, she gave Cynthia thumbs up, calling out, "We can hope!"

Rolling her cart down the hall of the top floor, she noted two of the doors had breakfast trays sitting out in the hall. Glad that the guests had already taken care of that, she pulled out her list to see who had checked out. Some guests stay until the last moment, not checking out until eleven AM, making it difficult to get the room cleaned and ready to turn over to a new guest by three PM. She found most people traveling for business had early flights to catch and would check out by breakfast.

Going to the first room that needed to be cleaned, she knew it would take extra time since it was a two-bedroom suite. Using her passkey, she stepped inside, and after a quick glance, breathed a sigh of relief. The room was clean, other than some trash in the trashcan and the beds obviously needing to be changed. A look into the bathroom showed her that they had already piled the soiled linens in the corner.

*Perfect!* It would be nice to think that all guests of the hotel would be so considerate. She often wondered if the messiest people were the same way in their own homes or if they simply chose to be completely lazy when staying somewhere else.

For the next three hours, she scrubbed bathrooms, mopped tiles, changed linens, dusted, and vacuumed. She made sure the coffee station was set up and all the toiletries lined up perfectly in the bathroom. She found several items that were left behind, so she tagged and placed them into a basket on her cart to be given to Carlos...sunglasses, an umbrella, and a book.

At the end of her shift, Carlos would take the items from each of the housekeepers and note them in his computer.

She was almost finished with her executive suites by lunch and headed back to the employee locker room to meet with the others. Lucy looked askance at Cynthia's cheese crackers and water, but it was Belinda who jumped in and said, "That can't be all you're eating!"

"Actually, I'm fine," she said. "I had a huge breakfast this morning." She looked back down at the table, avoiding their gazes, but she knew her face was turning red from the heat she could feel radiating from her cheeks. She should have known she could not hide anything.

"Well?"

Her gaze jumped up to Susan, finding her friend staring at her with unabashed curiosity. A quick glance around the table showed that Lucy and Belinda were equally as attentive. Smoothing her hand over her already neat hair, she said, "What? I just said I had a big breakfast."

"Girl, nobody blushes like that when they talk about food. They might get a dreamy look on their face if they had something really good to eat, or a miserable look on their face if they haven't had enough to eat. But nobody blushes when they talk about breakfast. Unless there was something else that happened at breakfast that made them blush, and I don't think that would be food!"

"It's nothing really," she protested. "I just met a really nice man, and we sat together and chatted, that's all."

After the words left her mouth, the silence around

the table was deafening. Sucking in her lips, she looked around at her friends.

Lucy's face softened, and she said, "Oh, honey, I know you're lonely, but meeting someone at the homeless shelter?"

Her spine stiffened, and she said, "It's not like I'm dating him! We just had breakfast and talked, that's all!"

"That may be all," Belinda began, "but from the look on your face, you really liked it."

Shoulders now slumping, she asked, "What's wrong with that? He was a nice man."

Lucy reached over the top of the table and wrapped her hand around Cynthia's. Giving a squeeze of support, she said, "Honey, right now you're so busy trying to keep your head above water that the last thing you need is some man—who may be a really nice man— dragging you down as he gets his life together."

Cynthia opened her mouth to protest again, but Lucy got there first. "I'm just saying, think about it. If he's at the homeless shelter that means his life situation right now is such that he's got a lot he's got to get straight before he'd be ready to take care of any woman, even an independent woman like yourself."

Cynthia lost all the steel in her spine as she slumped back in her chair. She was barely aware of Lucy squeezing her hand again as she slowly shook her head. "You're right, neither one of us are in a good place in our lives right now. It was just nice for a few minutes to pretend that my world wasn't crazy, and I was having breakfast with a handsome man who seemed to care."

"Oh, Cynthia, there's nothing wrong with enjoying

someone's company, especially if they're handsome and sweet," Belinda said, her eyes full of sympathy.

Her shoulders lifted then drooped in a shrug, and she said, "I know. But between work, holding back the creditors from the hospital, and finding a room to rent, I don't have time for anything else."

The women finished their lunch and moved back to their respective floors, but Cynthia found herself only going through the motions. Scrubbing toilets, vacuuming carpets, picking up the trash, changing linens. Cleaning up after other people. The same thing over and over, day in and day out.

## 7

Zeke stood in the kitchen of his house, looking around at the space. He had bought the small two-story, two-bedroom house in a neighborhood that was beginning to see renewal. He probably would have passed it up, but Cael had convinced him it was perfect. The house itself was in great condition, and with the help of his brothers, he had added on to the back, expanding the kitchen and creating a large den on the first floor and a master suite on the second. He had almost doubled the floor space, making the home perfect for resale or continuing to live in.

He had never worked construction, but the time spent with his brothers as they completed his house and helping them with theirs had been a great chance to continue their bond, plus see that they were each in homes they cared about.

Sipping his coffee as he leaned his hip against the counter, he thought about the two spare bedrooms upstairs. One he used as both an office and a home gym, and the other was set up like a guestroom. He snorted, thinking that he had never had a guest stay there. But there was a double bed, a dresser, and a comfy chair in the corner with a floor lamp nearby, perfect for someone to curl up and read.

He closed his eyes and could see Cynthia in that chair, her long blonde hair out of the braid waving about her shoulders. She would be lounging in something comfortable, a book in her lap as she relaxed. Jerking his eyes open, he wondered why that image had slammed into him.

Shaking his head slowly, wondering if he was crazy, the idea of asking her if she would like to rent that room from him moved through his mind. *No, that would be crazy. It's too soon. But, maybe...just maybe, there's an alternative.*

The idea was ludicrous, but, as with so many ideas, once it took root, it began to grow. He downed the rest of his coffee, rinsed out his cup, and left it in the dryer rack. Grabbing his phone and wallet from the counter, he snagged his keys and headed out the door. He had no idea if he would bring his idea up to her, but he could not wait to see her again.

---

Zeke kept an eye on the clock in the dining hall, wondering if he should say anything to Cynthia. Like the previous two days, she showed at breakfast, jumped in to help, and now he was once again enjoying her company as they finished eating. She had not even asked, but when she finished her breakfast, she slid her plate closer to him, and he had no problem polishing it off.

They had chatted easily, not broaching any heavy subjects, but he found he could listen to her talk about the weather with as much interest as he would listen to most people talk about a huge event in their lives. Finally, afraid that she had lost track of time and not wanting her to be late for work, he said, "I hate to bring it up, but don't you have to leave for work soon?"

She smiled widely, and he felt that beam straight through to his heart. Her mouth was moving, but he heard no words, his entire being focused on the energy that seemed to be radiating from her. She reached out and touched his arm, and he jolted. Glad that his beard hid most of his blush, he said, "I'm sorry, what did you say?"

She laughed and said, "I just said that I don't have to go to work today. It's my day off. Instead, I'm going to be catching the bus around to different places in the city to check out rooms to rent."

Eyes wide, he said, "Have you narrowed the list down?"

Nodding, she said, "I have to be able to catch a bus to get to work and that knocks out a lot of the outer neighborhoods. So, I took the bus routes and compared them to the people that were looking to rent rooms. Then I narrowed it even more." She crinkled her nose as she added, "I really don't like cigarette smoke, so when someone advertised that they did not mind having a smoker, my assumption was the place was going to smell like cigarettes, so I crossed them off. I sent messages to several of them and had six who responded, so I'm going to check them out today."

He hesitated, wanting to tell her that he knew of a room but held back, afraid of scaring her away. Instead, he asked, "How would you like company? I mean, I know you don't know me very well, but I can go along for a second opinion…or protection…or for…uh…"

"How about just as a companion?" she asked, her smile wide again.

"Yeah, that sounds perfect." He couldn't believe she agreed to let him tag along, but he was thrilled. The chance to spend the day with her was more than he expected.

Her brows lowered as she nibbled on her bottom lip, then asked, "But what about work? I hate for you to spend the day traipsing around the city with me when you should probably be working."

He had not told her that he owned a business, just that he had a job. Somehow, it had seemed like bragging, and he did not want to say anything to make her feel self-conscious. "No worries, it's my day off, too."

Her smile once again beamed toward him. Pushing his chair back, he gathered their plates and said, "Let's go."

They exited the shelter, and she started toward the bus stop. He reached out and placed his hand on her arm and said, "We can take my truck."

"You have a truck?"

Nodding, he added, "It's nothing fancy, but it'll get us there."

"I can pay you for gas—"

He brushed her words aside as they came to a stop next to his truck. He wished he had taken time to clean it, but she seemed thrilled to climb up into the passenger side. Closing the door with an order for her to buckle up, he rounded the front. Starting the engine, he pulled away from the sidewalk, and with a glance toward her, he thought she looked perfect sitting next to him.

Cynthia had woken that morning with both a sense of dread and excitement at looking for a room to rent. Excitement, because she wanted to be independent. But dread, because she knew she would miss seeing Zeke, even though she had only met him a few days before. Now, sitting in his truck, the thought of spending the day with him felt almost like a date. She knew that was foolish…he was just being friendly, but it had been a long time since she had had anything close to resembling a date.

He handled his truck with ease as they moved through traffic, and she gave him the directions to the first place on her list. "I know the first one isn't in a great neighborhood, but when I talked to the girl, she said that she always felt safe."

Zeke only grunted as they drove down a street that housed brick buildings, garbage cans stacked along the sidewalk, and rusted railings on the stairs. He parked along the sidewalk, and she peered out of her window toward the building.

Zeke got out of the truck, opened her door, and assisted her down, saying, "Stay right with me."

Looking up at him, she said, "Zeke, if I live here, I'll be coming and going by myself."

He only grunted again, and she assumed that meant he was not giving it his seal of approval yet. They walked up the steps together and pressed the security button.

"Yeah?"

"I'm Cynthia, here to see the room."

"Oh, yeah. Come on up. Apartment twenty-three, second floor."

Pushing open the front door, Zeke held it for her, and they moved into the dimly-lit hallway. The elevator had a sign on it declaring it out of order, and he grunted again as they walked up the stairwell. Sighing, she was so far unimpressed.

Knocking on the door, they only had to wait a moment before it was thrown open and a woman was standing inside. Her gaze went from Cynthia up to Zeke, and she said, "This room is only for a single person."

"Oh, I know. This is my friend who is looking at places with me."

The woman stepped back, and Cynthia and Zeke walked into the living room. The tenant appeared to be in her early thirties, bleached blonde hair, and it appeared she had not washed her makeup off before going to bed the previous night if her raccoon-mascara eyes were any indication. Cynthia glanced around, pleased that the area was neat, although small. Turning around, she observed the woman's eyes glued to Zeke, drinking him in as though he was the last lemonade on a hot summer day.

"Although," the woman said, walking closer to him, "we're all adults. I would have no problem with a *friend* coming to visit." Sticking out her hand toward Zeke, she said, "I'm Rita, by the way."

Bristling, Cynthia said, "May I please see the bedroom now?" She heard the strident tone in her voice but forced a smile on her face. She could not believe jealousy was an emotion passing through her when she had only known him a few days. Sucking in a deep breath, she let it out slowly as she followed the woman out of the living room.

"Kitchen's on the right, my bedroom is next, and the bathroom's across the hall. Here's the room. It's a little small. I think it was probably used as a nursery or child's bedroom."

Cynthia stepped in, blinking at the tiny size. The room held a twin size bed and a small chest of drawers. She opened the only other door and peered into a minuscule closet. Heart sinking, she knew the price fit her budget, but the room was way too small. Doable if absolutely necessary, but only if she could not find anything else.

She turned around and slammed into Zeke, not having heard him walk in behind her. He reached out and steadied her, his hands resting on her upper arms.

His voice low, he said, "This place is too fuckin' small."

She nodded, sucking in her lips, disappointment snaking through her. "I'll keep it on my list in case I can't find anything else." She could have sworn she had seen displeasure move through his eyes but decided it must have been her imagination. Forcing a smile onto her face again, she said, "We have others to look at."

They walked back out into the living room where she thanked the woman and said that she would let her know soon. The woman barely gave her a glance, her eyes focused entirely on Zeke.

Cynthia could not help but grin as Zeke put his arm around her, pulled her in close, and led her out of the apartment.

Once back in his truck, she sighed, and Zeke turned to look toward her. "I suppose I could make that work if I don't find anything else better—"

"Cynthia, no. That room would've made a kid's room only. There's no way you would have been comfortable there."

"I just need a room, Zeke. I mean, it would be nice to have something that was bigger and nicer, but I can't completely cross it off my list just because the room was small." Under her breath, she mumbled, "Or because *Rita* looked man hungry."

Barking out a laugh, Zeke offered a visible shiver, causing her to laugh as well. Giving him the directions to the next place, she settled back in the seat, enjoying the ride as well as the driver.

The next apartment appeared to be in a better

section of town, and Cynthia's hopes were high as they got off the elevator and knocked on the door. This time, a young woman answered, her smile bright.

"Hi, nice to meet you. Come on in."

As soon she and Zeke stepped across the threshold, the odor of cigarette smoke hit her, and her eyes began to water. She took a step back, running into Zeke's body, and his arms settled on her shoulders, offering a comforting squeeze.

Before she had a chance to speak, Zeke rumbled, "Your ad doesn't mention anything about smoking."

The young woman blinked, and said, "Oh, I don't smoke. It's my boyfriend."

"Your ad doesn't mention anything about someone else living here besides you," Zeke continued.

Cynthia elbowed him in the ribs, hearing a slight 'umph' leave his lips before she said, "I'm sorry, but I'm afraid the smoking just won't work for me."

The woman huffed and said, "Don't you even want to see the room? I mean, my boyfriend isn't here all the time."

"Thank you, but no. Good luck with finding someone to take the room." The words had barely left her mouth before Zeke was moving backward, pulling her with him. Once they made it back outside, he led her directly to his truck, threw open the passenger door, and began digging around in his glove compartment. He pulled out a small box of Kleenex and handed it to her.

"I wish I had some eye drops or something for you,"

he said, bending to watch as she dabbed her watering eyes.

Shaking her head, she said, "I'll be fine. It'll just take a few minutes for my eyes to clear." She sighed once again and said, "This is going to be a lot harder than I thought."

After they climbed back into his truck, he asked, "Have you ever had to share an apartment with strangers before?"

She stared out of the windshield for a moment, then said, "No. I've lived with friends, but I haven't had to do this before." She twisted around to look at him and said, "I know beggars can't be choosers, but I don't want to make a mistake. I'd like to find a place where I can live for a while and not just a friend's couch to sleep on."

She felt the sting of tears hit her eyes and hoped that it was disguised behind the cigarette irritation.

"How about a break for a cup of coffee?" he asked.

His voice was soft and gentle, soothing over her, and she had a feeling she had not been successful in hiding her emotions. Nodding slowly, she smiled. "Sounds good. We'll have a little break and keep searching."

8

Zeke found a small coffee shop several blocks away and parked outside. Soon, he and Cynthia were ensconced at a small booth in the corner, sipping a cup of coffee and sharing a cinnamon bun.

He knew they had only been to two places but could feel her disappointment. The desire to comfort her was strong, but he felt like he needed to know her more before he could understand what she needed.

She had grown quiet, almost contemplative, and he hated to break into her musings but rushed ahead before he lost his nerve. "Tell me about yourself," he blurted. "Tell me how you ended up at the shelter." He winced as soon as the words left his mouth. *Smooth, Zeke, real smooth. Way to make her feel self-conscious.*

Her gaze jumped up to his, a look of fear passing through her eyes, followed by resignation. She sucked in her lips as she appeared to consider what she wanted to expose. He wanted to pull the words back but had no idea how to do so without making the moment more awkward.

"Have you ever wondered how things can just seem to keep going wrong?" she began.

Her words had described his life before he ended up with Miss Ethel, so he nodded his understanding.

She looked back down and began fiddling with her coffee cup, and he gave that time to her, knowing whatever her story was, she needed to pull her thoughts together. Finally, looking back up, she said, "I had great parents. I was an only child, but my parents and I were happy. School was fun. I had piano lessons and dance classes. We would take vacations in the summer. And then one day, it all changed. I was ten years old when my mom was in a car accident and died. I was devastated, but my dad and I grew closer. Looking back, I know he wanted to do anything he could to help. I think that's why he remarried...thinking I needed a mother when, honestly, I really just needed him." She shrugged, before adding, "They hadn't even dated very long. But before I knew it, I had a stepmom and two stepsisters. Dad seemed so pleased, like he was giving me an instant family to take the place of Mom being gone."

"I take it that didn't turn out to be such a good thing," he said. Reaching across the table, he placed his hand on hers, pleased when she turned her palm up, and they linked fingers.

"I tried to make it a good thing," she said. "But it was evident from the beginning that I seemed to be the baggage that went along with my dad instead of a bonus."

"What do you mean?"

"Eileen never really warmed to me. She was always polite when my dad was around, but very sharp when he wasn't. Her two daughters, Marabelle and Sarabelle, took their cues from their mom. Sweet as sugar when Dad was around, mean as snakes when he wasn't."

Zeke blinked, uncertain that he had heard correctly. He knew what she was telling him was important, but a chuckle erupted that he was unable to hold back. "I'm sorry, Cynthia. I know this isn't funny, but are you seriously telling me that their names were Marabelle and Sarabelle?"

Her blue eyes danced, and a giggle slipped from her lips as well. Her smile was bright as she nodded her head, and he was glad she was not offended. "Yes, that's honest to God truth."

Shaking his head ruefully, he said, "No wonder they were mean."

She squeezed his fingers, her smile still bright. "Thank you for that, Zeke. I used to think the same thing but could never say it."

He was glad he gave that to her and waited to hear the rest of her tale.

She sighed once again and said, "Things were bearable for several years, then, when I was sixteen, my dad had a heart attack and died. It's not that he didn't care for Eileen, but even I could tell she never filled the void that my mom had left. Again, I often wondered if he married her just because he thought I needed a mom." Shrugging, she said, "With my dad gone, Eileen had no reason to pretend to like me anymore. I lived in the house but was expected to work. I got a job at a fast-food restaurant and worked until I graduated from high school. I mean, it wasn't like I was opposed to working. I'd always helped out with house-work and laundry, but somehow, I was expected to do the bulk of it for all of them. Marabelle and Sarabelle never had to. But I had a roof over my head and food in my stom-ach, so I figured this was just what I needed to do...at least that was what I was constantly told. On my eighteenth birthday, she informed me that I was no longer welcome and that since I was a legal adult, I was on my own."

"What a fuckin' bitch," Zeke breathed, hating that she had to endure that.

Her eyes sought his again, and she said, "It sucked because she was living in what had been my family home. The home where I had memories of both my mom and my dad, and now it was her home, and I was being kicked out."

"What did you do? Where did you go?"

"One of the ladies that worked at the restaurant with me took me in. I was only sleeping on her couch, but her family was nice. She was in the process of applying as a housekeeper for the Prince Hotel and encouraged me to apply as well. I did but had no idea if I would get the job. I went in for an interview, and the Head of Housekeeping was really nice. She ended up hiring us both. We have a new Head of Housekeeping now, and he's a good supervisor, also."

"And you've been working there ever since?"

Nodding, she said, "Yes. I've been working there for seven years."

He had not asked Cynthia her age but quickly calculated that she was close to twenty-five years old.

"Working for minimum wage was never going to allow me to have a place of my own, but I moved in with a friend. I bounced around for a couple of years, renting a room or a couch with one friend or another. I finally landed a room with a friend I had met at the hotel. She was nice, and I liked her boyfriend well enough. They had one bedroom, and I moved into the other one. I was finally in a place that felt a little bit more like my own."

She had grown quiet, and Zeke carefully observed as shadows moved through her eyes. He held his breath, various scenarios moving through his head, waiting to see what she would say next. Her eyes were focused on her coffee cup again, and he gave her hand a little squeeze.

She looked up, her lips curving in a tight smile that did not reach her eyes. "I ended up getting sick, and that's when everything fell apart."

Sucking in a quick breath, he said, "Oh, Cynthia, I'm so sorry."

"I'm fine now. At least it's not something that can come back," she said. "I was at work and began feeling ill. Abdominal pain, back pain, and nausea. I had no idea what was wrong until I was practically on the floor in tears. I didn't want to go to the hospital but had no choice. As it turns out, my appendix had ruptured, and I was rushed into emergency surgery."

He was glad when her fingers squeezed his back, not ready to lose their connection. "You had to miss work." His words were more than just stating the obvious but indicated he understood the financial implications of what she was saying.

"I missed two full weeks of work. They wanted me to miss more, but I convinced the doctor that I was ready to go back. Honestly, if it wasn't for Carlos and my coworkers, I would've been fired. I couldn't work a full shift, couldn't push my cart, could barely bend over and move. But everyone jumped in to help, and I managed to slowly get stronger without losing my job." She frowned, saying, "Without health insurance, the hospital bills wiped out my savings. The hospital social worker assisted me with the paperwork so that because of my low income some of the debt was dissolved, which helped. But I just couldn't afford the room I was renting anymore."

Brows lowering, he asked, "I thought she was your friend? She couldn't reduce your rent even for a little while until you caught back up?"

"I assumed the apartment was in their names, but actually it was only in her boyfriend's name. They had started having a lot of arguments, and at one point, I heard them arguing about me. He wanted his money and my friend was trying to tell him that I didn't have it. So," she shrugged, "he suggested an alternate form of payment."

It took several seconds for those words to penetrate Zeke's understanding, and when they did, his hand flexed in anger, and he realized he was squeezing her fingers. Releasing them, he found it difficult to drag air into his lungs when his entire body was vibrating with anger. Voice shaking as much as his body, he growled, "Let me get this straight. You're telling me that he was offering to let you stay there in exchange for sex?"

Her eyes held his, but her lips sucked in tightly, as though she were afraid to confirm his understanding.

"Am I getting that right, Cynthia?"

She jerked her head up and down, and he reached out, grabbing her hand again, this time careful to not squeeze.

"Zeke, it's over and done with. It was two weeks ago, they had a huge blowout fight, and they broke up. He kicked her out, and I had to get out, too. Not that I would've stayed there with him anyway!"

A shudder ran through her body, and he fought to keep from finding out the guy's name and tearing his head off. Uncertain he could speak at the moment, he remained quiet, letting her finish her story.

"My girlfriend ended up on somebody's couch, but they didn't have room for me. I pretty much bounced between couches, unable to afford anything. I didn't even have a car I could sleep in. I called the homeless shelter, and they said they'd let me know when they had an available bed. As soon as they did, I came in."

Snorting, she added, "Believe it or not, I actually got hold of my stepmom, told her my situation and asked if I could move back in with them until I got on my feet."

Thinking her story could not get any worse, he dropped his chin and shook his head. "Let me guess, she said no?"

"Bingo, you win the prize," Cynthia quipped, but he could hear the pain behind her attempt at levity. Lifting her hand to tuck a strand of hair behind her ear, she said, "That was it for me. I decided no more contact with Eileen and the two 'belles.'"

Zeke fought to keep from snorting, holding her attention instead.

"They took everything they could from me. My parents' house. Their money. I managed to make it out with a pair of diamond earrings that belonged to my mother."

"They can't take your memories, babe," he said softly and was immediately rewarded with her gentle smile.

"You're right. I have those." Her eyes brightened and she exclaimed, "My mother used to read poetry to me. Anne Bronte wrote, 'Well, let them seize on all they can, One treasure still is mine, A heart that loves to think on thee, And feels the worth of thine.'"

He sucked in a hasty breath hearing her quote poetry. He longed to share Miss Ethel's gift but remained quiet. This needed to be about Cynthia, not him. They finished their coffee and the cinnamon bun, and he said the only words he could think of, hating how pathetic they were. "I'm so sorry, babe."

Her eyes met his once again, and she shrugged, "Most of us never realize we are only one disaster away from being in serious financial difficulty. But I've got a steady job, even if it doesn't pay much. I've saved up just enough that I should be able to rent a room from someone if we can find somebody trustworthy. I know

I'm going to make it if I can just get a couple of lucky breaks."

Standing, Zeke held out his hand and assisted her to her feet. They made their way back to the truck, and once again she gave him directions. He knew how much she wanted to be able to find a room to rent, but he could not help but hope that they did not find one today.

*Maybe, just maybe, I can be her lucky break.*

---

Cynthia sighed heavily. Two hours later, she had crossed off two more possibilities from her list. The first room they checked out after their coffee break was in a house that resembled a frat house near a college campus. Empty beer cans were stacked on the windowsills, and the distinct odor of pot wafted from one of the bedrooms. She could tell Zeke bristled as soon one of the young men who was also renting a room walked in, gave her head to toe scan, then never took his eyes off her breasts.

The next one seemed to have possibilities. A house in a nice neighborhood set back slightly from the road. When they went inside, they met the owners of the house, an attractive, middle-aged couple. They showed her the bedroom, and she became excited. It was a decent size, fully furnished, and while the rent was at the upper level of what she felt she could pay, she was willing to forgo any extras in her life to make this work.

Afraid to let someone else come in and rent the

room before her, she was almost ready to sign a contract when the wife said, "We are very sociable, and do host quite a few parties. I hope that won't be a problem."

Cynthia thought it was a strange thing to mention and was about ready to say that parties did not bother her when Zeke's body stiffened next to her, and he asked, "What kind of parties?"

She twisted her head around to look up at him, bugging her eyes out, hoping to indicate that she did not want him to interfere with her getting the room.

"We have a very open marriage," the woman said, "and socialize with other couples that are like-minded."

Swinging her head back around to the couple, her mouth dropped open, uncertainty moving through her. "Uh…open?"

The lady laughed and said, "We don't believe in monogamy. Please understand that we would never force our lifestyle on anyone else, certainly not someone who is staying with us. But our lifestyle is very freeing, and you might feel that the two of you would enjoy that as well."

If she thought Zeke had growled at the frat house, she could not begin to describe the sound that emitted from deep within his chest as he grabbed her hand and pulled her toward the front door. Halfway down the front walk toward his truck, she managed to get out, "Zeke! Slow down!"

He rounded on her, his face tight with anger, and said, "This is ridiculous! You can't stay in any of these places!"

He gently assisted her into his truck, then slammed the door as he stomped around the front. She noticed that even when he was angry, he still treated her with care.

Once inside, he sat with his hands on the steering wheel, his knuckles white as he gripped tightly. She reached over, placed her hand on his, and said, "This is just the first day. I had one more to visit, but why don't we just stop for today?"

He looked toward her and said, "I'm sorry, Cynthia. I want you to have your space, but I'm just not willing to compromise your safety for that."

She knew what it was like to have people care… Carlos, Lucy, Belinda, Susan. But it was still nice to have this wonderful man watching out for her. He started up the truck, pulled out of the drive, and asked for the next directions. "Are you sure?" she asked. Receiving his nod, she gave him the directions for the last one she wanted to check out that day.

As they pulled up to the darling bungalow in a pleasant neighborhood, she tried not to get her hopes up. Ringing the doorbell, an elderly woman appeared, her smile wide as she looked up at Cynthia and Zeke.

"Oh, my! You must be the sweet girl who called about renting my extra room."

"Yes, ma'am. I'm Cynthia Ellison, and this is my friend Zeke."

"Come in, come in! I'm Bernadine Johnson."

Stepping into the small living room, Cynthia's first thought was that it was as quaint as a picture in a fairy-tale book. Before she had a chance to look around further, she sneezed. And sneezed. And sneezed. Still having some of Zeke's tissues in her purse, she grabbed one and held it to her nose.

"Oh, I hope you aren't allergic to my little dears," Bernadine said.

Stepping further into the room, Cynthia was able to count four cats sleeping on the sofa and chairs. Sneezing again, she watched as two more cats walked down the back hall toward her.

"Would you like to see the room now?" Bernadine asked. "It only has a twin-sized bed, but that still accommodates a few of the cats who will probably sleep at your feet."

Sneezing once more, she wanted to cry. "Thank you, but no, Ms. Johnson." She sneezed. "I'm usually good with one, but I'm afraid the whole group of them is too much for me."

Bernadine's face fell, and she said, "I probably should put that in my advertisement, shouldn't I?"

Trying to offer a sympathetic smile in between fits of sneezing, Cynthia said her goodbyes as Zeke wrapped his arm around her and led her out of the house. This time, neither spoke, and she was grateful. All she wanted to do was go back to the homeless shelter, take a shower, and have a good cry.

## 9

Zeke knew that Cynthia was disheartened. She continued to sniffle, and he was not sure if it was from tears or from the cats. He could tell she had been excited when she first saw Ms. Johnson's bungalow, but with that many cats, it would never work.

She did not seem to pay attention to where he was driving, for which he was glad. He parked outside of Grimm's and glanced over to see her dab her eyes and blow her nose before she leaned forward and peered out of the front windshield. Her face scrunched as she looked at him and asked, "Where are we?"

"Come on," he said. "Let's get something to eat." He felt sure that she must be hungry, and for himself, he wanted a little fortification for the proposal he hoped to make that afternoon.

"I haven't been to a restaurant in a long time," she admitted. "Are you sure this place is safe?"

He chuckled and said, "I assure you Grimm's is completely safe."

Leaving her to ponder his declaration, he walked around the front of the truck and pulled open the passenger door. He could still see the doubt on her face, and as he lifted his hand to her, palm up, he asked, "Do you trust me?" He watched as a flash of doubt moved through her eyes and then was quickly gone. She placed her hand in his as her answer, and he assisted her down from his truck. With his hand still firmly wrapped around hers, he escorted her inside.

She stumbled slightly when they entered, and he knew it would take a moment for her eyes to adjust to the dim interior.

A voice from the back called out, "Hey, Zeke!"

"Hey, Lynn." The woman came closer, and he continued, "I'd like you to meet my friend, Cynthia."

He watched as Lynn's face brightened into a wide smile as she took in Cynthia. Glancing down, he saw her face smile in return.

"Nice to meet a friend of Zeke's!" Lynn said.

"Thank you," Cynthia said.

"You here to work or eat?" Lynn asked.

"We're here to eat," he answered. "Can you get us some wings?"

"Sure thing, boss," Lynn said easily. "What you want to drink?"

He looked down at Cynthia, who turned her wide-eyed gaze up to his. She whispered, "Um…just soda." He nodded and called out, "Two Pepsis."

Lynn headed to the bar, and he escorted Cynthia to a table on the side. There was not a large lunch crowd, but he was glad to see people were coming in. As they sat down, Cynthia's face held confusion and she cocked her head to the side, asking, "She asked if you are working? And then she called you 'boss'?"

Sighing, he had hoped to start their conversation a little slower but wanted her to have his honesty. "This place was owned by my oldest brother. When he got out of the service, he bought this old building, and, with the help of some of my other brothers, turned it into a bar. Soon after, I got out of the service and didn't know what I wanted to do. Zander helped me by giving me a job here. I was a bouncer for a couple of years."

"And now?" she asked. When he hesitated, she continued, "I have a feeling there's a lot more to you than meets the eye, Zeke Kemp."

Self-conscious, he shrugged and said, "I was a cook in the Army. After working here for a while, I thought that Zander should be serving food. Simple food, not like a full restaurant. But I kept bugging him, and we finally were able to get the building next door and turn that into the kitchen."

"So you're a cook here at Grimm's?"

Nodding, he said, "Yes." He squirmed in his seat, knowing that he was not offering full disclosure. Forcing his gaze to stay on hers, he added, "The truth is that Zander and I are now partners. I'm a co-owner of Grimm's."

She jerked slightly, her eyes widening, and he was uncertain what she thought of his revelation. A wide smile moved across her face, and he felt the air rush from his lungs.

"Oh, my goodness," she exclaimed, reaching over and

placing her hand on his arm. "That's amazing!" Then, slowly, her brow furrowed, and she asked, "But why do you live at the shelter?"

"Cynthia," he sighed heavily, his slight subterfuge weighing heavily. "I haven't been completely forthcoming with you. I don't live at the homeless shelter. I volunteer there."

Her brow scrunched even further, and her head shook slightly back and forth as she said, "I...I don't understand."

"Another brother of mine, Asher, worked to get the grants to assist the homeless shelter. I started volunteering there from the beginning, cooking some of their meals before I would come work here as a bouncer in the evenings. Even when I became a partner at Grimm's and opened the kitchen here, I kept going to the homeless shelter for the breakfast service." Shrugging, he added, "It just means a lot to me."

Her mouth opened and closed several times, but nothing came out, so he continued, "It never occurred to me when we first met that you assumed I was a resident. I would never want to do or say anything that made you feel self-conscious. Everybody has their reasons for ending up in a shelter, and no one should be judged for it. I was afraid that you'd think I was holding myself above you if I said anything."

"But didn't you think I'd find out eventually?" she asked, her hands nervously rolling a paper napkin into a small ball.

He stilled her hand, keeping his fingers wrapped around hers when he said, "Cynthia, I didn't expect us to become friends. I didn't think I'd ever see you again, although I hoped I would. I'm truly sorry for not telling you sooner."

He held his breath, his chest tight as he waited to see her reaction as she digested the information he had given.

Her blue eyes lifted to his, and she offered a slight smile. "There's really nothing to forgive, Zeke. I'm the one who made assumptions." She laughed as he leaned heavily back in his chair, his relief evident. "How ridiculous would I be if I was upset that you have a job and a place to live?"

With perfect timing, Lynn walked over and placed a large platter of wings between them, giving them two smaller saucers. She set several bowls of sauces on the table as well. "I know the boss is one of the few men who doesn't try to prove their manhood by eating the spiciest, hottest wings. But I wasn't sure about you."

Smiling up at Lynn, Cynthia said, "I can't handle spicy, either."

"Well, good, then you'll like everything I've got here."

"Yes," Cynthia said, her eyes now holding Zeke's, "I will,"

Heart lighter, he grinned as he forked wings over onto her saucer, serving her first.

---

Cynthia had relaxed during lunch, finding the wings delicious and the company delightful. She wanted to know more about the brothers he mentioned but hesitated, wanting him to share when he was ready. As the meal came to a close, her heart felt heavy, knowing that she had not found a room to rent.

Her fingers were sticky from the sauce on the wings, and she excused herself to go to the ladies' room. Washing her hands, she stared into the mirror and could not help but wonder what it must be like to run a successful business. Zeke had mentioned that he did not live at the shelter, but he did not mention his home. Grinning, she imagined a bachelor pad apartment somewhere. As soon as that thought moved through her mind, she wondered about the dates he probably went on that ended up there. She could hardly blame him; after all, women must throw themselves at him. Sighing, she closed her eyes and gave her head a little shake. *He's being a good friend, that's all. It's ridiculous to feel jealousy when there's nothing to be jealous over.*

As she walked back into the bar, she observed him sliding his phone into his pocket, a smile playing about his lips. Curious, she simply said, "I guess it's time to call it a day. I'll do some more looking and see what other rental rooms I can check out."

He reached down and linked his fingers with hers again, and she could not deny the thrill she felt from the warmth of his hand.

"I've got somewhere I want to take you first," he said.

She cocked her head to the side, but that was all he said as he led her back out into the bright sunshine and over to his truck. A few minutes later, they drove into an older neighborhood, the houses neat and the yards trimmed. At the end of a cul-de-sac, there was a large two-story home, beautiful rose bushes all around the house, and a picket fence in the front.

"Who lives here?" she asked. Before he had a chance to reply, she saw an older woman step onto the front porch. Her hair was more white than gray, pulled back into a bun. She was thin with a soft pink dress adorning her body. But what Cynthia noticed most was the welcoming smile on the woman's face.

Still with no explanation, Zeke linked fingers with her again, and they walked toward the porch. The woman clapped her hands in glee, and Zeke let go of Cynthia's fingers long enough to wrap his arms around the woman, kissing her on her cheek.

"I was delighted to get your call!" the woman said. She turned her gaze then toward Cynthia, her smile even brighter.

"Miss Ethel, I'd like you to meet my friend, Cynthia. Cynthia, this is my mom, Miss Ethel."

She was immediately engulfed in the woman's hug as she said, "It's nice to meet you." She wondered why he called his mom Miss Ethel but did not ask. It was obvious true affection abounded between the two, so what he chose to call her was inconsequential.

Miss Ethel leaned back, still holding Cynthia's hands, and said, "I'm delighted to welcome you into my home. I understand from Zeke you've just had lunch, but I had put on some tea. Would you like some?"

Still full from lunch, she was never going to turn down such an offer and smiled. "I'd be delighted."

Miss Ethel led them into the living room, and once

Cynthia was seated on the comfortable sofa, Zeke said, "I'll help you with the tea tray."

The two of them left the room, and Cynthia, curiosity abounding, glanced around. From her position on the sofa, she could see some framed pictures on the bookshelves of a younger Miss Ethel, surrounded by young boys. *Oh, my, she had a lot of children.*

Miss Ethel walked back into the room, followed by Zeke, his hands full of a tray. She could not help but smile at the sight of the large, rough-looking Zeke holding the tray with the delicate cups.

He set it on the coffee table before sitting next to her on the sofa, and it did not escape her attention that he sat closely so that their legs were brushing together. Once Miss Ethel had poured the tea, they settled back, sipping appreciatively.

Zeke began, "I've mentioned my oldest brother, Zander, and another brother, Asher, but there were quite a few of us that lived here. I actually have many brothers."

She glanced to the side, but it was Miss Ethel who explained. "I was a foster mother. I began taking in boys after my husband passed away and felt like I had a possible use. I had a large house—"

"And a large heart," Zeke interrupted, his voice gentle.

Smiling her appreciation, Miss Ethel nodded and said, "Yes, I did have a heart with enough love for all my boys."

Cynthia wanted to know more but was uncertain

what to ask. She was grateful when Miss Ethel continued.

"Each of my boys came to me for special reasons, but we created our own family. I'm sure Zeke will tell you his story at some time, but suffice it to say that he was my very special helper in the kitchen."

Nodding, Zeke said, "I had never cooked anything in my life until I came here. Miss Ethel's food was so good that I was determined to find out how she did it. I learned from the best."

"Well, if those wings at Grimm's were any indication, I'd say you learned very well," she said.

"Oh, yes!" Miss Ethel agreed. "He uses my secret fried chicken recipe for his wings."

After several more minutes of lighter conversation, Zeke shared a look with Miss Ethel before turning to Cynthia. "Would you like to see the rest of the house?"

"Absolutely," she enthused, wanting to see more of where Zeke had grown up.

He gave her a tour of the downstairs, including the large dining room and kitchen. "Miss Ethel's bedroom is also down here," he said, and she peeked into a sunny bedroom filled with comfortable furniture and soft pastel colors.

"I'll show you upstairs," he said, linking fingers with her and leading her back toward the front of the house and up the stairs.

He opened doors and showed her the rooms where he and his brothers used to sleep, describing the bunk beds and how they read at night, discussing books.

Her heart began to ache as she thought of the

possible reasons that led Zeke to need a foster home, and yet viewing all around her was thrilled that he had been led to Miss Ethel.

Opening the last door, he showed her a bedroom with a single bed covered in a lovely floral bedspread and a light blue rug on the wooden floors. A chest of drawers stood against one wall near a comfortable chair and reading lamp. He indicated another door, leading into a small bathroom. "This room was used when she had someone temporary coming or maybe a young boy that had a lot of fright being around all of us. By the time I came, Zander was the oldest, and he moved in here so that he would have some privacy." Chuckling, he added, "Zander and I were very close, and I spent a lot of time in here as well."

She turned to face him, her feet directly in front of his, and reached down to grab his other hand. Holding them both tightly, she stared up into his face. "I'm so honored you showed me your home, Zeke," she said.

His eyes bored into hers as though trying to send a message that she was unable to receive.

Finally, he said, "I hope you like it, Cynthia. It's your new room."

Gasping, not understanding, she asked, "My...my room?"

He lifted their hands and pressed them between their chests, saying, "Miss Ethel has these rooms available. She doesn't foster anymore and doesn't rent them out because she doesn't need the money. They're basically for family and friends."

Her eyes tore from his, jerking around to gaze at the

beautiful room once again, immediately imagining herself here. Soft footsteps coming from behind Zeke had her looking toward the door, seeing Miss Ethel standing there.

"It's true, my dear," Miss Ethel said. "It seems ridiculous to have the rooms sit empty when someone could use them. Rosalie, before she became Zander's wife, stayed here for a bit. In fact, I often have my boys' women around. You would certainly have some visitors besides just keeping company with an old woman."

Giving her head a shake, still in shock, she rushed to say, "Oh, Miss Ethel, I would never consider you to be poor company! I'm...I just...well, I'm stunned!" Turning to face Miss Ethel fully, she asked, "Are you sure? You don't even know me. And Zeke only met me a couple of days ago."

Stepping closer, Miss Ethel assured, "I'm a good judge of character, Cynthia. And I raised my boys to also be good judges of character. The fact that you're here with Zeke tells me everything I need to know." Patting her arm, she said, "Avijeet Das once said, 'I meet people and they become chapters in my stories.' My dear, I'd like you to become a chapter in my story." Nodding toward Zeke, she added, "I'll let you two talk some more, but I truly hope you'll come to live with me. For a week, a month, or as long as you need, you'll be welcome." With that, she smiled toward both of them, turned, and walked back out of the room.

Before she had a chance to say anything else, Zeke said, "Think about it, Cynthia. You were going to rent a room from somebody that you did not know at all and didn't know you. How much better to be able to live with someone that you can trust?"

She nodded, then said, "I'd be an idiot to turn this down, Zeke, but I must insist that I pay something in rent."

Shrugging, he said, "You can take that up with Miss Ethel, but let's not worry about that now. The most important thing is getting you out of the shelter and into a home. Once you've caught up a little bit from the hospital bills, then we'll see."

He leaned forward, placing his lips on her forehead, kissing her lightly. She dragged in a shuddering breath as a tear slid down her face, gratitude coursing through her.

Zeke stared at the tear running down Cynthia's face and gave in to the desire to touch her soft skin. Cupping her face, he used his thumb to wipe away the tear, saying, "Please, don't cry."

She pinched her lips together, and he could see her strength as she pulled herself together. Giving a jerky nod, she said, "I feel so lucky."

"Everybody needs a little help at some time," he said. "And believe me, Miss Ethel will get as much out of this as you will."

By the time he escorted her back downstairs, he was grinning widely. Miss Ethel was waiting for them in the living room, and as soon as he announced that Cynthia would stay with her, Miss Ethel clapped her hands together, pulling Cynthia in for a hug. Having been the recipient of those hugs many times in his life, he knew the warmth that was offered.

Miss Ethel pulled back and asked, "When can you come? Can you come today?"

Cynthia swung her gaze back to Zeke, and he nodded. "No time like the present. I'll take you back to the shelter, and you can pack your bag, and we can come back here."

"I don't want to put you out," Cynthia said, her gaze back toward Miss Ethel.

"Oh, posh," Miss Ethel said, waving her hand dismissively. "The room is ready for an occupant, and fresh towels are hung in the bathroom. There's not a thing that I need to do."

He watched the smile spread across Cynthia's face as though her happiness was too much to be contained. Linking hands with her again, he said, "We'll head out now, and I'll bring her back later."

"No rush, take your time," Miss Ethel said.

Once they were back in his truck driving toward the shelter, he could feel Cynthia's nerves hitting again. Before giving her a chance to voice them, he said, "Stop worrying. Honestly, Miss Ethel would love the company. We all try to drop in and see her several times a week so she's never alone for long, but I know she's very excited to have you there."

Cynthia shook her head slowly and said, "This is like a dream come true. My morning started out as such a nightmare, and now it's all working out."

Laughing, he said, "You'll love Miss Ethel. She's the closest thing to a fairy godmother you'll ever meet!" It did not take long for them to make it back to the shelter, and Zeke walked into the director's office with Cynthia, listening as she gushed in her excitement.

Eyes wide, Ms. Fox said, "I know Miss Ethel. That will be a wonderful place for you to stay."

Cynthia reached across and took Ms. Fox's hand, saying, "Thank you so much for giving me a place to stay."

"That's what we're here for, Cynthia."

"I know Zeke comes and helps out with breakfast, and I don't know that I can do it all the time, but sometimes I'd like to come in and volunteer."

Her smile even wider, Ms. Fox said, "You're welcome anytime. We can use all the help we can get."

Walking back out, she looked at Zeke and said, "I don't think you're allowed in the women's wing—"

"No worries," he said, giving her hand a squeeze. "Go ahead and get your things, and I'll wait for you right here."

In fifteen minutes, she was back in the lobby, a suitcase in her hand and a stuffed backpack on her back. He was struck for an instant, remembering she looked very similar the first time he laid eyes on her a few days ago. *Could that have only been a few days ago?* It seemed like he had known her for so much longer.

Stepping forward quickly, he took the suitcase from her hand and pulled the backpack off her shoulders. She started to protest, but he said, "I know you can carry this, but when I'm with you, I'd like to do it."

He placed everything behind the seat in the truck, and as they started down the road, he said, "I know you're probably anxious to get settled, but I don't want our day together to end."

"I feel the same," she confessed.

Grinning in relief, he said, "Perfect. Then how about dinner? I've got something that I'd like to show you." Gaining her nod, he drove to a fast-food restaurant, ordered burgers, fries, and sodas, then headed to another part of town. He pulled into the parking lot of an old, brick building that did not appear to be occupied.

Grabbing the bag of food, he rounded the truck, assisted her down, and said, "Come on in."

Looking around, she asked, "What is this?"

"You'll see," he said with a grin.

He released her hand just long enough to pull a ring of keys from his pocket, flipped through until he came up with the right one, and then unlocked the front door. They stepped inside the dark interior, and he leaned around to flip on a light switch. The building had a tall ceiling, rough wooden floors, and was mostly open space. In the back corner was an L-shaped bar, and on the wall behind it was a dusty mirror. A door was next to the bar that led to the back, and as they walked further in, there was another hall that led to the left.

He walked in, spread his arms wide and turned around slowly before facing her again, and, trying to still his nerves, said, "Welcome to Grimm's Two."

She met his smile with one of her own. Her eyes opened even wider, and she said, "Grimm's Two? You're going to open another bar?"

Nodding, he said, "Yeah, Zander and I bought this building, and we're going to turn it into a second establishment for us. It'll take some work because it's been sitting empty for a while. With good cleaning, we should be able to get it up to the health inspector standards. The wiring is good, the plumbing is good, and the kitchen in the back is old but usable."

"This is amazing! I'm so excited for you," she said, stepping closer and placing her hands on his chest, looking up into his face. "You must be so proud."

It hit him how true her words were, the pride he felt at being able to own his own business while working with his brothers. He had not realized how much he cared about her opinion, but his relief was palpable. "Two of my brothers are in construction and will do a lot of the work with us. The others will help out as they can. Hell, their wives and fiancées will probably jump in and help, too."

"I would love to be able to help, also," she said before sucking in a quick breath, suddenly appearing nervous. "I mean, if you think there's anything that I could help with. I'm really good at cleaning, and this is no worse than some of the things I have to clean in the hotel."

"Just knowing that you'd like to be a part of this is fuckin' amazing," he said. He linked hands with her again and walked toward the bar. He and Zander had scrubbed it off several days ago, wanting to ascertain the condition, thrilled to find that it was in excellent shape.

Turning, he grasped her by the waist, lifting her easily to the bar top, her hands flying out to grab onto his shoulders for purchase.

He had set the bag of food and two sodas on the floor near the door when they came in, and he jogged back over to pick them up. Setting them on the bar next to her, he turned, and with his palms on the surface hefted himself up as well. Laughing, he said, "I should be ashamed, using this as the first place I ever take you to dinner, but then this means that you and I are christening Grimm's Two. We're the first people to eat here."

Laughing, she said, "I'm honored."

In no time at all, they had decimated the burgers and fries and slurped their sodas to the bottom of the cups. While they sat on the bar and ate, he continued to explain his vision.

"You've seen the original Grimm's, and this will be a lot like it. Neither Zander nor I want to change the concept, which is a comfortable bar for people to come to. We're not going to spend money on fancy shit, tons of decoration, a big dance floor, or music. The idea is to offer quality food and drinks and an atmosphere that people can be comfortable in. If they want a nightclub atmosphere, they can go somewhere else."

Her smile encouraged as she listened with rapt attention to all that he said. "How will you be able to handle the kitchens in two different places?" she asked.

Pleased with her interest, he said, "Zander and I talked a lot about that when we first had the idea. I'll be involved in the management of the two kitchens and certainly plan on being involved in some of the actual cooking but will also hire people to help us out. We also feel strongly that we both want to be involved in both endeavors."

She tucked her hair behind her ears and tilted her head slightly as she peered at him. "So it won't be like he's always running Grimm's and you're always running Grimm's Two?"

Nodding, he said, "Exactly. Sometimes he will be there, sometimes here. Same for me. But the key will be hiring people that we can trust to oversee various aspects."

Finished with their meal, he hefted himself down from the bar and turned, placing his hands on her waist. Lifting her easily, he brought her close, allowing her to glide gently to the floor. Once her feet were steady, his hands did not leave her waist, and he noticed with pleasure that hers stayed around his neck. Unable to resist, he leaned down and placed a gentle kiss on her lips.

Suddenly, he jerked his head back, his lips tight as her eyes widened. She gasped, "What's wrong?"

"I'm sorry," he said, giving his head a little shake.

He watched as her face blushed deep red, and her gaze dropped to his chest as her arms slid down to push away from him. Realizing he was making a mess of things, he said, "Please don't be embarrassed."

Her chin lifted as her eyes sought his again, now filled with confusion. "Zeke, I have no idea what's going on. I wanted you to kiss me, but was it so awful?"

"No, no! It's just that I don't want you to feel indebted."

"Why would I think that?"

Expelling the air from his lungs in a huge sigh, he said, "Jesus, I'm fucking this up." Staring into her eyes, he said, "Cynthia, I've been attracted to you since I first laid eyes on you at the shelter when you walked in soaking wet. And I know I've had a chance to help you some, but I just don't want you to think I'm taking advantage of you. I don't want you to feel like you owe me anything for a room at Miss Ethel's. If you kiss me, I want it to be because you really want to kiss me."

With a slow smile spreading across her face, she breathed, "Zeke? I want to kiss you."

Heart pounding, he slid his hands up to cup her cheeks, his thumbs brushing over the petal-soft skin, having wanted to do this since he first met her. Tilting her head ever so slightly as he stepped closer, he bent and sealed his lips over hers. They were just as soft as he expected, the taste just as intoxicating.

Her fingers clutched his shoulders, and she lifted up on her toes, drawing herself closer.

One hand slid down her back, pressing her tightly to him as he angled his head to take the kiss deeper. She sighed slightly, and he slid his tongue into her mouth, finding hers eagerly tangling with his. A roar rushed through his ears as he banded his arms tighter, lifting her slightly.

She wrapped her legs around his waist, her heat now pressed against his aching cock. Her breasts were crushed against his chest, and he lost all sense of time as the kiss continued.

He finally leaned back, finding it difficult to drag air into his lungs, feeling her chest heaving as well. "Damn, girl," he managed to say. Dropping his chin, he held her gaze as she loosened her legs from around his waist, and he slowly lowered her back to the floor.

"I've wanted to do that, too," she admitted.

Staring at her kiss-swollen lips, he said, "Thank God.

Because I'd like to do a whole lot more of that." Sighing again, he said, "As much as I would love to stay here continuing what we've started, we need to get you settled into Miss Ethel's."

Tucking her tightly next to him, they walked out of Grimm's Two, and he locked the door behind them. As they drove back to Miss Ethel's, he glanced to the side and watched her fingers rest lightly on her lips, a ghost of a smile on her face. He now wished he had offered her the room in his house. But he knew she would benefit from being around Miss Ethel, and it would give them a chance to develop their relationship. *Now if I can just convince my cock that was the right move.*

That night, after Zeke left, Cynthia sat on the sofa, an open book in her lap as Miss Ethel's knitting needles clicked in a fast rhythm. She wondered about life in the house when Zeke was little. As though her thoughts had been spoken aloud, Miss Ethel looked up and smiled.

"You are wondering what it was like to raise boys... boys who were not my biological children, but my children, nonetheless."

Blushing, she nodded. "Yes...I can't imagine what it was like."

Laughing, Miss Ethel replied, "I wanted to give them stability...a home that was warm, loving, accepting. My George and I wanted children, but it was not to be. I had accepted that after many years of trying, crying, and praying. And when he died, a large part of me died as well." She lay her needles down in her lap and grew quiet.

Cynthia remained silent, allowing Miss Ethel's thoughts to wander along the lanes of the past. Finally, Miss Ethel said, "My boys gave me back my life. They think I gave to them...but it's really the opposite."

Cynthia swallowed past the choking emotion in her throat and watched as the older woman's face settled into soft smile lines.

"You see, my dear," Miss Ethel said. "Family doesn't have to be who we're born to...family is who we surround ourselves with. Who uplifts us, holds us, comforts us, and provides for us. That...is family."

As she lay in bed later that night, Cynthia thought on Miss Ethel's words, a smile playing upon her lips as she thought of Zeke and hoped for their future.

## 11

Cynthia woke the next morning, blinking as the sunlight came through the blinds. She felt wonderfully rested, and it took no time at all to remember where she was. Miss Ethel's house...Zeke's mom. She rolled onto her back and stretched, her gaze taking in the cream-colored walls decorated with photographs of roses. She had not thought about it the night before but wondered if those were roses from Miss Ethel's own garden.

She climbed from the bed, quickly pulling up the floral bedspread, tucking it around the pillows. Her toes dug into the soft pile of the blue rug, which felt so much warmer than the cold tile of the shelter's floor. She had placed her clothes into the closet and dresser drawers and quickly grabbed what she needed for the day before heading into the bathroom. Not sure when Miss Ethel woke, she hurried through her shower and morning routine.

Dressed in her Prince Hotel uniform, she tiptoed

down the stairs, surprised to find Miss Ethel already in the kitchen scrambling eggs and frying bacon.

"Oh, my goodness. I didn't expect you up so early," she said.

"Good morning," Miss Ethel greeted. "I used to get up early with my husband to fix breakfast before he went to work. After I started taking in boys, I always wanted them to have a hearty breakfast before school. Now, I suppose it's just a habit." Setting two plates on the table, she ushered Cynthia to a chair. "Please, eat before you go to work."

Glancing at the clock on the stove, she determined she had just enough time to indulge before she needed to hurry to the bus stop she had seen down the road.

Politely attempting to shovel the food in, she looked up in surprise as Miss Ethel said, "There's no reason to hurry, my dear. Zeke will be along in a few minutes to take you to work."

Cynthia's fork halted on its way to her mouth, and she blinked in surprise. Swallowing, she said, "I didn't know he was coming by."

Miss Ethel smiled and said, "He told me last night before he left. I don't think he wanted you to have to take the bus."

As if on cue, the front door opened, and they heard Zeke's voice call out, "Good morning." Looking up quickly, she watched as he came into the dining room, bent to kiss Miss Ethel's cheek, and tossed a wink toward her.

Miss Ethel moved to the kitchen to get a cup of coffee for him as he settled into the chair next to

Cynthia. Leaning over, he kissed her lightly, asking, "How did you sleep?"

"I didn't know you were going to take me to work," she said instead of answering his question. "What about the breakfast at the shelter?"

"I've already been there and prepared food for them to serve. It wasn't too far to drive over here so that I could have a cup of coffee while you have breakfast. I thought you'd have more time in the mornings if you didn't have to make a couple of bus changes."

She sucked in her lips, then sighed. "Zeke, you've done so much for me. Honestly, you don't have to do this—"

He shushed her with another light kiss, then said, "I know I don't have to do it. But the idea of spending a few minutes with you first thing in the morning is exactly what I want to do."

She finished her breakfast as he sipped on a cup of coffee, both making small talk with Miss Ethel. Dashing upstairs to brush her teeth, she looked into the mirror. She knew he might not drive her every day to work, and that was okay. But on the days that he did, the money she would save on bus fare was just more money she could use to reduce her hospital bill faster.

Several minutes later, she stood on the front porch saying goodbye to Miss Ethel. The older woman gave her a hug and said, "I hope you have a wonderful day, Cynthia."

Suddenly overcome with emotion, she held on tightly. "Oh, Miss Ethel, I feel like things are looking up, and that's kind of scary."

"My dear, remember, 'This day is too dear, with its hopes and invitations, to waste a moment on the yesterdays.'"

Blinking away the threat of tears, she tilted her head to the side. "Who said that? It sounds familiar."

"Ralph Waldo Emerson," Miss Ethel replied. "No doubt you learned it in one of your English classes many years ago."

"I love it...it's perfect." Hesitating for a few seconds, she admitted, "My mother used to read poetry to me when I was little. I have little time for reading now, but I still love to lose myself in a good book."

With a final hug, she missed the expression that passed between Zeke and Miss Ethel. She hurried to Zeke's truck, and within ten minutes she was dropped off at the Prince Hotel. He kissed her lightly again, and with a wave goodbye, she watched as he drove away. Floating on air as she walked to the employee entrance, she whispered, "This day is too dear..."

---

Carlos had handed out the other floor assignments and was in the process of handing one to Cynthia when he pulled it back, his eyes scanning the contents. The other housekeepers headed on down the hall toward the service elevator while Cynthia waited patiently.

Pulling out a pen, Carlos mumbled, "I have no idea why this has you starting on the fifth floor. Your schedule always has you as you start on the sixth, and I can't see any reason why that should change today."

Scribbling a few notations, he handed her assignment sheet to her and said, "All of the guests that were on the sixth floor have now checked out. You can stick to your routine as always."

It took several minutes for the service elevator to come back down for her after dropping off the other housekeepers. Stepping out onto the sixth floor, she noted the doors with trays next to them and called down to the restaurant for them to be picked up. Moving to the far end, she quickly cleaned the first room, glad that it had been well kept by the guests. A ten-dollar tip had been left for her next to a thank you note on the desk. Thinking over her recent good luck, it was hard to keep Zeke from coming to mind. With an extra skip in her step, she practically danced through the dusting.

Still smiling, she went into the second room on the executive floor, finding it well kept as well. She was almost finished with its cleaning when she checked the safe. Opening it, she sighed as she discovered a manila envelope. Pulling it out, she saw that it was not sealed. Lifting the flap, she peeked inside, her eyes bugging as her gaze landed on a thick stack of bills. On top was a one-hundred-dollar bill, and if the rest of the stack was the same, she was staring at a great deal of money. *Shit!*

It was such a pain when someone left money in a room. The procedure required her to immediately call Carlos, who would then notify security. Both Carlos and the hotel's security would come, count the money, and then it would be taken to the hotel safe. All the while, she had to remain in the room, which would undoubtedly make her have to work through lunch to be able to finish the cleanings.

A piece of paper caught her eye, and she pulled it out slightly to see what it said. **First installment. More to come.**

She immediately pushed the paper and the bills deeper into the envelope, hating that she had even looked. She glanced around even though she was alone as though to make certain no one had seen her peek. Placing the envelope back into the safe, she walked toward her cart, startled when a figure suddenly appeared in front of her.

Stumbling backward, a hand reached out and grabbed her upper arm tightly. Looking up, she recognized Bob Shelton, the hotel owner's assistant. "Mr. Shelton, I'm sorry. I didn't see you there."

She looked into his face which appeared to register irritation, but she was uncertain why. His gaze looked behind her into the room before coming back to rest on her. "I was just getting ready to call security—"

"Why?" he bit out sharply.

Glancing down at his hand which was still banded tightly around her upper arm, she was relieved when he suddenly let her go. "The previous guest left an envelope in the safe."

His face appeared blank, neither registering surprise nor distress. Instead, he calmly asked, "And did you look inside the envelope?"

Nodding, she said, "Yes. I needed to know which procedure to follow." He did not say anything in reply but continued to stare, giving her the impression that he wanted her to continue. "As soon as I saw there was money inside the envelope, I placed it back in the safe and was getting ready to call security and Carlos."

Still not speaking, he brushed past her and moved to the safe. Pulling out the envelope, he looked inside before his eyes darted back over to her. "Did you pull it out of the envelope? Did you take a look to see how much money was there or if there was a note?"

It was not in Cynthia's nature to lie, but the exchange was making her uncomfortable. Holding his gaze, she lifted her chin slightly and said, "No, I didn't. As soon as I saw there was money, I replaced it and was heading to my cart for my radio when I ran into you."

She saw no emotion on his face, but he gave a curt nod. Uncertain what she should do, she asked, "Uh…do you want me to call them?"

"No, that won't be necessary. You may go on to your next room, and I'll call them now."

Licking her dry lips, she nodded and moved out of the room, hesitating at her cart only long enough to hear him radio for both Carlos and security. Giving her head a little shake, she hurried down the hall to the next room she needed to clean, trying without success to forget the note that was tied around the bundle of money.

At the end of her shift, she was back in the basement, loading her cart with the supplies for the next day. For the first time in a long time, she was looking forward to going home after work. The idea of returning to Miss Ethel's house was so much more uplifting than the idea of the shelter or someone's couch.

Carlos appeared in the doorway, and the chattering of her coworkers came to a stop as they all looked up at their boss. His gaze moved through the room until landing on Cynthia, and his smile widened. "Cynthia, I want you to know that I have nominated you for an Exceptional Employee Award."

Startling, she barely heard the congratulations pouring in from the other housekeepers as she stared dumbly at him. "Really? Why?"

"Mr. Shelton had the hotel security and me witness the count of the money that was in the envelope that you found left in one of the safes. It was a substantial amount of money, and I was very impressed, although not surprised, with your actions."

She wondered what he thought of the note but did not want to say anything, not giving away that she had actually seen it. Blushing, she said, "I didn't do anything exceptional, Carlos."

Lucy snorted and said, "Girl, you know some of the losers we've had come through here. They would have stolen that money without blinking!"

Nodding, Carlos agreed. "Not everyone is as honest as you, and I think it's high time that someone from housekeeping was recognized." He walked over and patted her shoulder, adding, "I think you're an exceptional employee every day, Cynthia. It's just time that the higher-ups realize it."

She was energized with his praise and was anxious to share her good news with Zeke. When he had dropped her off at the hotel that morning, he said he would have loved to be able to take her home at the end of her shift but was uncertain if he could get away. He had seemed so disappointed, and she had rushed to assure him that taking the bus to Miss Ethel's neighborhood was much shorter than her previous bus route.

Sitting on the bus, she still felt the excitement of the impending award. Occasionally the words of her stepmother still rattled around her mind. *"You'll never amount to anything." "You have your mother's looks, which is so unfortunate for you." "My daughters will achieve greatness. You? Doubtful!" "You've taken all from me you'll ever get. It was only your father who wanted you around, and with him gone, you need to leave as well."* Pressing her hand over her heart, she stilled the words and focused on Carlos' praise instead. Her parents had always been quick to applaud her efforts, but it had been many years since she heard their voices. Straightening in her seat, she smiled. *I am exceptional.*

She soon arrived at Miss Ethel's house, smiling as she stepped inside. It appeared Miss Ethel had been pruning her rose bushes because several vases of beautiful roses filled the house. Greeting her new landlady, she hurried upstairs to shower and change out of her Prince Hotel uniform.

Back downstairs, she spent the next hour in the kitchen with Miss Ethel, chatting as they cooked together. Dinner was a small roast with carrots and potatoes, homemade biscuits, and topped off with peach cobbler.

"Oh, my goodness. If I eat like this all the time, I'll have to take up running to work off the calories."

Miss Ethel laughed and said, "It took a long time for

me to get used to cooking for one after having boys for so long."

Shaking her head as she set plates at the small table in the corner of the kitchen, she said, "How on earth did you feed all those boys?"

Miss Ethel's face was filled with a faraway expression, and Cynthia could tell that the older woman's mind cast back to years when she lovingly built her family.

"My husband and I were unable to have children, and once we paid off this house, we saved our money for our retirement years. Of course, he died, and I felt that I had more life to live and more heart to give. There was some money from the state per boy, but it would not have kept them fed the way I believe young boys needed to be fed." Shrugging, she added, "I certainly bought in bulk at the stores!"

Halfway through dinner, Zeke showed up, saying, "I wanted to make sure you were settled in."

Lifting an eyebrow, she replied, "The way you're shoveling in the peach cobbler, I think you came more for dessert than for me!"

Laughing, Miss Ethel said, "She's got you there, Zeke."

Over cobbler and coffee, Zeke and Miss Ethel continued their stories, entertaining her with visions of a house full of young boys, all learning to be a family. She watched the genuine affection between the two, hoping that one day he would trust her enough with the story of how he came into Miss Ethel's care.

He needed to get back to Grimm's, so they walked

hand-in-hand out to his truck. She quickly filled him in on the excitement of her day. The news of her impending award was tempered by the note that she had seen with the money.

"I'm glad you were able to get it to security as fast as you were," he said. "If there was anything funny about it, I'd hate to think that someone knew you had seen the note."

Biting her lip, she said, "I never lie, but I was so stunned, I didn't want anyone to know that I had seen it."

He leaned his back against his truck, pulling her up against him, tucking her in tightly into his embrace. "I don't blame you, Babe. I think under the circumstances that was the right thing to do. You found the money, turned it over to the right people, and now you can step back and not worry about who left it or why."

He kissed her goodbye, and just as with every other time, all thoughts were swept away as she focused on his arms around her, his lips teasing hers, and the moonlight beaming down on them. A few hours later, as she climbed into bed, she realized it was the best day she had had in a long time.

---

## 12

"So then, this guy shows up and says he'll handle it."

Zeke was in Grimm's Two along with Zander, Cael, Cas, and Asher. The space had been cleaned out, and an electrician had inspected the wiring, declaring it safe. Using ladders, they had replaced all the burned-out bulbs, and now that the room was fully illuminated, they stood around the bar, looking at the floor plan.

He had spent the night mulling over the story that Cynthia had told him and was now sharing it with the others. "She said she didn't feel weird about it because this guy is high up in the hotel organization. She wasn't sure of his exact title, but thinks he's second in command under Richard Prince, the owner."

"And what did the note say?" Zander asked, turning his attention from the floor plans to Zeke.

"She said it just had a few words on it. 'First installment. More to come.'"

"Sounds like somebody was staying in the hotel and left their payoff money in the safe," Cael said, his hands on his hips. Shaking his head, he added, "Man, whoever realized he checked out of the hotel and left his money has got to be fuckin' pissed."

"Or fuckin' dead," Asher commented. "If he was supposed to be making some kind of payoff and ended up leaving the money in a hotel, I can't imagine whoever was supposed to get the money is very happy."

"What kind of idiot would leave that much money behind? Especially a payoff. He must've been in a rush," Zander said.

Shrugging, Zeke added, "When you put it like that, it sounds like a bad movie plot. Well, one way or the other, it's over for Cynthia. She turned in the money the way she was supposed to. The only thing she didn't do was admit that she'd seen the note."

Cas rubbed his chin and asked, "Did she say why she lied about that?"

"She said she just had a bad feeling. Maybe it was the way the boss man was looking at her. She said as soon as she said that she had not read it, he seemed more relaxed. I told her to go with her gut, and if her gut said not to admit she saw the note, then that was probably best."

Zander nodded slowly before saying, "Whoever left that money is not going to be happy. The less people they know who may have seen it, the better."

Chuckling, Cael said, "There used to be some show on TV about stupid criminals. I can't help but think about that when I think of somebody in town to make some kind of payoff and they leave the money in the hotel safe instead."

The others laughed along with him before turning their attention back to the floor plans. After the inspection, they realized how much easier it would be to turn this building into Grimm's Two than it was for the original Grimm's. This building was in good shape, but Zeke knew the kitchen would need a complete overhaul.

"What do you think about opening the bar first and adding the food later like we did with the original Grimm's?" Zander asked.

Pondering the question, Zeke admitted, "On the one hand, I hate not being able to offer the food here when it opens. But since this building is in such good shape, it'll be much quicker to get the bar up and running now and longer for the kitchen."

"What will you need out here?" Asher asked, looking around the space.

"Cas is measuring for the bar, agreeing to build a solid wood, one-of-a-kind bartop. Out here, we just need tables and chairs, barstools, and to get the bar outfitted. Once we have that, we can have the health inspector come around. We've already applied for the liquor license and should have that soon."

"So, what do you need in the kitchen?" Asher continued to ask, this time directing his question to Zeke.

Zeke led the others through the door into the kitchen. Looking around, he said, "There's nothing wrong with the cabinets, but the old appliances have to go. I'll need a new refrigerator and freezer, new stovetops and ovens. The countertops will need to be replaced as well."

Looking back down at Zeke's designs, Cael pulled out a pencil, and they all began to toss ideas around, working to make Zeke's vision come true. An hour later, Zander and Zeke shared a smile.

"As far as I'm concerned, you can go ahead and order what you need," Zander said.

The idea that he could create the kitchen of his dreams from scratch shot through Zeke and he clapped Zander on the back. "I've already got a list of things I'd like to get. I'll work up a priority order, and we'll go over it together. That way we can agree on the price, and I'll get you to sign off on it as well."

The two brothers shook hands while the others looked on, smiling. The front door cracked open, and Zeke looked over his shoulder to see who was entering. Stunned, he saw Cynthia's head pop through the door and watched as her eyes scanned the area before landing on him.

"Oh!" she squeaked. "I'm sorry. I didn't realize anyone else would be here."

"Cynthia!" he called out, jogging toward her. "Come in, come in!" He made it to her and could see that she was still in her Prince Hotel uniform. "How'd you get here?"

As he reached her and took her hands in his own, she looked up, and he saw the hesitancy in her eyes. Her glance darted to the side where he knew his brothers were watching, curious. "Miss Ethel told me she had visiting to do this afternoon, so I thought I'd come by and see you. I took the bus here. I should've known you were busy, I'm so sorry—"

"No, no," he insisted. "This is perfect. Come on, I'd like you to meet some of my brothers." He could have sworn he heard her squeak again as he grabbed her hand and pulled her along with him toward the bar.

"Guys, I'd like you to meet Cynthia. Cynthia Ellison." He placed his arm around her shoulders, giving her a comforting squeeze. "Cynthia, this giant is one of my brothers, Cael. This is Asher. And this is my oldest brother and business partner, Zander. And this is the creator of the wooden bar, my brother, Cas." Her smile was warm, but he could see the barest trembling of her lips.

"It's so nice to meet all of you," she said, shaking each of their hands. "I knew that Zeke would be here, but I'm embarrassed that I didn't think that I'd be interrupting a meeting."

"I assure you the pleasure is all ours," Zander said. "We've been anxious to meet Zeke's new...um...friend."

"Actually, we were just finishing up," Cael said. He smiled down at Cynthia and added, "My Regina has been interested in meeting you. I have a feeling this weekend will include a get-together."

She tilted her head slightly to the side and repeated, "A get-together?"

"We still get together with Miss Ethel whenever we can, and that involves our women," Zander explained. "They'll be anxious to meet you."

With goodbyes said, Zeke watched his brothers head out of the building before he turned and looked back at

Cynthia. Seeing her scrunched brow, he said, "Don't worry. Everyone's going to love you." Looking toward the kitchen, he said, "Can I show you something?"

Another smile replaced her worry lines, and she said, "Absolutely."

---

*You can show me anything you want to.* As Cynthia watched Zeke lead her into the kitchen, she admired the way his jeans fit across his ass. His long hair was pulled back into a low ponytail, and her fingers twitched with the desire to pull out the band and run her fingers through his tresses.

As they entered the area for the kitchen, her attention jerked back to more than his ass and his hair as he swung his arms around and began to explain his design.

"I'm ordering stainless steel appliances and counter-tops," he began. "The refrigerator and freezer will go here," and moving to another section, said, "and the ovens and stovetops will be here." Walking to the center of the space, he threw his arms out again and continued, "There will be plenty of space for the cooks to work without running into each other constantly."

His eyes were bright and his face full of excitement, and she could not help but grin in response. As his gaze landed back on her, he blushed.

"I guess I sound stupid, don't I?"

Giggling, she shook her head. "Not at all! Zeke, I love seeing you this excited." She walked toward him and placed her palms against his chest, feeling the steely muscles underneath her fingertips. Still holding his gaze, she added, "This is your dream. You're doing what you love to do, and this time, you get to design it from the ground up."

He nodded slowly and brought his hands up to cup her cheeks. Tilting her head back slightly, he bent and took her lips, which she gave eagerly.

It only took an instant for the kiss to go from sweet to wild, and her fingers curled to clutch the material of his shirt. His tongue swept inside her mouth, its velvet softness sending tingles throughout her body before settling in her core. One of his arms slid over her shoulder and down her back, pressing her tightly against him, and she could feel the rock-hard evidence of his arousal.

Dragging his lips away, he sucked in air before saying, "I want you so fuckin' bad. But I want to do this so fuckin' right."

The air burned as she pulled it into her lungs and whispered, "Then take me."

Their gazes held, long and hard, before he linked fingers with her and began stalking toward the door. She raced to keep up, not knowing where they were going but trusting him completely.

Ten minutes later, they had driven to another quaint neighborhood. He parked outside the two-story house. She stared out the window, noting two trees flanked the house on the front, casting shade on the small front porch. Before she knew it, he was at her door, helping her down. Once more, he linked fingers with her and led her to the front door.

Inside, her gaze quickly took in the living room, large eat-in kitchen, and the den. A sliding glass door opened onto a trellis covered patio. He turned and cupped her face once more, stopping a whisper away from her lips and said, "Welcome to my home, Cynthia."

Her heart overflowed as she saw hesitancy mixed with pride in his eyes, and said, "Your home is beautiful, Zeke. Just like you."

Relief filled his face as he closed the scant distance and sealed her lips with his own.

## 13

Zeke lifted her easily into his arms, and as she wrapped her legs around his waist, he banded one arm around her back and the other one supported her ass. Managing to do this without breaking the kiss, he continued to devour her lips as he stalked to the stairs. Rounding the post, he forced himself to slow, setting her gently to the floor and lifting his head from hers.

He saw uncertainty pass through her eyes but quickly said, "I don't want to make any assumptions. I want to do this right."

The crinkle in her brow erased, and she grabbed the front of his shirt in her fingers again, saying, "Make no mistake, Zeke. I want you. Now." With a grin, she whirled around and started up the stairs.

Only a second behind her, he quickly captured her, and she twisted, plopping onto one of the steps as he covered her body with his own. She grabbed his face in her hands and brought her lips back to his, sucking his tongue into her mouth, tangling it with her own.

At the feel of her silky tongue and the heady taste of her, his cock ached to be freed from its confines, the threat of permanent indentations from his zipper passing through his mind.

His hand slid to the bottom of her smock, then slowly lifted the material to expose her pale skin. Using his fingertips to explore, he discovered her uniform pants were simple elastic waist pull-ons, allowing easy access to the hidden treasures he sought.

So engrossed in his discoveries, he blinked in awareness as he felt her push against his shoulders. Pulling back, he did not have time to question before she shimmied up a step, reached to the bottom of her smock and jerked it over her head. Her breasts were not large but perfectly proportioned to her size and spilled over the tops of her plain cotton bra.

He bent and ran his tongue over the soft mounds, dipping into her cleavage as he unsnapped the front closure, allowing them to spill forth. Her breasts were as pale as the rest of her, tipped with dark, rosy, hard-budded nipples, begging to be sucked. And he obliged, pulling first one deep into his mouth before kissing his way over to the other. Her fingers clutched his shoulders as she arched her back, offering more of her luscious body to him.

He kissed his way down her stomach, shifting on the stairs so that he could grasp her elastic waistband and drag it down her legs, snagging her panties as he went. She scooted up one more step and lifted her legs, allowing him to pull off her sneakers and pants. He stared down at her naked beauty, not believing he was given such a gift.

With his hands on her thighs, he lifted her legs over his shoulders and nuzzled the soft skin below her mound, his nostrils filled with the scent of her arousal. With the flat of his tongue, he licked her slit before sucking on her clit.

Her fingers dug into his shoulders, but he was heedless of anything but wanting to give her continued pleasure. Lapping her as he plunged his tongue inside, he knew she was the woman of his dreams. Inserting one finger deep inside her core, he found the exact spot that caused her hips to buck off the stairs. Lifting his gaze, he observed her peering down at him as she rested her upper body on her elbows.

He felt her core tightening and, sucking her clit into his mouth once more, grinned as her orgasm rushed over her. She cried out his name as her fingernails dug deeper into his back.

As awareness slowly took the place of the intoxication of her, he hated that he had just given her an orgasm while she was lying back on the hard stairs. Bending, he scooped her body easily into his arms and carried her the rest of the way up the stairs and into his bedroom.

"That was...that was..."

"Painful?" he asked, dreading her agreement.

Her eyes widened, and she shook her head sharply. "No, you big goof. That was amazing!"

He held her gaze and admitted, "It was amazing,

Babe, but I'm sorry I didn't get you to the bed first. There's no way those stairs could have felt good."

Her lips curved into a smile, and she pulled her naked body closer to him as he lowered her feet to the floor. "When you're floating on air, you don't feel the stairs underneath you."

Her words scored through him, and he kissed her once again. He knew she could taste her arousal on his tongue, and that only furthered to have him take the kiss deeper. Finally aware that her fingers were fumbling with the bottom of his shirt, he stepped back.

Reaching behind him, he grabbed the soft material in his fist and pulled it over his head, tossing it to the floor. As she sat on the bed and scooted back, her eyes remained latched onto his body as he shucked his jeans after kicking off his boots. His cock rejoiced at being free, bobbing forward toward her, and he almost laughed at the thought that his cock knew exactly where he needed to be.

He bent and snagged his wallet from his jeans, pulling out a condom packet. Ripping it open, he rolled it over his erection before moving to the bed and crawling over her body. Pushing into her tight, warm sex, he began to move deliberately, refusing to give in to the desire to rush. His cock dragged along the inside of her core, and he watched as her eyes partially closed, hooded with lust.

Cynthia opened her legs wider to accommodate his body, and her legs wrapped around his waist, her heels digging into his muscular ass. He was barely aware of her fingernails, once again digging into his shoulders as his thrusts increased in speed.

"Come on, babe," he begged. "Come with me." He could tell his orgasm was imminent and wanted her to fly apart with him. Still thrusting, he bent and sucked a taut nipple into his mouth, biting lightly as he tugged on the sensitive bud.

She cried out, and he roared through his own climax, her core milking him until the last drop was wrung from his body. His arms quivered as they continued to hold him up as he dragged in one raspy gasp after another. He had no idea what it was about this woman that caused his heart to race, but he wanted to wrap her up and keep her with him. Finally, he collapsed onto her waiting body, barely able to roll to the side, pulling her with him.

For several long moments they lay, euphoria washing over them as they fought to catch their breaths, their bodies still crushed together, slick with sweat, heartbeat pressed against heartbeat.

Neither spoke, words not seeming necessary. Finally, he kissed her forehead and said, "Be right back." On legs that felt like Jell-O, he made his way into the bathroom to dispose of the condom. Walking back into the bedroom, he saw that she was lying on her side, her elbow crooked and her hand propping up her head. Her gaze was pinned on him, her eyes moving from his head down to his toes.

"Like what you see?"

A Cheshire-cat grin was her answer, and she patted the mattress next to her. He obliged readily, but not until he scooped her up, jerked the comforter back, and settled them both on the cool sheets before pulling the covers up again. With the pillows propped behind them, he turned her so that her head was resting on his shoulder, their arms around each other and their legs tangled.

The late afternoon sun was still coming through the windows, and he loved the halo effect as it highlighted her blonde hair. His fingers drifted gently over her shoulders and back, and he felt her slight weight as she rested on him.

She lifted her face, her eyes searching his, and he asked, "Whatcha thinking, babe?"

Uncertainty passed through her eyes, and his gaze dropped to where her teeth nibbled her bottom lip. She spoke hesitantly, saying, "I looked at the pictures of you and your brothers at Miss Ethel's. I loved seeing you as a younger boy but couldn't help but wonder how you came to live with her."

He did not answer right away, and she rushed to say, "Never mind. It's none of my business—"

Shushing her, he said, "Yes, it is your business, Cynthia. You're not just anyone...you're someone special to me."

Her face softened as her lips curved into a smile, and she nestled closely against his chest. It had been a long time since he had spoken about his family, generally preferring to think of his life beginning at the age of thirteen when he found Miss Ethel and his brothers. But it was Miss Ethel who had taught him that we are all a combination of the elements of our upbringing.

And it is only as we mature that we become the adults we choose to be.

"My dad was a big guy, but I guess that comes as no surprise. To be truthful, he was bigger than I am now. He had a temper, but he never raised a hand against my mom or me when I was little. But when he was angry, he could hit with words, and we'd feel each blow."

Her fingers had been tracing the pattern of his tattoos on his arms, and as he spoke, he felt her hands halt for a few seconds before slowly soothing over his skin again.

"I think my mom loved him, or at least she did at one time, but she grew weary of him coming home half-drunk with blood on his clothes. At first, I think she tried to hide that from me, but by the time I was about eight years old, it was no longer hidden. Considering that he might only have a bruise or two or a split lip, it didn't take long to figure out that whoever he was fighting with must've bled a lot more. The police would come around to question him, but one look from him and Mama would lie, saying he was at home the whole evening."

Her fingers continued to trace soothing patterns on his skin, and he felt the tension ease. Sucking in a deep breath, he continued. "As I got older, he thought that teaching me to be a good man was teaching me how to fight. And I learned. I learned to fight from the best. When he trained, he trained like a prize fighter, and I had to fight back just to keep him from beating me to a pulp."

"Oh, Zeke, I'm so sorry," she said, lifting up on her

elbow to peer down at him. Her hand moved from his shoulder to his face, cupping his cheek, rubbing her thumb over his beard.

"Crazy thing is, he just wanted me to learn how to fight."

"But that's still abuse," she argued.

Nodding, he said, "Oh, believe me, I get it."

"And your mom?"

"She left. I was eleven years old, and she left." He heard Cynthia suck in a sharp breath but was glad that she remained quiet as his thoughts slid back to that time. Finally, he said, "I got in trouble at school. Another kid had teased me, and I reacted in the way that my dad always taught me that I should. I reared back, hit the kid square in the face, and broke his nose. My mom was hysterical, and my dad got angry at her, saying I was just being a man. They had a huge fight, and for the first time, I actually felt angry at Mom. I didn't understand how she couldn't see that I had handled the situation the way that Dad would have."

"And she just left you? Knowing what your dad was capable of, she just left you?"

"At that moment, I think my mom looked at me and saw someone that was turning out to be just like the man she married. I think she figured any good influence she had over me was gone. I didn't understand it at the time, but I think she walked out the door out of self-preservation."

Shaking her head, her blonde hair flying back and forth, Cynthia argued, "Parents don't give up on their children. If she saw what an influence your father was, then she should have worked harder in the opposite direction."

He looked at her, seeing the righteous indignation on her face, and brushed his hand over her cheeks, sliding his fingers through her hair at the sight of her head. "Somehow I think you'd be that kind of mom," he said, leaning forward to place a kiss on her forehead.

"Of course, I would! Self-preservation is all well and good but not at the risk of your children."

They were quiet again for another moment before she gently asked, "Did your dad leave too? Is that how you ended up with Miss Ethel?"

"In a way," he said, heaving a sigh. "The next couple of years, I stayed out of trouble in school, but it wasn't easy. Every time I got angry, I could feel the rage building. Somehow, I suppose my mom's influence must have still been ingrained because while I might get into a fight, I didn't let it get the best of me again. The same cannot be said for my dad."

Shifting slightly so that he could peer into her face, he wanted to see the effects of the words that would follow. Holding her gaze, he said, "One night my dad didn't come home from the bar. The police showed up at the house and told me that my dad had gotten into a bar fight. He had ended up hitting a man that was much smaller than himself, and when the man fell backward, he was dead."

Cynthia gasped, but her eyes never wavered from Zeke's. He stared, wondering what effect his words would have.

"Oh, Zeke, I'm so sorry," she said, her breath

catching as she spoke. "How horrible for you. I know I should also say how horrible for the family of the other man, but all I can think of is you, all alone, having to carry that burden."

The air left his lungs in a rush, and he bent to take her lips once again. This kiss was soft and gentle, the sharing of souls exposed, the feeling of redemption passing between them.

"Where is he now?" she asked, wondering if his father tried to insert himself into Zeke's adult life.

Shaking his head slowly, he replied, "Died in prison. Fittingly, he was killed in a fight."

Sucking in a sharp breath, she turned the conversation away from his father. "And so, you ended up with Miss Ethel."

Nodding slowly, he added, "The social worker contacted my mom, but she had become ill and no longer felt like she could care for me. I became a ward of the state and ended up on Miss Ethel's front porch. Pissed and scared but trying to hide it. Ended up with six brothers and a woman who was more of a parent to me than my own.

"On a practical note, with her and Zander's tutelage, I caught back up in my schoolwork and developed an appreciation for the literature that abounded in her home. I learned to talk out disagreements and what it means to truly have someone's back. I learned to work through my frustrations by chopping vegetables and discovered that cooking was not only something I was interested in because I wanted to eat well, but it provided a creative outlet at the same time. But more than that, Miss Ethel taught me that the sins of my father are not my own."

Cynthia shifted her body, bringing her knees up so that she straddled Zeke's hips. Her breasts were a distraction, but he kept his eyes on her face as she said, "It matters not how strait the gate, How charged with punishments the scroll..."

His breath caught in his throat as he continued with her, both quoting from the poem by William Henley. "I am the master of my fate. I am the captain of my soul."

Grinning, he said, "She taught me that whatever I am, I can be that because of me."

She leaned forward, her lips sealing over his, and he opened his mouth, allowing her tongue to sweep inside. He let her take control until his cock ached with need. Rolling her beneath him, he barely took the time to sheathe himself with the condom before sheathing himself in her body.

This time, the movements were slow and languid as they both tried to draw out as much as they could before their orgasms crashed over them. As he continued to hold her body tightly to his, the words pounded in his head, "I am the master of my fate..."

## 1 4

Waking up the next morning in Miss Ethel's house, Cynthia lay in bed for several minutes pondering what Zeke had told her the previous evening about his family. She thought about his mom who walked away from her son that she could have continued to parent, and his dad who had been killed while in prison during a fight with another inmate. She had always noticed the strength in him but now understood the gentleness as well.

She had today off from work but wanted to help Miss Ethel with her roses. It had been so long since she had had a garden to tend. She thought back to Zeke's house and could not keep the smile from her face at the thought that she would love to plant more flowers in his yard.

Climbing from the bed, a giggle slipped out at the thought of Zeke surrounded by flowers. With her hair pulled back in a loose ponytail and dressed in shorts and a T-shirt, she hurried down the stairs and into the kitchen. She hated that Miss Ethel was always awake before her but understood how much the older woman loved preparing food for someone else. Cooking had always been a necessity for Cynthia but never a pleasure. Watching Miss Ethel in the kitchen, she could easily see how young Zeke would be entranced by the process.

Miss Ethel never appeared to be in a hurry but worked steadily, smiling and talking as she scrambled eggs, flipped sausage patties on the griddle, and kneaded homemade biscuits. It was calming and the perfect start to a day.

"Do you have plans for your day off?" Miss Ethel asked.

"You had mentioned that you needed to prune your roses and I thought I would help you. I know so little about gardens and certainly nothing about different flowers."

"Oh, that would be lovely," Miss Ethel said. "We'll get started right after breakfast."

Soon, they were once again ensconced at the small table in the kitchen, their plates full and their teacups filled to the brim. After the breakfast dishes were cleaned, she followed Miss Ethel out into the backyard after sliding on gardening gloves.

"I'm certainly not an expert on gardening," Miss Ethel said, "but I do know how to take care of what's in my yard."

As they walked around, Miss Ethel pointed out various plants. "Over here are my hostas. They do particularly well in the shade, although they can take some sun. Every couple of years, I have to divide them."

Eyebrows lifted, she asked, "Divide them?"

"They grow so thickly that the roots began to choke out each other. You can take a spade, push it straight down through the plant, and separate the roots. I started many years ago with only four hostas, and as you can see, I now have them all over my yard." Miss Ethel waved her arm toward the front fence and said, "Over there are my forsythia bushes. They bloom with bright yellow flowers in the early spring and then need to be pruned afterward."

Cynthia's head was reeling with the information but loved what she was learning. Pointing to some bright orange flowers on tall stalks, she asked, "And what are these?"

"Those are my daylilies. They're called that because they open up to full bloom during the daylight and close at night in the dark."

Shaking her head, Cynthia said, "That just seems so weird to me."

Chuckling, Miss Ethel said, "Plants, like people, are all different. Just like I need to know how to care for the different plants in my yard, that's how I needed to find out about each of my boys and what they needed."

She nodded, nibbling her bottom lip as she thought back to the previous evening. "Zeke told me about his parents last night."

Miss Ethel turned her warm, grey eyes to her and smiled gently. "I was hoping he would. I'm glad that he trusted you with that. I think it's good for him to think on the past, knowing that's where he can leave it."

Shooting Miss Ethel a grin, Cynthia asked, "Do you have a fitting quote for that?"

Chuckling again, Miss Ethel said, "Oh, I suppose Zeke has told you for my penchant for quoting literature."

"My mother used to read poetry to me, and I have a few passages I can quote. Zeke, on the other hand, has so many quotes memorized!"

Her accepting smile bright, Miss Ethel explained, "My grandfather was a voracious reader. My grandmother was too, but she pored over the Bible while my grandfather devoured any book he could get his hands on from the library. He was one of the few men I ever met in my life with a photographic memory. Once he read something, he could remember it. And he found it to be a great comfort to be able to quote passages that were pertinent to what was going on at the time."

"I think that's wonderful," she said, honored that Miss Ethel was sharing a bit of her past with her.

"I, on the other hand, do not have a photographic memory," Miss Ethel admitted. "But I do have the ability to memorize. Over the years, I suppose it's gotten easier." Winking, she said, "Now let me see. Søren Kierkegaard wrote 'Life can only be understood backward; but it must be lived forwards.' I think that is apropos when thinking of Zeke. He can see how far he has come when he looks backward, but only he determines how to live as he goes forward."

"I know this is only from George Harrison," Cynthia admitted, "but he said, 'It's being here, and now that's important.'" Blushing, she said, "I really need to read more!"

Smiling widely, Miss Ethel's eyes danced. "Never apologize for applying someone's words of wisdom to your own life."

The sound of car doors slamming caught their attention and they walked around the corner of the house. Miss Ethel clapped her hands in glee at the sight, but Cynthia's feet stuttered to a halt as she watched six beautiful women walking toward the house. Tall, short, blonde, brunette, redhead, slender, curvaceous…it was a strange conglomeration of beauties. And intimidating in spite of their friendly faces.

The women swarmed around Miss Ethel, each hugging her warmly before turning their attention to Cynthia. A pretty blonde walked over, and before she had a chance to react, the woman pulled her into a hug and said, "I'm so glad to meet you. I'm Rosalie, Zander's wife. He told me he got to meet you, and I was jealous that I had not had a chance to be with you yet." Uncertain if the woman was being facetious, as she pulled back and stared into her eyes, she realized Rosalie appeared completely sincere.

A slender brunette stepped forward next and said, "I get to meet you before my husband does. I'm Eleanor, and my husband is Rafe."

"It's nice to meet you, too," she said, but her words were barely out of her mouth before a tall, curvy, pregnant redhead reached down and offered her a hug.

"I'm Regina. You met my husband Cael at Grimm's Two, I believe."

Nodding, she said, "Yes, I did. I also met Asher."

"Ooh, then it's my turn to meet you next," said a slender woman with dark blonde hair. She had a slight limp and used a cane. Offering a one-armed hug, she said, "I'm Penny."

"You haven't met our husbands yet," said a dark-haired, athletic, also pregnant woman. "I'm Morgan, and my husband is Jaxon. His twin is Jayden, and this is his wife, Ruby."

She received hugs from the last two women, blinking in surprise at their friendly curiosity. Miss Ethel walked over and patted her arm, saying, "As soon as the girls heard that Zeke had someone special in his life, I'm surprised they waited this long to come over."

"Well, we've decided that an impromptu picnic is in order," Rosalie said. "We've already texted the men and told them to come here for lunch." Looking at Miss Ethel, she said, "You don't need to do a thing…we've already joined together, and everything is planned."

Rosalie linked arms with Cynthia as they walked around the side of the house. "I've known Zeke as long as I've known Zander, and I can't tell you how excited I am that he's found someone special."

She felt the heat of blush on her face, and said, "I feel like this may be rushed. After all, he and I just started seeing each other."

"Honey, the fact that he has you here with Miss Ethel tells us everything we need to know," Eleanor stated. "Her boys would never have just anyone here. That's how we knew how important you were to him."

Uncertain what to say, she was glad that it did not

appear she needed to respond. For the next hour, she continued to learn about pruning rosebushes from Miss Ethel as she also listened to the genuine camaraderie amongst the women.

She discovered that Rosalie had been injured outside of Grimm's, something that both Zander and Zeke felt responsible for. In the end, it was Zander's dedication at her hospital bedside that caused them to fall in love. Eleanor ran a burn clinic for veterans, something she had also suffered with from her time in the military, and Rafe worked there with her. Morgan, a former Olympic hopeful swimmer who had suffered a career-ending injury, now worked at Eleanor's clinic as well. Penny, a victim of a childhood car accident, worked for a real estate office. Ruby, currently working for Jayden, used to be a private housekeeper. It was a strange way to bond, but she found that they had a great deal in common. Regina rounded out the group, her job sounding interesting as she described restoring old films.

As they all managed to work in Miss Ethel's kitchen preparing lunch, she was struck with the ease of their conversations as well as a genuine interest in each other's lives. They formed a sisterhood that contrasted greatly with the relationship she had with her stepsisters. *This is how a family should be*, she thought. Knowing that she would never have that with her stepmother or sisters, she smiled as they included her in their bond.

Soon, the men began to arrive, and she anxiously waited for Zeke. Pleased to be able to greet Cael, Asher, and Zander since she had met them before, she was also introduced to Rafe, and the twins, Jaxon and Jayden, and Cas.

Finally, Zeke walked through the front door, his gaze scanning over everyone before landing on her. She watched him smile widely as he stalked to her, pulling her in for a hug. He leaned down and whispered, "I'm sorry you got ambushed by all of them. I had no idea the women were planning this."

She leaned back and smiled. "It's okay. I was super nervous at first, but they're all so nice."

Because it was such a lovely day, they began taking the platters of food out to the two picnic tables in the yard. She wondered if the dynamics would change now that the men were around, but the feeling of family continued. Joking and laughter abounded as well as a genuine interest in each other.

"Cynthia, I understand you had an interesting discovery this past week at work."

She looked up in mid-swallow to see one of the twins speaking to her. She was uncertain which one it was until she noted Morgan sitting next to him.

"That's right. Someone left a great deal of money in a room safe at the Prince Hotel, where I'm a housekeeper."

Ruby looked over at her and said, "Because I cleaned houses, everything in the house belongs to the owner. I never thought about what you might find in a hotel room."

Nodding, Cynthia said, "There are all kinds of things that people leave in the rooms. A lot of it is mundane, like sunglasses, books, chargers for phones, even keys. But there have been some really odd things as well."

Seeing the others staring at her in anticipation, she continued, "Jewelry, a mobility scooter which made us wonder how they actually left the room, artwork, train or plane tickets, even pets. It doesn't happen a lot, but we have found urns of someone's ashes."

"Oh, my God!" was uttered by several of the others, while Miss Ethel exclaimed, "My goodness! Do they come back to get them?"

"I assume so. Our procedure is that I tag them with the room number and the time and date that I found them. The Head of Housekeeping takes them, logs them into his book, and keeps them locked in the hotel safe. Well...not the pets. I believe that the guest is contacted if they left a phone number or address for certain items, like the pets or the remains. Anything else, it's left up to the owner to contact the hotel."

The various conversations resumed around the table, and Miss Ethel brought out a large chocolate sheet cake with whipped vanilla frosting. By the time the group was beginning to disband, Cynthia felt as though she were not only amongst friends but family.

As she walked Zeke back to his truck, she asked, "Are you working late tonight?"

He turned and wrapped his arms around her, pulling her in tightly to his chest. Kissing the top of her head, he left his lips in her hair as he said, "Yeah, I am. And you have to work tomorrow, don't you?"

She leaned her head back and nodded. "I'll be

nervous. Tomorrow is the day that the head of the hotel is supposed to present me with a certificate."

"You deserve it, babe. You take it, and you own it."

"I've only seen Mr. Prince a couple of times in the hotel. His office is on the top floor, but not near the suites I clean. I think Carlos told me that he'll take me to Mr. Prince's office. I'm glad Carlos will be with me. Otherwise, the knocking of my knees might sound too loud!"

"I don't have to work tomorrow night," Zeke said, holding her gaze. "How about I take you to dinner, and we can celebrate your award?"

Squeezing his waist, she grinned. "I'd love that."

He nuzzled her neck and whispered, "And maybe we can go back to my house after dinner for another kind of celebration."

At that, a bolt of lust shot through her and she squeezed him even tighter. "I'd love that even more." After waving as he drove down the road, she jogged back into Miss Ethel's house, excited for what tomorrow would bring.

15

Cynthia stood in the employee workroom, checking her reflection in the mirror for what felt like the millionth time that morning. She never went to work with a wrinkled uniform, but that morning she had ironed her Prince Hotel housekeeping uniform, taking extra care to make sure it was perfect. Her makeup was light, although she had added an extra swipe of mascara and a touch of pale pink lip gloss. Her hair was smoothed back from her face, but instead of the tight bun, Lucy and Belinda had convinced her to let her beautiful waves hang down her back in a low ponytail. She did not want to wipe her sweaty palms on her uniform, so she clutched a paper towel in her hands instead.

"Girl, stop fidgeting," Lucy admonished. "You're beautiful."

Just then, Carlos appeared at the doorway, his eyes scanning the room. When they landed on her, he smiled and asked, "Are you ready?"

Releasing a held breath, she nodded. "As ready as I'll ever be."

With 'good lucks' and 'congratulations' ringing in her ears, she fell into step next to Carlos as they walked down the hall and rode the service elevator to the top floor. Walking down the hall, they came to a tall wooden door. Carlos knocked once, and, receiving an invitation to enter, he opened the door and motioned for Cynthia to proceed before him.

She realized she was still clutching the paper towel in her palms and quickly slid it into her pants pocket. Sucking in a deep breath, she lifted her head high and walked in. It appeared she was in a smaller outer office, the deep burgundy carpet masking their footsteps. A wooden desk sat to one side, the leather chair empty.

One of the doors in the room opened, and Bob Shelton walked out to greet them. He nodded first to Carlos and then turned his attention to Cynthia. Smiling, he said, "Please, come this way."

He walked to another large, wooden door at the back of the room and opened it. He moved into the room and Carlos looked down at her, giving a slight nod. She followed Bob into the next office, glad for Carlos' presence behind her back.

The same deep burgundy carpet continued into this much larger office. Dark paneled walls gave the room an old-world feel. One wall was covered with built-in bookcases, many filled with leather-bound novels. At the back of the room were an ornate wooden desk and plush leather chair. Behind that, underneath the window, stood a wooden credenza.

A sitting area was in the opposite corner, consisting of a leather loveseat and two leather chairs surrounding a coffee table. The lighting was soft, eschewing fluorescent lights, instead lit by numerous lamps.

Standing by one of the windows was a man dressed in an impeccable suit. While Cynthia did not move in circles for people dressed in expensive clothing, she nonetheless knew that his suit cost more than she could imagine. The black suit was well complemented with a pale blue shirt and a royal blue silk tie.

The man was tall, his dark hair trimmed neatly, and while not slicked back, it was held in place with a product that neither looked overdone nor too casual. His blue eyes were deep-set, and his square jaw was cleanly shaven. He was as handsome in person as the pictures she had seen. Her internet searches had often found images of him in a tux with a variety of beautiful women on his arm, attending functions around town.

His gaze moved over her with an air of curiosity before he stepped toward her with a wide smile on his face. Mr. Shelton stepped in quickly and said, "Mr. Prince, this is Cynthia Ellison, from housekeeping. She's here today for—"

"Welcome, I'm Richard Prince. And I know exactly why you're here," Richard said, his smooth voice warm.

He reached out his hand for hers and took it in his own, giving it a friendly shake. She hoped her voice did not quiver as she greeted, "It's nice to meet you, Mr. Prince."

His eyes moved to the side, and his smile stayed firmly on his face as he nodded and greeted Carlos.

Lifting his free hand, he waved toward the small sitting area and invited, "Let's sit down."

She and Carlos took the small sofa while Richard and Bob each settled in one of the leather chairs facing them. She noticed a coffee service on the coffee table and said, "Would you like me to pour?"

Richard smiled and said, "If you don't mind. That really should be my job, or Bob's, since you are our honored guest, but I'm afraid either of us might make a mess."

She doubted very seriously if either one of them would have trouble pouring coffee but quickly filled their cups. Too nervous to drink any herself, she sat and only had a small sip for appearance's sake.

After a moment of small talk, Richard asked, "Where do you live, Cynthia?"

Head held high, she replied, "Currently, I'm renting a room from a lovely woman who has a large home and beautiful gardens."

"My mother had beautiful flower gardens," Richard said, smiling as he nodded. "She would never let the gardener take care of the flowers right next to the patio, insisting that she wanted to do them herself."

Finding herself relaxing, she said, "She also loves to quote literature, and yesterday, I was learning quite a bit about gardening and gardening quotes."

Eyes wide, Richard asked, "Any wisdom that you can pass on?"

Smiling, she said, "Gardens are not made by singing, 'Oh, how beautiful!' And sitting in the shade...that was by Rudyard Kipling."

"A maid quoting literature," Bob mumbled, his lips tight.

Blushing slightly, she said, "I think it's apropos for my job, don't you think? After all, this hotel would not be beautiful if no one was willing to do the work to make it so."

Richard laughed aloud, clapping his hands as he said, "Well played, well played."

He looked over at Bob and no words passed between them, but it appeared Bob knew what was expected. He moved to the credenza and picked up a picture frame which he handed to Richard.

Richard turned it around and showed the certificate to Cynthia. It read, "Prince Hotel Employee Excellence Award is presented to Cynthia Ellison in recognition of your exemplary performance and work ethic."

He stood, and she quickly came to her feet as well as he ordered, "Bob, pictures."

Bob immediately pulled out his phone and began clicking several pictures of her and Richard both holding the certificate between them and several with him shaking her hand. Richard asked Carlos to join them, and Bob began another round of pictures.

Her facial muscles felt tight from smiling so widely but she was afraid to drop her smile in case Bob clicked another picture. When he finally slid his phone back into his pocket, she sucked in a breath and forced her body to relax. She thought that she and Carlos would now be leaving, and it appeared Bob thought the same as he started for the door, but Richard said, "Let's sit back down. I have a proposition to offer."

Her gaze jumped to Carlos, and at a quick glance, she could tell he was not expecting anything. Sliding her eyes to Bob, it was equally obvious that he had no idea what his boss was up to. Uncertain what to do, she waited until the others moved back to their seats and she followed. Perching nervously on the edge of the sofa with her hands clasped together in her lap, she waited.

"As I'm sure you noticed when you came into the outer office, I am without a receptionist. Mrs. Smithwick has taken a month of leave to be with her grandchildren due to her daughter having surgery. She has only been gone for two days, and Bob and I are quite lost."

Bob opened his mouth as though to speak, but when Richard sent a sharp glare his way, Bob snapped it shut. It was obvious he was not happy with Richard's assessment but equally as obvious that he would not argue with him in front of others.

She felt Carlos' body tense next to hers and wondered where Richard was going with his comments.

"It's my understanding that you've been handling the executive suites as well as another floor. You are obviously very trustworthy, and I like to reward those I trust. I would like to suggest that for the next month you take Mrs. Smithwick's place and serve as my receptionist."

She sat in stunned silence, something that did not appear to be a problem with Bob as he sputtered "Her? She's a maid!"

Anger poured off of Carlos at Bob's words, and she

rushed to say, "It's true, I work in Housekeeping. I'm not ashamed of the job, but I'm not a receptionist."

Waving his hand dismissively, Richard said, "You would make a perfect receptionist. Bob is my administrative assistant and handles all the business end of that position. I need someone who can answer the phone, greet visitors, serve coffee when needed...that sort of thing. I think you'd be perfect for filling in for the job for the next month."

The idea of working in his beautiful office held a great deal of sway, but she cast a gaze toward Carlos, trusting his instincts. Before either of them had a chance to answer, Richard said, "it would, of course, include a raise, but I realize it's something you would need to consider. Perhaps you can think it over and let me know tomorrow."

Richard stood again, and everyone quickly took to their feet as well. He reached his hand out to take hers, his strong fingers wrapped around her cold ones, and said, "I think you would be an asset and hope you will strongly consider working in this office."

Returning his smile, she said, "I'm extremely flattered, Mr. Prince, and will be more than happy to let you know tomorrow."

She stepped to the side as he and Carlos shook hands, then followed Carlos out of the office, through the smaller outer office, and back into the hall. Neither said anything as they rode the elevator down and walked toward the lobby.

As they approached Carlos' office, he said, "Come with me."

Following, she stepped inside his smaller, utilitarian office. He waved her to his seat, and she sank into it, thoughts of the last thirty minutes swirling in her mind. "I take it you were surprised by Mr. Prince's offer?"

He nodded and said, "Yes, I was. Nothing has been said to me beforehand or I assure you, I would have given you a heads up."

"What do you think?"

His eyebrows lifted as he turned the question back around, "I think it's more important what you think."

Nibbling on her bottom lip, she said, "I'm flattered to be asked and would probably be a fool to turn it down." She lifted her gaze to his, but his blank face gave her no indication of what he was thinking. Continuing, she said, "A raise would be incredible right now because I'm still paying off my hospital bill. I was forced into the homeless shelter last week but now have a room with a nice elderly woman. A month with a significant raise would go a long way to helping my situation."

Hearing that, he nodded slowly and said, "I think you're right."

Tilting her head to the side, she asked, "What is making you hesitate?"

"You are more than capable of handling a job like what he is offering. You're smart and learn quickly. As to his motives? He works most of his days with Bob Shelton and Sheila Smithwick. Both excellent at their jobs, but neither as nice to look at as you."

Now it was her time to lift her eyebrows, and she said, "You think he's making the offer because of my looks?"

"I think he had any number of people he could've asked to fill in for her, but within a few minutes of being with you, he made the offer."

"It appeared that Mr. Shelton was surprised by his offer."

Snorting, Carlos said, "Bob, in my opinion, oversteps his bounds at times. I'm sure he likes to think that he knows everything that Mr. Prince is doing before he even does it. I'm convinced that Mr. Prince is completely in charge of what's going on in his hotel. I think occasionally he likes to tweak Bob."

She nodded slowly, considering everything he had said. Looking up, she sighed. "I'd still like to know what you think. I value your opinion."

His face softened, and he said, "Cynthia, I would hate to lose you on the floors for a month because you're my best employee. But I can certainly make do and realize that for you to have a chance to work as a receptionist for the owner of the Prince Hotel is an opportunity that might not ever come around again. The money he's offering would be welcome, and I think it would be good for you."

Nodding, she stood, her hands still clutched around her award, and said, "I think so, too. I'll sleep on it tonight and talk to a friend and let you know tomorrow." With that, she said goodbye and hurried down to the employee workroom where she stowed her award in her locker. Pushing her cart to the service elevator, she rode to the top floor of executive suites and began her day of housekeeping.

## 16

Zeke had spent the morning serving breakfast at the homeless shelter before heading to Grimm's Two to check on the delivery of some of the kitchen appliances. Now it was afternoon, and he was back at Grimm's getting ready for the after-work rush. He finished in the kitchen, pleased with the line cook's ability to handle everything without his constant supervision, and headed to the office seeking Zander.

Zander was not in the office, so he moved down the hall to the stock room where he found Zander checking the alcohol. Seeing the clipboard in Zander's hand, he knew his brother was preparing for the next order.

Zander looked over his shoulder and greeted, "Hey, Zeke. What's up?"

"I got something I've been thinking about, but I don't want to interrupt your stock take. We can talk about it later."

Zander tossed the clipboard to the top of the stack

of cardboard boxes that held liquor and said, "Hell, no time like the present. It's not like I can't finish this later."

They stepped back across the hall to the office, each settling into the old creaky chairs. Zeke glanced around and said, "Looks like Rosalie's been in here again."

Chuckling, Zander shook his head. "During the school year when she's teaching, she only comes in occasionally. But two months during the summer, she likes to make use of her organizational skills. Of course, with Charity, she comes in a lot less."

Zeke laughed aloud at the exaggerated tone Zander used when he said the words *organizational skills* but knew that his brother loved having Rosalie around.

They were silent for a moment until Zander prodded, "What's on your mind?"

"I was thinking about something, but I can't decide if it's the right thing to do or not. Since it would involve you, I need your opinion."

Zander nodded and leaned back in his chair, giving a silent indication for Zeke to continue.

"I know it's time to start looking for some managerial help with Grimm's Two. We agreed that we wanted the partnership to include both places, neither one of us solely in control of the other. That means sometimes I'm there, and sometimes I'm here. Same with you. I didn't know if you had already started looking at someone to help out."

Zander peered at him carefully and said, "No, I haven't started looking yet. I don't know anyone offhand, and I guess I dread the whole advertising and interviewing process." Cocking his head slightly, he continued, "What about you?"

Rubbing his hand over his beard, he admitted, "I hadn't until just the last couple of days. I wondered about Cynthia." His gaze jumped up to Zander's, not sure what he would see in his brother's eyes. As usual, Zander gave very little away in his expression. "It was just a thought—"

"Not a bad thought at all," Zander said, leaning forward with his forearms resting on the desktop.

Encouraged, he continued, "She's smart and a hard worker. I know she doesn't know anything about this business, but I think she could easily learn."

Snorting, Zander said, "Hell, I didn't know anything about this business when I got started. Do you think she'd be interested?"

"I have no idea. I haven't even hinted at the subject since I wanted to bring it up to you first. I don't think she's unhappy at the Prince Hotel, but I know it's not her life's pursuit to clean up after others."

Zander leaned back in his seat and asked, "What about the two of you? Working with someone you care for has its own pitfalls."

"I thought about that," he admitted. "That's one of the reasons I haven't brought it up until now. We've moved from just being friendly to being a couple—"

"Congratulations," Zander said, his smile sincere.

Chuckling, Zeke said, "Thanks, man. I mean, it's all new, but I really like her."

"Liking someone and working with them while having a relationship are two different things. If we offer her a job here, and she takes it, and then you two break up…"

Zeke nodded slowly, his heart twisting at the thought of Cynthia not being around. "I know, and that's probably one of the things on my mind. But one way or the other, I'd like to see her in a job with a future. I want to be in that future, but I'm mostly concerned about her."

"Then it sounds like you already know what you want to do. You want my input? I say go for it. I've got no one in mind and dreaded the idea of hiring someone so much that I figured you and I could divide our time for a while. But if she's interested, you can feel her out and we'll get together and talk."

Heart lighter, he stood. The two shook hands, clapping each other on the back. "It's about time for the evening crowd to hit, so I'll make sure things are good in the kitchen before I take off. I'm taking her to dinner tonight to celebrate her Employee Award."

Heading back down the hall, he glanced at his watch, anxious for his evening to begin.

Two hours later, he and Cynthia were sitting next to each other in a corner booth of a local steak house, both enjoying their ribeye and mound of buttery mashed potatoes. At first, she had insisted that she could not eat the whole steak, but he had no doubt he would be able to finish off what she left.

"I'm incredibly proud of you, you know," he said. "But, you didn't need to get an award for me to know how exemplary you are." Her smile widened, and he leaned forward, kissing her, deciding that kissing her in the middle of a smile was one of the top favorite things he liked to do of all time.

"It was so surreal," she said, her hands moving about as she talked. "Carlos and I walked into a plush office that was so unlike anything I had seen except in movies. Thick carpet, dark wood paneling, built-in bookcases, and a massive wooden desk that looked so neat it made me wonder if he did any work at it."

Laughing, he asked, "So, you got to meet Mr. Prince and not just an underling?"

"Oh, yes, it was he who presented me with the award. And he had his assistant take our pictures."

"I'm glad, babe," he said. "You deserve it."

She sucked in her lips and turned her eyes toward his, and said, "He actually talked to me for a while and made me an offer. I talked to Carlos about it but wanted to talk to you before I let him know my answer tomorrow."

"An offer?" Zeke asked, curiosity taking hold.

"It seems his receptionist is on family leave for a month, and he asked if I would take that position temporarily."

Eyes wide, Zeke swallowed his mouthful, uncertain he had heard correctly. "Seriously?"

Nodding her head up and down quickly, she said, "I know! I was just as stunned. I mean, I don't have secretarial skills, but he assured me that Mr. Shelton is his assistant and that I would just be the receptionist."

"What would you do as that?"

"He said I would work in the outer office, answer the

phone, greet guests, probably serve coffee to anyone who came in to see him, that sort of thing."

For a moment, his heart plunged, knowing that as much as he had wanted to ask her if she would consider working at Grimm's, a bar could not compare to the lure of working for the owner of an exclusive business. But, seeing the light in her eyes, her hopefulness was palpable. Reaching over and taking her hand, he said, "It sounds great, babe."

"I talked to Carlos afterward, and he admitted that it would be a good opportunity. Mostly because for a month I would be paid a salary much above what I make as a housekeeper. As you know, any extra money can go straight to paying down my hospital bill."

He watched as a small crease settled between her eyebrows, and he reached over to gently rub his finger to smooth the line. "What are you worried about?"

"Obviously, I would need some clothes... I certainly can't wear my Prince Hotel Housekeeping uniform to work, and I surely don't have enough money to buy a new wardrobe, especially for one month."

"You're about the same size as Rosalie and Eleanor. I'll bet they have some clothes that you could borrow."

Hope flared again in her eyes, and she said, "Oh, I'd hate to be an imposition!"

He squeezed her hand and said, "I know my sisters-in-law, and they'd love to help." Holding her gaze, he asked, "Now, what else is holding you back?"

"Do you think it would be weird? Going from housekeeping to the receptionist for the head of the hotel?" Giving a little sigh, she said, "And then, at the end of the month, going back to housekeeping. That's kind of like being elevated for a short while only to be sent back into the dungeon."

"Maybe something else will come by the time your month is up," he said, thinking of the possible job at Grimm's. He knew that working with him and Zander could not compare to working for Mr. Prince, but maybe she wouldn't feel that it was too much of a step-down.

Shrugging, she said, "Maybe. But I have to admit, the biggest pull is the money. It would be so nice to come closer to paying the hospital bill in full. I just hope I can do the job."

"Cynthia, listen to me," he said, taking both of her hands in his. "You are so smart that you can learn anything you need to. You've got a beautiful smile, and that's probably one of the reasons Mr. Prince would like to have you be his receptionist. He knows anyone coming in to see him will immediately feel welcome. Take the job for a month until his other receptionist comes back, and then we can see what else is out there that you might want to do if you choose not to go back to housekeeping."

Tears filled her eyes as she held his gaze, and she said, "Oh, Zeke, you make me feel as though I can do anything." She leaned forward and kissed him lightly, glancing to the side to see if anyone else in the restaurant noticed, a blush teasing her cheeks. Glancing down at their plates, she said, "As soon as we're finished, could we go back to your house and continue our celebration?"

"Oh, hell yeah, babe. I can't wait for us to celebrate alone."

Later, as they lay basking in the glow of their lovemaking, he could feel the hope of change in the air for both of them. As his hand trailed over her back to the curve of her hip before making its return journey back to her shoulder, he thought of their future.

With her head resting on his chest, she said, "You're so quiet."

"I'm thinking of us."

She raised up slightly so that she could peer down at him. "Good thoughts?"

Patting her ass, he grinned. "Babe, all thoughts about us are good thoughts." She remained quiet, and he continued, "I'm just thinking that there are lots of changes happening to both of us, but I think that can only lead to good things. You've got a new job for a month, and I'm spending the next month working on getting Grimm's Two opened."

"I know it will be busy, but it's an exciting time," she said, dropping her head to nuzzle his jaw.

All other thoughts flew from his mind as she continued to nibble from his jaw down to his neck. With a flip, he rolled her under him and spread her thighs once more, burying himself to the hilt after rolling on a condom. Connected in every way possible, they made love once again.

## 17

The next morning, Cynthia walked down the hall toward the executive wing, hesitating in the outer office. Glancing over at the desk, it was hard to believe that could be hers, at least for a month. She looked around, uncertain how to let Mr. Prince know that she was interested in the job. Since she was not about to knock on his door, she turned, deciding to go to Carlos instead.

Another door opened, and Bob Shelton walked out, his eyes widening when he saw her standing there. His gaze moved over her, and she squirmed, knowing that she looked out of place in her housekeeping uniform. "Well?" he asked.

Ignoring his imperious tone, she said, "I came to let Mr. Prince know that I will be more than happy and very honored to take the position of receptionist until Mrs. Smithwick gets back."

"I'll be sure to let him know," Bob said. Sending his

gaze over her again, he asked, "I trust you have something more suitable to wear for this position?"

Stiffening, she forced a smile on her face. "Yes. I'll report tomorrow morning...appropriately garbed." Turning on her heel, she walked out of the office and back down the hall. It was obvious he did not like the idea of having her there. Since she had given him no reason to dislike her, she assumed it was because he felt that she was inferior for the position. *No matter, that just means I have to work harder to prove him wrong.*

She had already told her friends about the offer, and when she entered the housekeeping workroom, she was met with squeals of delights from Lucy, Belinda, and Susan.

"Girl, this is the start of something big for you," Lucy swore. "I can feel it in my bones, and my bones are never wrong!"

Laughing, she said, "Well, I don't know about your bones, but I am excited. I'm nervous but excited. It may only be for a month and then I'll be right back here cleaning rooms, but if he gets me closer to paying off my hospital bill, then it's worth it."

"What are you gonna do about clothes?" Susan asked.

"It seems that Zeke has already called a couple of his sisters-in-law and they're going to meet me at Miss Ethel's this afternoon after work. Two of them are about my size and have said they can easily offer some clothes for me to wear that would be appropriate for the office."

After double-checking her cart to make sure she

had everything she needed, they rolled out of the workroom, a train of carts and housekeepers single file for the service elevator. Carlos had given her the executive floors again, and as she said goodbye to her friends when they alighted on their respective floors, she tried to imagine what it would be like the next day.

Lucy was the last to get out, and she turned and waved. "Enjoy your last day house cleaning!"

Just as the door closed, she called out, "I'll be right back here in a month!" As the elevator moved up another floor, she wondered about her words. Would she be right back here in a month? And if so, would that be disappointing?

———

Cynthia was not used to undressing in front of a group of others, although, occasionally, if her uniform became soiled at work, she would have to quickly change and there might be other women in the workroom. But standing in her bedroom at Miss Ethel's, she was continually standing in her bra and panties in front of the other women who were all handing her different clothes to try on.

The camaraderie and delight from the others at her new temporary job kept her from feeling self-conscious as she slipped on blouses, skirts, slacks, and a few dresses.

"Believe me, on a teacher's salary, I can't afford a lot of high-end things," Rosalie said, "but, with some nice slacks and skirts, you can completely change your outfit with the various tops."

"You wear pink beautifully," Regina commented, holding up a pink blouse in front of Cynthia. "I know with red hair I'm supposed to be able to wear anything, but honestly, pink just isn't my color."

"I always liked red," Ruby said, and the others began to laugh.

"With a name like Ruby, of course, you'd like red!" Morgan said.

Morgan and Regina were definitely larger than Cynthia, but they provided moral support as well as commentary on the clothes she was trying on. Plus, she wondered if they just wanted to be part of the gathering. Once again, she was struck with the difference between these women who had formed their own sisterhood, as opposed to her real sisters who had gleefully abandoned her along with her stepmother.

Miss Ethel appeared at the door and said, "My goodness! How all of you can cram into this room, I'll never know. You should have used my bedroom for your trying-on session, my dear. It's not huge, but it would have fit everyone better than this room."

A couple of the women were sitting on the floor in the corner, two others were on the bed, another one in the chair, and Rosalie was standing next to Cynthia.

Eleanor, sitting on the floor, piped up, "Oh, don't worry, Miss Ethel. We all fit in here just fine."

The older woman chuckled and said, "Just like when my boys were younger. As big as they were, they could all pile into this room when Zander was a senior in high school. Somehow, as close as they were, I don't think they minded." She looked over at Cynthia, and the creases in her face deepened as her smile widened. "You're absolutely beautiful, Cynthia. But then, you're equally as beautiful when you were wearing your uniform. Remember, your true beauty is inside."

Miss Ethel turned to go back down the stairs, calling over her shoulder, "As soon as you're finished, come on down. We'll have some tea. In fact, with everyone here, we'll have a tea party."

Cynthia stared at the empty doorway and said softly, "It's hard to believe she's real. She truly is like a fairy godmother."

Laughing, Rosalie said, "We're not exactly dressing you for the ball, but you're right about Miss Ethel."

With her selections soon made and heartfelt thanks given for the clothes they were letting her borrow, the women made their way to the dining room where Miss Ethel had teacups, two teapots, and plates of scones and cookies waiting.

Once settled, Ruby asked, "What will you be doing in your new job?"

Licking the crumbs from her lips, she replied, "I don't think it's going to be very much. Mr. Prince mentioned answering the phone and greeting any of the visitors that come to see him. I'll probably be serving coffee to them. I'm not even sure I'll have access to a computer because I think his assistant, Mr. Shelton, handles that. I suppose, starting tomorrow, I'll find out more about it."

"Do you think it'll turn into something more permanent?" Penny asked, pouring another cup of tea.

"I doubt it. From what I know, Mrs. Smithwick has been with him for years. She's only taking family leave to be with her daughter who has had surgery so that she can help with the grandchildren. It's my understanding that she will be back in a month. My guess is that I'll go right back to housekeeping." She saw the looks the others were giving her and rushed to say, "I'm not dumb. I know it will be a letdown to go back to scrubbing toilets after having worked in such a plush environment, but honestly, it's about paying off the hospital bill. The extra money I make will go a long way to having that happen."

"Well, here's to tomorrow and all the wonderful things that it can bring," Miss Ethel said, lifting her teacup as though in a toast.

Laughing, the others agreed, lifting their teacups up as well. Looking around the room, filled with friends that were becoming sisters and a woman so like her own mother, she smiled.

Zeke stood at the back door of Grimm's along with Zander, both counting the stock of alcohol crates as they were brought off the truck and rolled into the storeroom. Multitasking as he ticked off the numbers on his clipboard, Zander asked, "So, what happened? Yesterday you were going to ask her to work for us, and today you're telling me that she's working for Mr. Prince."

He had already explained to Zander what had happened, but in response to the question just shrugged. "Not much else to say."

As the last cart was rolled off the truck, Zander signed off on the form before handing it back to the driver. Looking over at Zeke, he said, "If she was looking for a way to get out housekeeping, you could've made the offer for her to work here. That would've given her a choice."

"Seriously? Why would she want to work here, doing this," he emphasized with his hand sweeping around at the dusty cardboard boxes and wooden crates of alcohol that were now stacked in their storeroom, "when she can be working in an elegant office with Mr. Richard Prince, owner of the exclusive Prince Hotel?"

Planting his fists on his hips, Zander argued, "I don't know where she'd rather work. But you could've asked her."

Zeke hated to admit that after he and Cynthia had talked the previous evening he had internet stalked her new boss. Initially, he assumed it would be an older man, very grandfatherly, who just wanted to help an employee. Stunned as he flipped through image after image of a young, virile, handsome man in expensive suits and usually seen with an elegant woman on his arm, he realized that he had little to offer Cynthia. Dropping his chin, he stared at his boots and sighed.

"Hey, it's me," Zander said, his voice soft. "Talk to me."

He lifted his gaze and stared at his oldest brother, the one who first offered him a true glimpse of friendship and brotherhood. Scrubbing his hand over his face, feeling the scruff he rarely shaved off, he admitted, "Richard Prince has education. Family connections. A ton of money. I can't compete against that."

Brows drawn down, Zander asked, "Who said anything about a competition?"

"I know she cares for me, so it's not that. And, honestly, I doubt she's his type, considering it looks like he goes for wealthy socialites or famous models and actresses. But as far as workplaces go, Grimm's can't compete with a...a...fuckin' office like his."

Clapping him on the shoulder, Zander said, "Look, it's only for a month. When that month is over with and she's thinking about going back to housekeeping, you can let her know that if she wants a place with us, she can have it."

"Can we hold off that long?"

Grinning, Zander said, "Fuck, man. We can hold off longer. There's nothing we gotta do between now and then that you and I can't handle."

Pulling himself up to his full height, he sucked in a fortifying breath. "You're right. And if I don't get my ass in gear, we won't be able to handle it." With that, he tossed up a wave and headed back to the kitchen.

## 18

Walking into the Prince Hotel the next morning, Cynthia passed through the lobby, catching a reflection of herself in one of the large glass windows. Her pencil skirt was just short of her knees. Her black pumps gave her a few inches of height, and her pale pink blouse added a touch of feminism. Her hair was down, only pulled back at the top away from her face, but her blonde tresses hung down her back. With a little extra makeup, she hoped for a more professional appearance.

She had received an email from Mr. Shelton telling her to report to the hotel's HR office before she came to her new workspace. After filling out a few forms, she walked toward the back. Entering the plush office, she hesitated, uncertain what she should do first. Before she had a chance to look for Mr. Shelton, the large door in the back opened, and Mr. Prince walked through. His eyes widened as he took her in from head to toe, and his smile filled his face.

"I'm so glad to see you here this morning! And so

pleased that you decided to take me up on the offer. You're a beautiful asset to the Prince Hotel."

His words went a long way to ease her nerves, and she smiled in return. "Thank you. I appreciate your vote of confidence." Glancing around the office, she said, "I confess I'm nervous because I'm not sure what's expected of me."

He waved his arm toward the beautiful wooden desk near the corner and said, "This will be where you sit. You'll answer the phone and take notes, letting me know who calls and when. I'll let you know if there are visitors expected, and once they've arrived, you can let me know." He walked over to the desk and pointed to the intercom system. "I've already had HR set you up with email on the laptop, and we can communicate that way too if I'm not readily available. If the visitors are in my office or in the conference room, I'll also ask you to serve coffee. Occasionally, I might have you run an errand for me, but I'll try to keep those to a minimum."

Taking it all in, she met his eyes and quickly said, "I don't mind running errands at all, Mr. Prince. I would much rather do that than sit idle."

His smile continued as he said, "You're a woman after my own heart. I've always preferred being busy, as well."

Looking around the office, she noticed another table in the far corner with a coffee pot. "Would you like me to bring you some coffee now?"

"That would be lovely. I take it with just a dollop of cream and one sweetener packet, please." With that, he walked back into his office.

She walked over to Mrs. Smithwick's desk and found a drawer empty for her to stow her purse. Walking to the table, she brewed a pot of coffee and fixed a cup the way he had instructed. Carrying it carefully, she moved to his door and knocked. Upon gaining entrance, she saw that Mr. Shelton was already in with Mr. Prince. It had escaped her notice the other day that there was a door in the wall, similar to the paneling, that must connect the two men's offices.

She set the cup of coffee on Mr. Prince's desk before turning to Mr. Shelton. "Would you like a cup of coffee also, Mr. Shelton?"

Her question seemed to startle him, but before he had a chance to answer, Mr. Prince said, "In here, we are more informal. You may certainly call us by our first names...Richard and Bob."

She had no doubt that the older Mrs. Smithwick would have been given that liberty, but from the look on Bob's face, he was not expecting her to have the same familiarity. Nonetheless, if that's what Mr. Prince...Richard wanted, that was what she would use.

"Coffee, Bob?"

His face tight, he gave a curt reply. "Black."

With a polite inclination of her head, she walked back out and fixed a cup of coffee for Bob. Once she had delivered it to him, she headed back to the desk. Opening her laptop, she pulled up her email and found that, just like Richard had said, HR had set her up with a password. Smiling, she sent a notice to Carlos, letting him know that she was settling in on her first day.

She handled the phone calls that came in but realized that the hotel's switchboard diverted most of Richard's calls to Bob. She discovered that when she noticed his phone rang often and heard Bob setting up meetings.

Hoping that it was okay, she fixed herself a cup of coffee, mostly to give herself something to do. She noticed dust in the corner of the table behind the coffee pot and wondered about the night cleaners who were in charge of the executive offices.

Giving a little shake, she forced the thoughts of housekeeping out of her mind. Another hour passed with her only answering a few more phone calls, so when Richard called for her to come to his office, she almost jumped for joy.

Standing, she ran her hands down her skirt, straightening the wrinkles, and knocked on his door. He called for her to enter, and when she did, he said, "You don't have to knock when I've called for you, Cynthia."

"Oh, okay." She stood just inside his office, uncertain if she should approach or stay where she was. Even if the position was only temporary, she wanted to do everything right.

He chuckled, and her eyes jumped to his. "Please, come on in," he said. She approached, and he continued, "I can feel your nerves bouncing off the room. I want you to just relax. I promise I'm not an evil boss who will bite your head off."

"I'm sure you're not," she rushed. "I think it's just first-day jitters."

Nodding, he said, "Well, just relax, and we'll get along fine. The reason I called you in is because I'm going to be heading to lunch at noon. I'd like you to join me."

"Absolutely, that'll be fine," she said, breathing easier now that she knew what he wanted. "Do I need to bring anything with me to take notes?"

Shaking his head, he said, "No, nothing at all. It won't be a business lunch. But we both need to eat, and it'll give us a chance to get to know each other a little bit."

Since that seemed to be all he wanted, she turned and went back to her desk. Glancing at the clock, she realized she had another hour to go before they would be leaving for lunch. A few more phone calls later, she overheard Bob say, "Richard, do you want to get lunch today?"

She sucked in her lips, wondering if Bob was going to be joining them for lunch. His animosity toward her was so obvious, she almost hoped that he would not. She could not hear what Richard said, but assumed he answered in the negative when she heard Bob say, "You're kidding. Her?"

Cynthia could feel the heat of blush from her chest to the roots of her hair. *Well, it appears he won't be joining us for lunch! Good!*

At precisely noon, Richard walked out of his office and looked toward Cynthia. With a smile, he asked, "Ready?"

She had actually been ready for the past forty-five minutes, mostly twiddling her thumbs with nothing to do, but she did not want to give off the vibe of having been bored. She closed her laptop, pulled out her purse, and stood. Walking around her desk toward him, she nodded and returned his smile. "Absolutely."

They walked out of the offices and through the lobby. With a quick glance, she noticed the workers behind the reception desk seemed to snap to attention as he walked past. Their eyes landed on her, and she felt a combination of excitement and embarrassment. *Just two days ago, I was scrubbing the toilets here, and now, I'm walking out with the owner!*

"There's a new Indian restaurant that has just opened up nearby," he said. "Would that be acceptable to you?"

She had never eaten Indian food but was not about to tell him that. "I'm sure it'll be lovely," she said, hoping her noncommittal answer would satisfy him. She hesitated to see which way he would turn as they left the building, assuming they would walk since he said it was nearby. Instead, he lifted his hand, and she saw a black sedan pull up to the curb just in front of the hotel.

Realizing he had a ride and his own driver, she blinked in surprise as he held the door for her. Sliding into the buttery softness of the leather interior, she scooted all the way over, giving him plenty of room to sit. He gave directions to his driver, and they were there in a minute.

She sucked in her lips, thinking of the wasted gasoline for a one-minute drive, but kept her mouth shut. He offered her a hand to assist her as she alighted from the vehicle, then remained a respectable distance from her as they walked together into the restaurant. There was a line at the hostess desk, and she realized the new restaurant must be very popular. Wondering how long they would have to wait, she was once more surprised as the hostess looked up at Richard and immediately lifted her hand to call over a server.

They bypassed the others, and the hostess greeted, "Mr. Prince, we're so glad to see you again. Please, follow Jonathan to your table."

She noticed several patrons' eyes followed them as they walked to their table. Once seated, she leaned forward and whispered, "I can't believe we were able to bypass the crowd trying to get in!"

Richard chuckled and said, "Being the owner of an exclusive hotel has its perks. I try not to overuse them, but since they know that I will send business their way, they are more than happy to seat me when I show up." Smiling, he inclined his head toward her and added, "And the fact that I have a lovely lunch guest does not hurt."

She rolled her eyes and laughed, then stared at the menu. She had no idea what any of the dishes were and knew that pretending was foolish. Setting the menu down, she looked up and said, "I have to be honest with you, Richard. I've never eaten Indian food before and have no idea what to order."

His eyes warmed as they looked at her, and he said, "How refreshing to have someone be so honest. Tell me...do you like chicken?"

Nodding, she said, "Yes."

"Mild or spicy?" he continued.

"Mild."

With that information, he ordered for her and then

said, "I have no doubt that you will find your meal delicious."

As they waited for their meal to be prepared, he asked, "So, Cynthia, do you have family in the area?"

Shaking her head, she said, "No. My mother died when I was a teenager, and my father died a few years later."

His eyes opened wide, and he said, "I'm so sorry."

"Thank you," she said. "I had a stepmother and stepsisters, but we're not close. In fact, I haven't seen them for several years. I have a group of friends that I'm finding to be much more sisterly than my stepsisters ever were." Tilting her head slightly, she asked, "What about your family?"

"My family is still all alive and well. My father is the president of Prince Hotels International, and my oldest brother is his second in command. I guess you could say I was brought up in the hospitality business. But, instead of working for our international company, I preferred to be the owner of one of the hotels."

Their food was delivered, interrupting their conversation, and true to his word, she found the butter chicken to be delicious. When the meal was complete, he signed the bill using his company credit card.

Dabbing her lips with her napkin, she said, "Thank you so much for lunch. It was a nice way to enjoy my first day."

"I don't always have a chance to eat out for lunch," he said. "Many days, I will simply have the hotel's restaurant send something. In fact, that will be one of your duties. You can check with me in the mornings to see what my lunch plans are, and if I'm having the hotel restaurant prepare my lunch, I'll let you order."

Settling back in his sedan, she readily agreed. "Absolutely. In fact, Richard, I truly would like to help while Mrs. Smithwick is out. So if there's anything you need me to do, just let me know."

"I take it Bob is probably handling all of my calls, isn't he?" Richard asked, a smile playing about his lips.

Nodding, she blushed. "I don't think he's very happy that I'm filling in for her."

"Don't worry about Bob. Like I said, I think you're a delightful asset, and the office is brighter just having you there."

It once again only took a moment to get to the hotel, and as Richard headed back to his office, she slipped into the ladies' room. Now, staring at her reflection, she smiled. The job might seem a little boring, but at least her boss was nice. She pulled out her phone and sent Zeke a text. **Having a great first day. Can't wait to see you.**

With that, she headed back down the hall to her office, much more relaxed than she had been that morning.

## 19

Zeke had been glad to get Cynthia's text, happy that her day was going well. He wished he could have said the same about his own. He had spent most of the day at Grimm's Two overseeing the delivery of furniture and equipment.

The tables and chairs had been delivered, but neither he nor Zander realized that the table legs would have to be screwed on. That morning, as he stared at the round wooden tabletops with their legs wrapped in plastic taped to the underside, he dropped his head in frustration. By the time lunch had rolled around, he only had some of them put together because of the constant interruptions of other deliveries.

Finally leaving the tables, he focused his concentration on the kitchen. The electrician had shown up, but the equipment had not yet been delivered. It was close to noon when the truck rolled into the alley for the delivery, but the electrician had gone on to another job.

Sucking in a deep breath, he let it out slowly, signing

off as the stovetops, ovens, refrigerator, and freezer were placed in the kitchen. When the electrician came back, they made sure everything was hooked up correctly and within the fire codes.

Standing back, he wiped the sweat from his brow and grinned. For the first time that day, it seemed as though something was finally going right. There was still a lot of smaller equipment to be delivered, but the kitchen was finally looking the way he wanted.

By late afternoon, he had received more deliveries, rejected a few that were incorrect, and spent time on the phone with suppliers. His hair had been pulled up into a man bun on top of his head as he sweat profusely in the heat.

He heard the front door open and wondered what he was going to have to deal with next. Lifting his gaze, he spied Cynthia standing in the doorway, backlit by the outside sunlight. Her trim legs looked amazing in the skirt that hugged her hips and thighs. The pink blouse was not revealing but soft and feminine. Her hair, generally pulled back in a tight bun, was flowing about her shoulders.

She stepped inside, the door behind her closing, allowing him to see her facial features more clearly. As soon as her eyes landed on him, they sparkled as she smiled widely. She was like the sunshine on a cloudy day, the calm in the middle of the storm.

Abandoning the still-not-put-together table and chairs, he stalked straight toward her, grinning as she gave a little hop and moved directly toward him as well. Reaching her, he wrapped his arms around her, pulling her in tightly. Her head leaned back as she lifted on her toes, and he met her seeking lips.

They both opened, their tongues tangling at the same time, and he felt his cock swell painfully in his pants. Pulling back regretfully, he sucked in a deep breath. "You're a sight for sore eyes, babe."

Her eyes moved over his face before sliding to the side, seeing the unfinished mess in the floor. Her brow crinkled as she asked, "What's going on here?"

"We thought we were getting a good deal on the tables and chairs but missed the part where we would have to put them all together. I got started on it, but then the kitchen deliveries came so I never got back to finishing."

Her gaze shot back to his, and she said, "I can help."

"I don't think so, babe, not looking like that."

She huffed and said, "But I want to help. I want to be a part of this with you."

Her words warmed him deeply, more than he could have imagined. "I want that too, but why don't you just sit here and keep me company while I put a few more of the tables together?"

"You don't think that sounds a little bit sexist?" she asked, her eyebrow lifted.

Chuckling, he shook his head. "I didn't mean it like that, babe. But I'd love to hear about your day. Pull up a chair, tell me all about it, and together we can get some of this done."

She grabbed a chair and pulled it over to the table he was working on. The top of the table was flat on the floor, face down, and she held each leg in place as he used the electric screwdriver to tighten and bolt in the screws.

"I know it was the first day, but it really was kind of boring. I'm supposed to answer the phone calls that come in for Richard--"

"Richard?" As soon as the name left his mouth, he could hear the roughness in his voice, coughing slightly, he asked, "He lets you call him by his first name?"

Nodding, she said, "He said in the office that I am to call him Richard and Mr. Shelton Bob. Like I was saying, I'm supposed to answer the phone calls, but I discovered that most of them seem to be routed to Bob. I don't think he's very happy with me being there, but I don't know why. It certainly not like it's a permanent position, and I'm not doing anything at all that could remotely seem like his job."

Taking a moment to get the screws tightened on the next table, he looked up and asked, "So, what else did you get to do today?"

Shrugging, she said, "Not much. I fetched coffee for him and Bob. Fiddled around some. Answered a few phone calls. Got them some more coffee and some for me. After lunch, he had a meeting in the conference room, and I got to fix some coffee for those people."

Shifting back on his heels, he stared, his brow crinkled. "That's all he wants you to do? Fetch coffee?"

Slumping slightly, she nodded. "Well, today was just my first day." Brightening, she added, "I did have a nice lunch."

"Did you go out somewhere?"

"Richard took me to an Indian restaurant. I wasn't

sure about the food, but he ordered for me, and it was pretty good."

The thought of Cynthia having lunch with her wealthy boss shot a bolt of jealousy straight through Zeke, and as he glanced down, he realized his hands were clenched into fists. Sucking in a deep breath and letting it out slowly, he forced his body to relax. *It's not a big deal...coworkers have lunch together all the time.*

"I'm glad it was good for you," he said. While the sentiment was true, he could not deny that he wished it had been he that had lunch with her. The table he was working on was finished, and they stood, flipping it over together.

"It's perfect!" she exclaimed, clapping her hands together as she beamed up at him.

Shrugging his heavy shoulders, he said, "It's just a table, babe."

She walked around from the other side of the round table, her fingers slowly dragging across the top as she approached. She did not stop until she was directly in front of him, and he felt her breasts pressing lightly against his chest. Her fingers left the table, and she walked them from his waistband up to his chest and said, "It involved screwing hard objects into tight holes." Tilting her head slightly, she held his gaze as she added, "And you do that perfectly."

"Fuck," he groaned.

Still smiling, she rose on her tiptoes and whispered, "That's the idea."

The jealousy he felt earlier was replaced with another bolt, this time of pure, white lust. As he enveloped her in his arms, he groaned again just before his lips slammed onto hers. As he lifted her up, she tried to swing her legs around his waist, but her straight skirt impeded the movement. Although, with his arm around her, he pressed her heat against his rock-hard cock.

"Fuck," he groaned again, turning and stalking toward the kitchen. Kicking the door shut, he fumbled with the lock until it flipped and then moved to the outer door, doing the same. It was no easy feat with her lips on his, her tongue in his mouth, her breasts pressed against his chest, and her hips grinding against his.

Placing her ass on the counter, he sucked on her tongue as his hands moved to her blouse. The buttons were tiny, and he did not want to rip the material, so he was glad when her fingers pushed his out of the way and she deftly unfastened the blouse before shaking her torso and letting the material pool behind her.

He flipped his shirt over his head before reaching forward and jerking the cups of her bra down, freeing her breasts. He eagerly watched as the cool air hardened her beckoning nipples.

He bent and sucked one deeply into his mouth, and her fingernails raked downward across his chest before she began tugging on the zipper of his jeans. He pulled back slightly, toed off his boots, and dropped his jeans and boxers to his ankles.

She took the opportunity to lay back on the counter, shimmying her skirt up to her hips to her waist. He reached forward and snagged her silky panties, jerking them off her legs. The scent of her arousal rose to greet him, and now that her thighs were free of the tight confines of the skirt, he spread her legs and dove in. His lips latched over her folds, licking and sucking as she writhed on top of the counter.

She was so primed and ready, it only took a moment of his tongue on her sex before his lips sucked on her clit, and she cried out her orgasm as her hips bucked upwards. Lapping her juices, he managed to get a condom rolled onto his eager cock.

Sliding her forward, he impaled her as he held her in his arms, twisting around. With her back pressed against the refrigerator door, he thrust upward, sheathing himself in her warm, slick sex. She met him thrust for thrust, her fingernails creating little crescents in the muscles of his back as she held on tightly.

With her lifted in his arms, her breasts bounced right in front of his face, and he wrapped his lips around one and tugged. Just as she began to fly apart for the second time, he buried himself to the hilt and roared. Flinging over the precipice at the same time, he saw white light behind his tightly-closed eyelids as he continued to drain every drop. Finally empty, he dropped his forehead to the cool metal of the refrigerator by her shoulder.

His strong arms and legs grew weak, and he regretfully pulled out of her heat before setting her feet steadily back on the floor. With his body still pressed up against hers, he was uncertain which one of them was holding the other up. Continuing to drag breath deep into his lungs, his heartbeat finally slowed and he opened his eyes, finding her staring up at him, a smile playing about her lips.

"Damn, girl," he managed to utter.

A giggle slipped between her lips, and she said, "Who knew that putting tables together would be so sexy?"

"Fuck, babe. I'll put furniture together for you every night if I thought you'd go wild like this."

A blush crossed her face, and her gaze dropped to his chest. Giving her head a little shake, she admitted, "I've never gone wild like that. Ever."

"I love hearing that. I love that you're honest enough to confess that, and I love I'm the first who's made you go wild." As much as he hated to move, he knew the cold refrigerator door could not be comfortable. He pulled her forward, sliding her bra cups back over her breasts. He bent and pulled up his boxers and jeans after removing the condom. Darting into the adjoining bathroom, he took care of himself. When he returned, her skirt was back in place, and she was tucking her now-buttoned blouse into the waistband. He did not see her panties on the floor, so he assumed she had retrieved them.

As she looked up at him, there was a hesitancy in her eyes, and he wanted to remove all traces of it. Opening his arms, he said, "Come here, babe." He was grateful when she rushed into his arms.

Holding her close, he looked over the top of her head toward the counter and chuckled. "I'll never look at this kitchen the same."

She leaned her head back, grinned widely and said, "Good. Whenever you're in here cooking, I want you to think of me."

"Cynthia, babe, I think of you all the time anyway."

She did not reply but tucked her head back underneath his chin and held him tightly with her cheek pressed against his heartbeat. Continuing his honesty, he said, "I was jealous when you told me that you had lunch with your boss."

Her head jerked back, and she rushed to say, "Zeke, that was nothing. Believe me, he is just a boss...the owner of the hotel where I work, nothing more."

He ran his nose along her forehead, down to her ear, nuzzling her soft skin, feeling her shiver. "You are so beautiful that unless he is completely blind he would crave your company."

"You are the one I want to be with. The only one I want to be with."

He lifted his head long enough to stare into her eyes, honesty beaming at him, spearing him through the heart. "And you are the only one I want to be with as well."

They soon headed back to Miss Ethel's, and he stayed to have dinner with both of them. Relaxed, he wondered how soon would be too soon for Cynthia to move in with him. It was on the tip of his tongue to say something that evening, but he did not want her to think it was a knee-jerk reaction to his jealousy. Plus, seeing Miss Ethel and Cynthia enjoy each other's company gave him pause. Willing to be patient, he could wait until the time was right.

But for now, he reached across the table and helped himself to another piece of peach pie.

---

Two days. Two days of fetching coffee. Ordering lunch. Forwarding a few emails. Answering a few calls. And yesterday, Richard had asked her to pick up his dry cleaning, which she jumped up to do eagerly, desperate for some task to accomplish.

Finally, today, he said that he was having a lunch meeting in the conference room and would like her to make sure the food from the restaurant was delivered. It was not much, but she was glad for a diversion.

At the appropriate time, she led several employees in white shirts and black pants as they rolled carts with domed dish covers toward the conference room. Knocking, she opened the door when beckoned, and stepped inside the room. "Mr. Prince, lunch is ready."

She had already been in the room earlier that morning serving coffee and knew that there were five people around the table with Richard and Bob. She had taken care to order exactly what he had asked for and stepped to the side to allow the servers to place the plates in front of each of the persons at the table.

The servers left, and she walked around the table, refilling the coffee cups.

"Where's Mrs. Smithwick?" one of the women asked.

"She's on family leave for a month," Richard replied, buttering his roll. He looked up and smiled at Cynthia and said, "Ms. Ellison was recently the recipient of the Prince Hotel Excellence Award, and I thought she would make a perfect replacement while Mrs. Smithwick is gone."

"Yes, quite the step up," Bob said. "In the blink of an eye, she's gone from being a maid to an assistant here in Richard's office."

Cynthia bristled, both at Bob's comment and the callous way in which she was being talked about while she was standing right there.

"Whoa," one of the other women said. "That is quite a jump."

Chuckling, the man sitting to Richard's left said, "One look at her, and you can see why she was elevated."

Richard's gaze jumped to her when she was unable to keep the slight gasp from leaving her lips. "Ms. Ellison, thank you. You may go have your lunch now. In fact, when we're finished, I'll ring for the restaurant servers to come back and clear away the plates."

With a tight-lipped smile, she inclined her head slightly and turned to walk out of the room, resisting the urge to slam the door.

She walked back to her desk, grabbed her purse

from the drawer, and walked out, not having any idea where she wanted to go. Beyond the lobby was the service elevator. Looking at her watch, she hoped the time was right. Going down to the basement, she walked to the housekeeping workroom, the familiar laughter emanating from inside already acting like a calming balm on her verbal stings.

Stepping inside, she saw Lucy, Belinda, and Susan sitting at a table eating their lunch. Lucy saw her before she had a chance to greet them and cried out, "Cynthia! Oh, my goodness, girl, you're a sight for sore eyes!"

The three women stood and moved toward her, each offering a heartfelt hug. "What are you doing down here?" Belinda asked, her gaze taking in Cynthia from head to toe. "Those clothes look a lot better on you than this old uniform!"

"I had a break, and Mr. Prince didn't need me, so I thought I'd come to see if you ladies were having lunch."

"Well, sit," Susan encouraged, and she readily took the available chair. "You do look gorgeous."

"I had some friends who loaned some work clothes to me," she admitted. "It didn't make any sense to spend money that I don't have on clothes that I won't wear beyond this month."

"Who knows? This job might lead to something else, and you won't need to come back to housekeeping," Susan said.

Shrugging, she mumbled, "Maybe." She saw her friends hesitate with their meals, and she said, "Keep eating, please. I know how short your lunch break is, and I'm getting something later."

Lucy eyed her carefully, then said, "So, how is it up in the world above?"

"It's fine," she said. "Mr. Prince is very nice, and Mr. Selton is...well, I'm not so sure he's thrilled with me being there, but he's been fine."

"Fine and nice aren't exactly exciting words," Lucy said, lifting an eyebrow.

Shoulders sagging, she admitted, "It's kind of lonely, which is weird to say. Because when I was on a floor cleaning, I was generally by myself unless one of us was sharing a floor. But I was always so busy."

"Yeah, busy cleaning up other people's messes!" Susan said. "Don't you think it's going to be hard to come back to this?"

Nibbling on her bottom lip, she shook her head, and said, "I don't know. I like to stay busy, and so far, I'm actually bored. Honestly, my days went a lot faster when I had a set schedule to keep to."

She watched the other women's expressions show a mixture of incredulity, and she realized it was unfair for her to cry 'poor me' when she was making more money and doing a lot less than they were. Moving the subjects to something lighter, they chatted for a few minutes until it was time for her friends to go back onto the floors.

As she wandered down the hall, she noted Carlos' office door was open, and she peeked in. He was sitting at his desk, his computer open, and a plate loaded with a large turkey club sandwich and chips nearby.

She lifted her hand to knock on his door frame, but

the movement caught his eye, and he smiled widely when he saw her standing there.

"Come in, come in," he said. As she entered his office, he stood and walked around the desk, his hand extended, greeting her warmly. "To what do I owe the honor of your visit? Surely, you're not ready to take your old job back after only a few days, are you?"

His wide smile indicated he was joking, and while she was not ready to return to housekeeping, the words from Mr. Prince's meeting still rung in her ears. Giving her head a little shake, she smiled in return. "No, no, everything's fine. Mr. Prince didn't need me right now, so I thought I would take a moment and check up with my friends downstairs. When their lunch was over, I just happened to wander by and thought I'd pop in to say hello to you, too."

"I'm glad you did," Carlos said enthusiastically, waving his hand toward a chair in his office.

Just like she did with her friends, she said, "Please, keep eating. I don't want to take up your lunchtime, and your sandwich will be so much better eaten fresh."

Tossing his hand dismissively in the air, he said, "Don't worry about it. I've actually been munching on that sandwich for about an hour now."

Laughing, she tilted her head down toward his computer and said, "Buried in work?"

"No rest for the weary," he joked, closing the laptop.

Settling in the chair, she thought about her former position. "I didn't ask Lucy and the others if things were going okay."

He said, "I have Lucy on the executive suites rotation. She's not as thorough as you were, but she has seniority and is almost as good. We have a couple of people, as you know, who we can call in for a temporary basis. They're doing fine for now."

"Well, I've only been gone a couple of days," she reminded. "In a little over three weeks, I'll be back."

He lifted his eyebrow, and she felt his penetrating stare. "Are you sure?"

"Carlos, you know this is only temporary. It seems as though everyone expects me to not want to come back to my job just because I'm out of the housekeeping rotation for a month."

Shaking his head, Carlos said, "There's nothing wrong with housekeeping. It's good, honest, necessary work. And you have always been an excellent employee. But it is physical labor. Many people do it for a while and then decide they want to try something else."

"Do you think because I'm wearing fancier clothes and work in a fancy office that I won't want to come back?"

Lifting his hands slightly to the side as he shrugged his shoulders, he said, "I don't know, Cynthia. You're incredibly smart, but I know your family situation made you feel like this type of labor was the only job you are qualified for. I also realize that working for Mr. Prince, you may decide that there's something else out there for you."

His words made sense, and yet it was hard for her to express how much she was finding her temporary job to be dissatisfying.

Continuing, he asked, "So, how do you like working for Mr. Prince in his office?"

Smiling, she said, "He's very nice. He's not demanding. In fact, I'm bored for much of the day. But he seems to be glad to have me around, and if I'm helping by just getting him coffee when he needs it, then that's fine too, I suppose."

"And Bob?" Carlos asked.

She could hear the sardonic tone to his question and said, "I think Bob would be very happy I was not anywhere around."

"Bob is a tough person to figure out," Carlos admitted.

"I get the feeling that he'd like to have Richard all to himself," she said. As soon as the words left her mouth, her fingers flew to her lips, and she blushed. "That didn't come out the way I meant!"

Laughing, Carlos nodded. "Don't worry, I know what you mean. I get the feeling that Bob wants to check up on everybody who works for Prince Hotel. I just wish he realized that some of us don't want or need anyone looking over our shoulders all the time."

"He looks over your shoulder?" she asked, her eyes blinking open wide.

"Well, Bob and I should be considered equals. I confess I resent when he tries to find out what's going on in housekeeping. I don't need him keeping tabs on me or my housekeepers." he looked at her carefully and added, "Just like when you found the money and he was questioning you to see if you had read the note."

Immediately uncomfortable at the memory that she

had lied to Bob—and everyone else, including Carlos—about the note, she fought the urge to squirm in her seat.

Carlos watched her carefully, then asked her, "Now that you're in the main office, you have the opportunity to see what Bob does with his time all day."

Shaking her head, she said, "Not really. His door stays shut most of the day. He has a separate door that goes directly into Mr. Prince's office so I never know when he's in there. Plus, I think he has all of Mr. Prince's phone calls and emails now rerouted to him because I'm getting very few to pass on."

Carlos' face went strangely hard, and he stated, "So, Bob remains mysterious."

His comment caught her off guard, and she shook her head slightly, saying, "I'm not sure I understand what you mean."

His face relaxed, and he said, "Nothing. Just ignore me. I suppose I'm resentful that the money you found should have been reported directly to me, and Bob jumped in first."

She wondered why it would matter that the money had not gone through Carlos' hands, but simply smiled and nodded as though she understood. Standing, she shook his hand and said goodbye, walking back down the hall toward the restaurant. As she ordered her sandwich and sat at a corner table nibbling, she thought back to the conversations that swirled around her that day. Finally, wiping her hands on her napkin, she thought, *Things were so much easier when I was just in housekeeping and my biggest worry was scrubbing the bathrooms.*

---

When she got off work that day, she caught the bus to the stop that was closest to Grimm's Two, anxious to surprise Zeke and wondering if they might have a repeat performance of their escapades from the other evening. Stepping inside, she was both disappointed to see that they were not alone, but excited to see some of his brothers and their women around.

As soon as Zeke saw her, he stopped what he was doing and jogged over, wrapping his arms around her and kissing her soundly.

"Babe, you're a sight for sore eyes," he said. Looking her up and down, he added, "You're gorgeous, but we're cleaning some of the back area, and I'm afraid your nice clothes will get dirty."

Lifting up on her toes, she whispered, "I was prepared to get *dirty* with you like we did the other night, but don't worry, I can get dirty in a whole new way."

He growled and lifted her in his arms, pressing her body next to his. "Damn, girl. You gotta go say something like that and get me all hard, but we've got other people around."

Laughing, she wiggled, and he set her down on the floor. With her bag slung over her shoulder, she waved to the others and headed directly to the bathroom. It only took a few minutes for her to emerge wearing a T-shirt, jeans, and sneakers. With her hair pulled back in a ponytail, she twirled in front of Zeke and the others, saying, "I'm ready to clean! Put me to work!"

Rosalie laughed, attired in a similar fashion, and said, "The guys already had the bar area clean, and, of course, Zeke's been working on the kitchen. But what we really need to do now is clean what will be the employee workroom and storeroom."

Throwing her hands up dramatically, Cynthia said, "Stand back, everyone. I am a professional!"

Laughter abounded as she followed Rosalie and Ruby toward the back. With the three women wiping the walls and shelves, then mopping the floors, it only took two hours for them to finish. Standing back, they slung their arms around each other, admiring the effects of their work.

Rosalie smiled and said, "I'm so glad you two helped. I was always impressed with how Zeke and Zander made Grimm's a family affair. And when they brought me on board, it was with that same sense of family."

"I had two stepsisters," Cynthia confessed, "but I never felt close to them. They never wanted to do anything with me. Quite frankly, they were so mean, that was fine. But it's been a lot of fun feeling like I've gained sisters through Zeke."

In spite of the dirt and dust covering the three women, they hugged before heading back out to the men. As they said their goodbyes, Cynthia realized that she enjoyed her time at Grimm's Two more than she had any of her times at the Prince Hotel.

While the physical layout of Grimm's Two was different than the original Grimm's, Zeke and Zander kept with the same organization. There was the bar area, the kitchen, the storeroom, an employee workroom, and a locked area for the stock of alcohol. In the office, they set up the desk, locked filing cabinets, shelving, and computer, as well as the safe.

Zeke was sitting at the desk and looked up as Zander walked in. Before his brother had a chance to ask, Zeke said, "We got the liquor license."

High-fiving, Zander grinned. "Good! I know you're working on the food service license from the health department."

Nodding, he said, "I've already hired two line-cooks, a dishwasher, and two people for food prep. They're taking the necessary course for the food handlers permits."

"Lynn said she would handle interviewing for servers," Zander said.

Raising his eyebrows, Zeke nodded enthusiastically. Lynn was one of the servers at Grimm's who had been working for him ever since Zander opened his first establishment. She was smart, dedicated, and knew her shit. A working mom, she often took the evening shift while her husband kept the kids. Having Lynn assist with hiring the servers would go a long way to taking some of the stress off of Zeke and Zander.

"And bartenders?" he asked.

"Same thing. Charlene and Joe are going to do the first round of interviews with prospective bartenders."

One of the things that always impressed Zeke about Grimm's was how Zander was a steady and fair boss. The employees were loyal, and now that a second Grimm's was opening, they were excited about helping to make it a success as well. Even though Zeke was no longer a bouncer for Grimm's, he knew one of the long-standing bouncers, Roscoe, had agreed to start at Grimm's Two and also train new bouncers.

Zander settled into the chair, and the two men looked at each other, silent understanding passing between them. Grinning, Zeke said, "I can't fuckin' believe it's all happening."

"Not long now," Zander said. "We're scheduled to open in a month, and it looks like we're going to hit that mark."

"I'm glad that Cynthia and Ruby were able to come and help Rosalie the other day," he said. "The place is looking really good."

Tilting his head to the side, Zander's deep-set blue

eyes bore straight into Zeke's. "How is she doing with her new temp position?"

Rubbing his hand over his beard, he shook his head and sighed. "I'm not really sure. She's finished her first week but doesn't say much about it."

"Are you still thinking about asking her if she would like to work here when her temporary position is over?"

"I guess that depends on what Richard Prince is going to offer her when it's over with. She talks about him in a very positive way, and it makes me wonder if he doesn't have some kind of plan for her when the other lady comes back."

Standing, Zander said, "Well, you know how I feel. From what I can tell, she'd be an asset if she'd like to work for us."

He watched his older brother walk out the office door and leaned back in his chair, his thoughts swirling. He loved the evenings when Cynthia came by and they had a chance to work side-by-side before heading to his house or taking her to Miss Ethel's. Since he showed his jealousy the first day that Cynthia told him she had had lunch with her boss, she had not said much about Richard Prince.

She might think that her boss was only interested in her work ethic, but Zeke knew that any red-blooded man would take one look at Cynthia and would love to keep her around. He just wondered when the temporary position was over what that might mean for her. She deserved the best, and while he wished it was working with him, he had to be honest. Richard Prince might have a better offer.

Giving his head a shake to clear his thoughts, he turned back to his computer, forcing his mind back to his own job.

---

Bob was out of the office for two days on a business trip, and Cynthia discovered how nice it was to have something to do. The phone calls came to her desk, and she fielded them with ease. She handled basic emails, quickly learning which ones Richard would need to deal with. And she found that she had more time with her boss, who was delightful company.

She walked in with the requisite cup of coffee, and as she placed it on Richard's desk, he looked up and smiled. "Would you like me to order lunch or make a reservation for you, Richard?"

He looked back down at his desk and scowled, saying, "I think I'll have to work through lunch, today," he said. "Perhaps you could order something for both of us."

"Absolutely," she said. She turned to leave when he called her back. Facing him again, she stood quietly, her hands clasped in front of her, and waited.

"The Prince Hotel is having an annual charity fundraiser in two weeks...I'm sure you've heard of it..."

Nodding, she replied, "Yes, I know that you had the event on your calendar."

"We have someone that handles all the details, but Mrs. Smithwick usually runs the final details by me. I just received the email from the event coordinator and wondered if you would mind going over it with me. We can make it a working lunch."

Excitement moved through her at the idea that she would have something to focus her energy on, and she nodded enthusiastically. "I'd be honored to help you, Richard. If you tell me what you'd like for lunch I'll order it, and then we can go over the details."

His face relaxed into a smile, and he nodded. "How about something from that bistro down the street? I'm in the mood for pasta."

"I'll take care of it now," she assured. "When it's delivered, I'll bring it in, and we can work on the fundraiser."

At his nodded acquiescence, her feet fairly danced back to her desk. Placing their order for lunch, she opened her laptop and searched the internet for information on past Prince Hotel annual fundraisers. She skimmed through a few articles, then clicked on images.

Held in the large, downtown art museum, the photographs showed men in tuxes, women in long gowns dripping in jewelry, politicians, starlets, professional athletes, and models. Sitting back in her seat, the air rushed from her lungs, and she wondered what it would take to plan such an event.

Glad that was not on her plate, she scrolled through more images to get an idea of what was expected. An hour later, one of the receptionists from the lobby brought the lunch order from the bistro. Stepping over to a side table, she opened the plastic containers and placed the food on china that she had from the hotel restaurant.

With the dishes and silverware arranged on the tray, she placed the tray on one of the cloth-covered rolling carts and knocked on Richard's door. Gaining entrance, she rolled the cart in.

His eyes widened in question, and she said, "I couldn't see having you eat out of plastic take-out containers. I hope you don't mind, but I borrowed these from the hotel restaurant."

Standing, he grinned widely as he motioned for her to place the items on the small table in the corner of his office. She had often seen him and Bob sitting at that table going over paperwork, but it was now cleaned off and ready for them to use for lunch.

As they ate, she found the conversation easy, very much like the first time they went to lunch. He talked about his family and mentioned that they would be coming to the fundraiser.

A rare blush crossed his cheeks as he admitted, "I suppose that's why I want all the details right. Perhaps it's the younger brother syndrome, but I always feel as though my father and older brother are watching."

"The event looks amazing, at least from what I've seen from the past." He tilted his head in question, and she explained, "When you asked me to assist, I went on the Internet to see what I could find. I knew it would be lovely, but I had no idea it would be such a big deal."

He shrugged and said, "It was something my mother started many years ago when Prince Hotels were first started. I can't say that my parents started from humble beginnings because they didn't. Both of my parents came from money, but the hotel industry was something that my father was interested in. He bought out a hotel chain, revamped them, and turned them into exclusive, private hotels. That attracted a certain type of clientele, and even when the economy was rough, we still made an excellent profit. My mother always felt that it was important to give back to the community, so the idea of the fundraiser was created."

"It seems like an excellent way to raise money," she said, although as the words left her mouth, she felt like a pretender. She had never been to a fundraiser and had no idea how they operated.

Chuckling, he said, "At a thousand dollars a plate, most of the guests just see it as a tax write-off. They could care less about what the money is going for. They like a night out, they like to show off their money, and they like being seen in society pages."

Her mouth was still hanging open at the idea of anyone spending a thousand dollars for a plate of food. "Oh...yes...I see," she mumbled.

As they finished their lunch, she stood and placed the plates and cutlery onto the restaurant's cart. She rolled it back into the outer office and placed a call for someone to come retrieve it. Making her way back into Richard's office, she hesitated, not knowing where he might want her to sit.

He moved to the leather sofa, placing a large folder on the coffee table. Looking up, he said, "You can bring our tea over here, and we'll take a look at the fundraising plans."

Once their glasses of iced tea were placed on coasters in front of them, he opened up his folder and handed a packet of papers to her.

"I've got the same information in front of me, and I thought we'd go through them page by page."

She nodded, tamping down her nervousness again. She must not have been successful, because she glanced up, finding him staring at her.

"Are you okay, Cynthia?"

Sighing, she admitted, "Richard, I'll help you with anything I can, but you must know, I've never been to a function like this. I'm uncertain what help I can be to you."

Waving his hand dismissively, he said, "You're very smart and detail-oriented. I have no doubt that as we go through it, you'll be able to catch any differences between what we did last year and what's on the list for this year."

That sounded simple enough, and she nodded. Opening her papers, she saw there was a list of everything that had been organized for last year's and this year's fundraisers.

They ran down the menu and alcohol orders, decorations, information for a silent auction, the band, the venue accommodations, and by the time they were finished, Cynthia was impressed with the detail that Richard had exhibited.

"Don't you have an event planner that does all this for you?" she asked.

Eyes wide, he nodded. "Oh, absolutely! This isn't my thing at all, but I don't like leaving things to chance. I have full confidence in the event planner, but I know that if one thing isn't right, I'll hear about it from my mother. And after she picks it apart, I'll hear about it from my father!"

The idea that this powerful man was still nervous about what his parents thought of him had her giggling.

Scowling, he said, "Hey, it's not nice to laugh at the boss."

With her hand pressing against her lips, she continued to smile. "It's just hard to imagine that you feel like you have a bar to measure up to."

He nodded slowly, then asked, "Do you? Did you have a family bar to measure up to?"

Continuing with honesty, she said, "With my parents, no. With my stepmother, yes. And she always let me know that I did not measure up to her own daughters—at all."

"What did you do about it?".

Shrugging, she said, "I finally decided I didn't care what they thought. I moved on with my own life, made my own choices, and now I don't have anyone to live up to except myself."

He leaned back and huffed, capturing her attention. "I admire that, Cynthia. I really do. I'm afraid I'm still doing anything and everything I can to make sure that I live up to the Prince name."

As they finished looking over the event, she admitted, "I don't see anything here that seems unprepared. I think you and the event coordinator have covered everything."

He shifted on the sofa and faced her, saying, "Mrs. Smithwick always comes to the event as my guest. I've never needed her for anything, but she's there in case something comes up. I'd like you to be my guest this year."

Gasping, she shook her head. "That's a lovely gesture, Richard, but I couldn't."

Brows lowered, he shook his head. "You couldn't? I don't understand."

"Surely you must realize that someone who works in housekeeping would never have an outfit for an event like this."

He had the good grace to blush, then said, "Cynthia, I really want you to come. I'll provide everything. The dress, the shoes, the limo. Don't worry about the cost, it's just a tax write off as a business expense. All you have to do is show up, and don't worry about the event. The coordinator does everything, but if there's something that I need, it would be nice to have you there. Please."

Uncertainty filled her, but a thread of excitement began to move through her. A beautiful dress. A limo ride. A chance to stand on the perimeter and watch, even if it's just to be an assistant.

Knowing she would never have an opportunity like this again, she wiped her hands on her napkin and said, "Thank you, I would be honored to go and help you."

Nodding, he smiled, saying, "Excellent." He stood,

gathering the papers from the coffee table and walked back over to his desk.

She took the opportunity to take the iced tea glasses back to the outer office before moving to her desk. She hurried over to her computer and opened it once again, looking at the images from the past fundraisers. She knew she would be nervous, but the excitement was growing.

## 22

Zeke was working late, and Cynthia took the opportunity to sit with Miss Ethel after they had eaten dinner and tell her about Richard's offer.

"It sounds like a lovely evening," Miss Ethel said. "Why do you seem so reticent?"

"I won't know anyone there," she said, "even though that won't really matter. I'm there to work, not socialize. Or, at least, I'm there for the potential of work. I think in the past Richard has used Mrs. Smithwick as someone to go between him and the event planner if needed. Otherwise, I think she probably just stayed out of the way."

"And he said he would take care of your outfit?"

"I have nothing to wear to a formal event, but I confess that makes me a little nervous, also." Seeing Miss Ethel's questioning gaze, she added, "It feels weird having the Prince Hotel be responsible for my outfit for the evening."

"Well, I certainly don't pretend to understand how some businesses work, but I would say that is probably not that uncommon."

They sat quietly for a few more minutes, the clicking of Miss Ethel's knitting needles tapping out a rhythm.

"I suppose," she finally confessed, "that I'll feel like such a pretender. The maid pretending to be a princess."

Laying her knitting needles down, Miss Ethel said, "My dear, don't you realize that all of the other people that are there will be pretending as well? No one walks around every day in ball gowns, dripping in jewels. That's one of the reasons parties are so much fun. It gives adults a chance to play dress-up."

A giggle burst forth from deep inside, and she said, "You're right."

Miss Ethel's brow scrunched for a moment before she blinked and said, "Oh, dear, sometimes I find that my mind is no longer able to grasp a quote that I'm searching for quite as easily as when I was younger." Giving her head a shake, she continued, "There was an English writer in the early 1800s. William Hazlett. I remember having to study him once and read just a few of his literary critiques. He once said, 'Man is a make-believe animal. He is never so truly himself as when he is acting a part.' I believe that you'll find many people playing make-believe at the fundraiser."

With renewed enthusiasm, she leaned back against the sofa cushions and continued reading the book she had started. Hearing the truck in the driveway, she turned and looked at the headlights. "Oh, good! Zeke is here."

Tucking her knitting away, Miss Ethel said, "I believe I'll turn in now. I'm sure you two have lots to talk about." With that, she walked down the hall toward her bedroom, leaving Cynthia bouncing on her toes at the open front door.

---

Zeke knew that he needed to focus on the word *assistant*, but the only thing he could see in his mind was Cynthia, looking like a princess, standing next to Richard Prince.

He tried to relax his face into a smile, but his muscles were so tense they hurt. Cynthia had met him at the door of Miss Ethel's, bouncing with excitement, and he had swooped in, picked her up, and gave her a twirl. Then when she told him what her boss had asked of her and what he was going to do for her, he found his enthusiasm waned as hers shot upward.

While his mind wrestled with these thoughts, he realized she had grown quiet. Staring at her pensive face, he sighed.

"What's wrong, Zeke?" she asked, her face registering hurt. "I thought you'd be excited for me. It's not a very big job, but I'll be the liaison between Richard and the event coordinator in case anything is going on during the evening that one of them needs to know about. It means he trusts me."

The last thing he wanted to do was hurt her, but as he shook his head, she reached out and placed her hand on his arm, giving a little squeeze. "Please, be honest with me," she begged.

They sat on the sofa, their legs touching, their bodies angled toward each other, his arm wrapped around her shoulders and his other hand holding onto hers. Sighing again, he said, "I'm sorry, babe. I know you're excited, and I'm messing this up for you."

Shaking her head, she said, "No, you're not messing it up for me, Zeke. But I just can't tell what you're thinking."

"I'm thinking how beautiful you'll be at this event, every man staring at you, wondering who you are, and I won't be there with you. You'll be with someone else."

Eyes wide, she shook her head, causing her hair to fling about her shoulders. "No, Zeke! It's not like that at all. I won't be there with anyone. I'll just be there in case my boss needs me. It's not a date. It's just my job."

"I know, I know," he said, holding her gaze. "And I'm sorry. I'm raining on your parade and fucking up your excitement."

Her fingers jerked against his hand and said, "Zeke, honey, you're not fucking anything up."

"I'm not really used to jealousy," he said. "I guess that's because I've never had anybody I cared about before. But now that we're together, it's hard for me to think of you being there without me."

She tilted her head slightly and asked, "Have you ever thought what it's like for me? When you're at Grimm's?"

Not understanding her question, his brows lowered as he grunted, "Huh?"

She rolled her eyes and said, "I've been at Grimm's and seen the way other women look at you. You might not realize it, but with your long hair, big body, and tats, you've got women—often drunk women—who are panting after you."

When he was working at Grimm's, he never paid attention to the women that were around, focusing instead on his job. First, as a bouncer, he needed to keep his wits about him and his eyes on the crowd. Then he wanted to make sure that Zander took him seriously as they considered a partnership. And now, with Cynthia at his side, no other woman entered his mind.

"Babe, I don't have women who--"

"I've seen it with my own eyes, Zeke," she interrupted.

"Nobody looks at me that way," he argued.

"I get it. You're gorgeous, and any normal female would notice. But that's your job. That's your place of business. So when you're there, I trust you to do your job and not be swayed by the women that would like to take you into a back room. Or if they can't get you into a back room, they'd like to dry hump you on the dance floor. Hell, I don't blame them. That's what I want to do."

Barking out a laugh, he shook his head. "Fuck, girl, how you can make me laugh in the middle of a fit of jealousy."

She smiled in return, nudging his shoulder with her own. "But seriously, Zeke, it's no different. I can't lock you away just because you work in an area where there are drunk, scantily clad women ogling you."

He lifted his hand and gently rubbed his thumb over her cheeks before leaning in to place a light kiss on her lips. "You're right. This is your job, and your boss would like you to go. Do I still wish I could be the one on your arm? Fuck, yeah. But I know you'll go and just by being you look like the princess of Prince Hotel."

"In a few weeks, I go back to being a housekeeper for the hotel. Unless there's another job that he thinks I would be suited for, I go back to the basement and the cleaning cart. I don't have any other job prospects, and honestly, I haven't been looking. This event, though, gives me a chance to show that I can do something besides just clean hotel bathrooms."

She laid her head on his shoulder, and they continued to sit for a few minutes, each to their own thoughts. When he had driven to Miss Ethel's that evening, there was something on his mind, but he no longer was certain that it was the appropriate time to bring it up with Cynthia.

"Hey," she said, her voice now whisper-soft. "What are you thinking about now?"

He continued to battle for just a moment over whether it was the right time to bring this up, but staring into her beautiful blue eyes, he knew he had to tell her what was in his heart. "I know we haven't known each other that long, but I know what I feel, and I know what I want." Cupping her face again, he said, "What I feel for you is love. What I want with you is for us to be together."

Eyes widening, her breath caught in her throat as she choked, "You...you love me?"

"Yeah, babe. I do. I know you're the first thing I think of when I wake up in the morning, and you're the last thing I think about when I close my eyes at night. I find myself thinking about you all during the day, sometimes so anxious to see you just to tell you something mundane or to find out how your day is going. I know it doesn't matter to me whether you work as a housekeeper in a hotel or an assistant to an owner or any other career you want to have. I knew the first time I laid eyes on you, dripping wet, standing in the lobby of the homeless shelter, that there was something about you that just drew me in. And I've continued to be bewitched every day since that moment. If that's not love, babe, I don't know what is."

Before he had a chance to say another word, she sucked in a sob just before moving in, latching onto his lips. He met her, emotion for emotion, pouring everything he had into the kiss. All of his hopes for the future, dreams about her, and desire to be with her every day for the rest of his life filled the meeting of their lips.

He tasted the sweetness of her essence and the salt of her tears. With his hands sliding to her waist, she shifted around so that she was straddling his lap. With her knees at his hips and her breasts pressing against his chest, he pulled her in tightly, heartbeat next to heartbeat.

After a moment, she leaned back, raggedly sucking in air, and with his thumbs, he gently wiped the moisture from her cheeks.

"I've never had anybody speak to me so sweetly," she said.

"I meant every word, babe," he assured. "But, to be honest, there was more."

Tilting her head to the side, she asked, "More?"

"When I came here tonight, I wanted to ask you to consider us taking our relationship deeper." Seeing her lowered-brow expression of uncertainty, he continued, "I know living with Miss Ethel gave you a room to rent and a way out of the homeless shelter. But I'd really like you to consider moving in with me. You're over at my place all the time, but I'd like to tuck you in at night after we make love and know that you'll be there first thing in the morning when I wake up."

Her head jerked up and down as more tears slid from her eyes. "Yes, yes, I want that, too. I want to go to sleep with you curled around me like a warm shield protecting me."

"Really?" he asked, unable to keep the excitement from his voice or his face.

Her smile widened as she continued to nod. Her brow crinkled as she appeared to be thinking, and she nibbled on her bottom lip. "Only give me a few more days with Miss Ethel. She's been so good to me. Let me get this event over with, and then I can focus on just us."

"Babe, as long as we're on the same page, I don't mind waiting. I want us to do it right, together. We can buy some things that'll make it feel more like our place."

"Sweetie, we don't have to buy anything. As long as we're together, it will feel like our place." She kissed him sweetly and whispered against his lips, "And for the record, I love you, too."

Hearing those words, he pulled her tighter, his heart soaring with the knowledge that they were moving forward...in love.

23

---

The weekend was coming, and Cynthia was still floating on air while battling nerves thinking about the upcoming gala. True to his word, Richard sent her to one of the exclusive boutiques near the hotel where she was instructed to buy a dress.

As soon as she saw the price tags she felt light-headed, but the saleswoman assured her that Mr. Prince had already left instructions for her to purchase any of the dresses that she might be interested in. She had no doubt that she disappointed the woman when she continued to look at the previous year's designs that had been marked down. Even though their price tag was far more than she could imagine paying for a dress, she simply could not bring herself to pay full price.

Uncertain what might look the best on her, she tried on any that were brought to her. All beautiful, she rejected them one after the other. The red one made her feel as though she would be trying to stand out when what she really wanted to do was simply blend into the background. The black one, with a deep V in the front, showed off too much cleavage. The sparkly silver gown had a slit up the leg that was much higher than she was comfortable with.

The saleswoman finally entered with a beautiful gown in a baby blue color. The neckline draped, showing only a hint of cleavage. The dress was fitted through the bodice, then flared with yards of material over her hips to the floor. It was simple. It was elegant.

"That dress makes you look like a princess," the saleswoman whispered as though in awe. "I don't think I've ever said that to a customer before."

Giving a little twirl, she loved the way the material swirled around her legs. Grinning widely, she agreed, "It's beautiful. I know the other dresses may have looked more worldly, but this one...this one is perfect."

"I've got just the right shoes for this gown," the saleswoman said, clapping her hands, and she disappeared to the back of the store. In a moment, she returned holding a delicate pair of strappy silver high-heeled shoes with little blue crystals embedded in the straps that went across the toes.

Trying them on, Cynthia had to admit that they complimented the dress perfectly. Deciding to ignore the price tags, she had the woman charge the dress and the shoes to the card Richard had provided.

Entering the office back at the hotel, she hung the garment bag on the back of the door so that it would be out of the way. Still giddy, she hurried to see if Richard or Bob needed anything from her. Lifting her hand to knock on the door, she could hear Bob's loud voice from inside.

"I can't believe you asked her to go to the fundraising gala!"

"And I don't see what your problem is," Richard replied.

She knew she should not eavesdrop, but curiosity won out, and she leaned forward, placing her ear against the door to Richard's office.

"I know Mrs. Smithwick went," Bob continued ranting. "But she worked with the event coordinator. She needed to be there in case there was something that the coordinator couldn't handle. Cynthia hasn't been involved at all so she would have no purpose."

"It's good will," Richard argued.

"Good will? Is that what you call it? I can't imagine why you need another pair of tits and legs to look at because there'll be plenty of willing women there."

"Yes, and so will my parents and brother. Always looking to see if I'm fucking something up. So, I can introduce them to a nice woman who is taking Mrs. Smithwick's temporary place. Having elevated someone from housekeeping they'll see it as a generous gesture."

Cynthia jerked back from the door, no longer wanting to hear their conversation. Her lips were pinched together, although she had to admit that she was not really hurt. Bob had never welcomed her into the office, and she was not surprised that he hated to see anything good come her way, even an evening out. And as far as Richard was concerned, his suggestion that she fill in for Mrs. Smithwick was nothing more than a congenial gesture, and she knew that from the beginning.

Sucking in a deep breath through her nose, she let it out slowly. Not wanting Bob or Richard to come out seeing her in the office and wonder if she had overheard them, she grabbed the garment bag off the back of the door and headed out of the office. She waited several minutes, pacing the hallway, hoping that their conversation had come to an end. When she felt that she had given them plenty of time, she walked back into the outer office holding her cell phone up to her ear as though talking to someone.

"I'm back in my office now so I have to go. I'll talk to you later."

Richard's door opened and Bob walked out, his gaze immediately going to the garment bag she held in one hand. She stuffed her phone into her purse and offered him a smile as she hung the bag on the back of the door.

"Is there anything that I can get you?" she asked with a smile.

He grunted, and she took that for a negative answer. Tossing her purse into the drawer in the desk, she moved to Richard's door and knocked.

He looked up from his desk and smiled. "I hope you found something that you liked."

Nodding, she replied, "Yes, I did. Thank you very much."

"I'd like you to go over these items with the event coordinator today. I'm going to leave this in your capable hands, and you can let me know if there's anything you need help with."

When Bob had been gone for those few days and Richard had her work on the plans for the gala, he had been turning more over to her. Now, with Bob back, she was thankful to be doing more than just fetching coffee and eagerly reached for the papers in his hand.

"I'll get right on this and let you know if there's anything you need to be aware of." With another smile and nod, she left his office and went back to her desk, determined to take any of the burden of the gala off of his shoulders.

---

It was Zeke's night to work at Grimm's, but when he walked out of the back hall from the office to the bar, he was surprised to see Zander and Rosalie. Walking over, he kissed her cheek, clapped Zander on the back and asked, "What the hell are you doing here tonight?"

"We have a babysitter for Charity, but our reservation for dinner isn't for another hour," Rosalie replied. "So, Zander thought we'd stop by so he'd have a chance to ask Roscoe how the bouncer interviews had gone this afternoon."

"He said they went well, but he's over near the back. I'll keep Rosalie company if you want to go talk to him."

With a kiss to his wife and a chin lift to Zeke, Zander headed toward the back wall where Roscoe was keeping an eye on the weekend crowd. As he watched his older brother move through the throngs of people, he noticed some of the women turn their heads and follow him, lust obvious on their faces. Glancing down the bar, he noticed two women looking at him in a similar fashion.

"Hey, what's with the serious expression?" Rosalie asked. "What on earth are you thinking about?"

He sighed and scrubbed his hand over his beard. Looking up at her, he asked, "Can I ask you a question? Like a really weird-ass question?"

Laughing, she said, "Now you've really got my curiosity up! Please, ask away."

"Are you ever aware that women look at Zander?"

Blinking, she glanced toward the back where Zander was now talking to Roscoe before turning her attention back to Zeke. "Huh?"

Tugging at the neckline of his T-shirt, he felt the heat of embarrassment and was glad most of it was hidden by his beard. "Oh, never mind."

She reached out and grabbed his arm and shook her head. "Oh, no, you don't. I tell my high school English students that whatever they have to say, they need to say it."

Placing his arms on the bar, he leaned his weight into them and said, "Does it bother you that where your husband works there are sometimes drunk women that would like to put the moves on him."

"I'm not sure what you're getting at, Zeke, but if you want the honest truth, then yes. I mean, I know I've married a gorgeous man, and it doesn't bother me that other women *appreciate* that. They can look all they want, but they better keep their hands to themselves! And I think women would notice his looks no matter where he worked. Although you're right, working in a bar does mean he's around a lot more people whose inhibitions are not what they should be." Shrugging, she added, "But it also comes down to trust. I completely trust Zander, so I know if a woman gets out of hand, he'll shut it down."

She peered at him as he remained silent and then gasped, "Oh, is this about Cynthia? Is she concerned about dating someone who works in a bar?"

Shaking his head, he admitted, "No. It's really more about me. I know she's beautiful, and she's going to the Prince Hotel's fundraising event, and I was surprised at how the jealousy hit me knowing that every man there will be staring at her."

"Oh, that's right. We girls were over at Miss Ethel's the other evening, and she was telling us about it. I saw her dress, and I swear she's going to look like a princess."

Scowling, he said, "That's not helping, Rosalie."

"You can stop fretting," she laughed, this time poking him in the shoulder. After a moment, she said, "Zeke, Cynthia is crazy about you. I know she's excited about the event just because she's never done anything like this before. Most women would love the chance to get all prettied up and wear a fancy dress. But for her, this is work. That's all, just work." Jerking her head toward the back, she said, "Just like what you and Zander do here."

He grinned and said, "I'm glad Zander's got you, Rosalie. You're as smart as you are beautiful." He bent forward and kissed her cheek, jumping back as Zander's hand landed on his shoulder.

"I'm gone for a moment and you put the moves on my wife," Zander joked.

Rosalie leaned over and kissed Zander on the lips before saying, "The only man for me is you, babe. Now, if you're finished here, how about taking me to dinner?"

Zeke said goodbye and watched them walk out together. Until he had met Cynthia, he had not understood the pull for being with just one woman. Now, she was all he wanted.

## 24

The women had stopped by earlier, both to help Cynthia get ready and to distract her from being so nervous. Ruby had buffed and polished her fingernails while Penny did the same for her toes. Eleanor had curled her hair before Regina ran her fingers through the lengths of her tresses, creating waves that hung down her back. They pulled the very top of her hair away from her face and clipped it with a sparkly barrette. Staring into the mirror, it almost looked as though she was wearing a tiara.

Rosalie and Morgan had purchased new lingerie for her to wear under the dress. Once she had slipped it on, they all stood back and looked at their handiwork. As they took their leave one by one, she received hugs of friendship and whispers of well wishes.

Now she was alone in the little room at the top of Miss Ethel's house, wondering what she was doing. She tried to remember Miss Ethel's words about how everyone pretends, but she also knew that almost everybody at the gala tonight would not be new to that world. This kind of pretense, for her, would be the first time.

She glanced around the room, accepting how familiar it had become to her. Thinking about Zeke's declaration of love and desire for her to move in with him, she smiled. She heard a soft step at the doorway and turned to see Miss Ethel's gaze roaming warmly over her before settling on her eyes.

"My dear, Cynthia, you are a vision."

Attempting a smile through trembling lips, she said, "Thank you."

"You seemed lost in thought when I approached."

Turning back toward the mirror, she nodded. "I was thinking about what you said about everyone pretending, trying to psych myself up for this event. It almost seems silly that we go to so much trouble to try to make ourselves into something we're not."

Miss Ethel stepped into the room, walking until she was standing right next to Cynthia. The two women stared together into the mirror, and Miss Ethel said, "Each society has its own standards for what they consider to be beautiful. And, of course, that has changed throughout the ages. But it's very common for we humans to want to adorn ourselves, hoping for outward beauty."

Capturing her eyes in the reflection of the mirror, Miss Ethel continued, "Suzy Kassem says that 'True beauty is measured by the number of pearls within you, not those around your neck.' Perhaps not a very original quote, and I confess the cover of the book seemed very strange to me, but as a poet and philosopher, I found that I agreed with many of her sayings. Another one of hers that's very apropos is 'Doubt kills more dreams than failure ever will'. I sometimes wish I had had her book when I was raising my boys. Her words are startlingly true."

Smiling at the older woman who had taken the place of the mother she missed so much, she asked, "Is there one that spoke to you? Just to you?"

Smiling, Miss Ethel patted her hand, and said, "'Laugh, I tell you, And you will turn back the hands of time...' I suppose, if that was true, then I would not have the wrinkles on my face."

Her heart clenched in love for Miss Ethel, and she threw her arms around her, hugging her tightly. She had not said anything to her about moving to Zeke's, worried about leaving Miss Ethel alone.

They separated, still holding each other's hands, and Miss Ethel said, "Never worry about me. I have lived and loved and still love. A mother knows that all her children move on, and this is a good thing. And if they move on in health, and happiness, and especially love, that is a very good thing. Remember, saying goodbye is part of life. But the ties of love will always bind us together."

She sucked in a quick breath and felt her chest quiver but blinked to keep the tears at bay.

Miss Ethel reached up and patted her cheek and smiled. "It's almost time for you to leave, my dear. The limo will be here soon, but Zeke is downstairs. He'd like to see you and wish you well before you go tonight."

With that, Miss Ethel turned and walked out of the room, her soft footsteps heard on the stairs.

Grabbing a tissue, she dabbed at the corners of her eyes and sucked in a fortifying breath before letting it out slowly, staring once again in the mirror. The diamond stud earrings sparkled, and it was impossible to keep her lips from curving. Her mother had had several pieces of jewelry but wore these earrings whenever they had a special occasion they were celebrating. When she died, her father had given them to Cynthia.

Her smile slid from her face as she remembered her stepmother eagerly taking all of her mother's jewelry for herself. After her father died, she sneaked into her stepmother's bedroom and looked through her jewelry box, only interested in the pieces that had once belonged to her mother. Eileen discovered her and slapped her for daring to steal the pieces. Her protestations fell on deaf ears and she received another slap for her troubles.

*Well, if you could see me now, Eileen.* Closing her eyes for a moment, she willed thoughts of Eileen from her mind. Hearing voices coming from downstairs, she lifted her gaze, patting her hair, and let out a deep breath. Snagging her evening purse from the top of the dresser, she turned to follow her heart.

---

Zeke paced the living room nervously, his eyes shooting upward as Miss Ethel descended, one hand on the banister. He moved forward quickly, jogging up the first couple of steps until he could take her other hand, making sure she was steady.

"Thank you, Ezekiel," she said. "She'll be down in just a moment."

He followed her into the living room, watching as she settled in her chair. Instead of picking up her knitting, she placed her hands in her lap and smiled up at him.

"Do you remember the first night you were with me?"

Blinking in surprise, he nodded and said, "Yes. Of course, I do."

"I told you what your name meant," she said softly.

His lips curved as he said, "I remember. I've always remembered what you said. You told me that it meant a strong warrior or champion."

"And I was right. You are a strong champion. You always have been."

Shaking his head, he said, "Oh, Miss Ethel, I was a jerk back then, and you know it."

Her head shot up, and her eyes bore straight into him. With a sharp voice, she said, "You were never a jerk, Zeke. You had simply been raised by a man who thought strength only came from a show of force."

"Sometimes I was jealous of the others," he said, his voice barely above a whisper. He saw her tilt her head in question, and he explained, "They had you so much earlier than me."

Her face softened, and for a second, it was as though the years fell away and he was staring into the face of the kind woman who took him in that first night.

"Oh, sweet boy. While I would've loved to have had you longer, I firmly believe that each of my boys came to me at the time they needed me most. You needed someone to show you the different kinds of strengths, and you would not have understood that if you had not seen how your father misused his. But my heart always ached for the suffering you had to endure...that all my boys had to endure before they came to me."

The ticking of the clock on the mantle was the only sound heard for a few minutes, both lost to their own thoughts and memories but connected by a strong thread of emotion.

"You not only taught me the true meaning of strength," he said, "but also the true meaning of love."

Bending to pick up her knitting, she smiled, then suddenly changed subjects and said, "I let Cynthia know that whenever she was ready to move in with you she did not need to worry about me."

He stood, staring dumbly at Miss Ethel, wondering how she knew that they had talked about Cynthia moving in with him. A sound on the stairs captured his attention, and he turned to see Cynthia gliding toward him. She was a vision, the pale blue dress swirling around her legs as she walked, allowing a peek at jeweled shoes. Her hair, pulled back from her face at the top, cascaded in waves down her back. Her makeup, heavier than normal, only served to play up her perfect complexion and brilliant blue eyes.

He stepped toward her, holding out his arms, barely able to catch his breath. "You are beautiful, Cynthia."

His simple compliment had her smiling widely as

she stared up at him. He bent to kiss her cheek, not wanting to mess up her lip gloss, but she turned her head, making sure their lips met. He kissed her soundly, hoping he poured all of his emotion into their touch. Leaning back, he grinned at her kiss-swollen lips just as the limo pulled into the driveway.

"It looks like your chariot is here," he said.

She glanced toward the window, and he could feel her body quivering with nerves. "You're going to be fine, babe. You'll be the most beautiful woman there, and Mr. Prince is lucky to have you helping him out tonight."

Her eyes searched his, and she must have been comforted with what she saw. Her lips curved, and she whispered, "I love you, Zeke."

With that, he walked her out the front door to the limo. Seeing her settled inside, he waved until she was out of sight. He sighed and walked back into Miss Ethel's house. Slumping onto the sofa, he sighed heavily again.

Lifting her eyebrow, Miss Ethel said, "Did you have any special plans tonight?"

Shaking his head, he said, "No, ma'am. I thought I might go to Grimm's and hang out some."

"I'm sure Grimm's will do just fine without you being there tonight, drowning your misery in alcohol."

Wincing, he said, "I was just going to check on things." Looking up, he asked, "Would you like me to hang out here with you tonight?"

She laid her knitting in her lap and pierced him with her stare. "Ezekiel, I never mind having your company, but the idea of spending the evening with your morose sighing all evening is not what I call quality time."

In spite of her accurate assessment, he could not help but chuckle, shaking his head. "You always knew how to call a spade a spade."

Smiling, she said, "I think you want to drive to the museum. I know you'd like to be close to where Cynthia is, and you could always use the time reading."

"The museum where the gala is being held? Why would I want to sit outside of there?"

Her voice softened, and she said, "You never know when Cynthia might need you. As excited as she is, she feels very much out of her element. Perhaps she won't need you, and you will just have a chance to catch up on your reading and know that you were nearby."

He stared at her for a moment, but she had picked her knitting back up, the needles clicking away once again. "Do you know something, Miss Ethel? Do you know if she might need me?"

She peered at him from over the top of her glasses, and her lips curved slightly. "Oh, my dear boy, don't be fanciful. How on earth would I know something like that?"

He sat for a moment pondering his actions, then realized that he would feel better being closer to Cynthia, even if she was never aware that he was outside. Standing, he moved to Miss Ethel, bent to kiss her soft cheek, and murmured, "I love you, Miss Ethel."

"Love you too, dear boy," she whispered back. He walked out of her house, missing the smile that graced her face.

## 25

Cynthia wondered if she should enter through the back of the museum, giving her a chance to check with the planner, Christine. The event had been in the planning stages for six months, and while she had only been involved for the past week, she still felt a sense of pride in knowing that all of Christine's hard work aligned with Richard's vision.

As she peeked out the window of the limousine, she realized the driver was letting her out at the very front. Before she had a chance to say anything to him, he parked, climbed out, and walked around to open her door. She offered him her hand, and he assisted her in alighting from the limo, keeping her steady as she shook out her skirt. With a smile and her thanks, he moved away, and she stared up at the steps leading to the beautiful building.

Once she had climbed the steps, she entered through the glass doors and stuttered at the glittering world spread out before her. Even though she was early, some guests had already arrived. The men in tuxes appeared dashing next to the women in their ball gowns, all in a swirl of colors.

Uncertainty filled her, but then she saw Christine at the entrance to a hall near the back and walked toward her. She noticed some people looked up from their conversations, peering at her, but she assumed they just wondered if perhaps they knew her. A slight grin tempted her lips as she thought, *What would they say if they knew I was a housekeeper?*

Walking steadily toward Christine, she greeted the planner and asked if there was anything she needed.

"I'm so glad to see you here," Christine said, her gaze drifting over Cynthia. "You're absolutely beautiful."

"I'm sure you have everything well in hand, but just remember that I'm here if you need me."

Christine said, "I was just going to check on the banner that's hanging over the table in the next room for the silent auction, but I need to start the hors d'oeuvre service. Can you just walk into the next room and make sure the banner is displayed?"

"Absolutely," she said, glad to have something to do. She moved into the room, seeing the white linen-covered tables lining the walls filled with items for the silent auction. As she walked along, she could not help but notice some of the displays. Decorative coupons for free stays at one of the Prince International Hotels. Jewelry, dinners at exclusive restaurants, a city bar crawl, signed memorabilia, golf lessons, custom artwork, and a behind the scenes tour of the Richmond Art Museum. There were many others, but she was curious at how much money could possibly be raised with such wonderful items. Turning around, she looked at the large banner on the wall that displayed where the money for the fundraiser would go.

Blinking, she was shocked to see pictures of several buildings, one of them being the shelter. The banner proudly announced that the recipient of the Prince Hotel Fundraising Gala would be the city's various homeless shelters. It dawned on her that while she had helped to keep Richard updated on the practical aspects of the fundraiser, she had never asked what the money would be used for.

Smiling widely, she walked over, her hand lifting slightly to touch the image of the shelter that had kept her off the streets. Suddenly invigorated to be part of such an event, she turned quickly, her skirt swirling about her ankles.

She did not realize there was someone behind her, and she stumbled as hands reached out to steady her. Her gaze landed on an older gentleman, tall and distinguished with his silver hair and mustache. Blushing from her neck to the roots of her hair, she said, "Oh, my goodness, please forgive me. I wasn't watching where I was going."

"Not at all," he said, his voice smooth. His eyes went beyond her to the banner on the wall, and he said, "A worthy cause."

Nodding, she said, "I agree. I'm so pleased to see the shelters be the recipients of the fundraiser."

The gentleman looked at the tables and said, "I hope that there are lots of bids this year."

"I was just admiring all the donated items," she said. "It appears the winners will have lovely prizes."

"Did you find anything you wanted to bid on?" he asked.

Laughing, she shook her head and replied, "I'm afraid bidding is not for me. I actually work for--"

"Cynthia," came a voice from the side, and she turned her head to see Richard walking toward her. Just as she was ready to greet him, he smiled at the man standing next to her and said, "Dad. I'm glad you've already met Cynthia."

He stepped in front of her, took her hands in his and held them out to the side, saying, "My God, you are beautiful."

She felt the heat rush over her and hoped her deodorant was working overtime considering how nervous she was. Thanking him, her gaze jumped back to the older man who was now staring at both of them.

"Are you going to introduce me to this charming woman?" the elder Mr. Prince asked.

"Dad, meet Cynthia Ellison. She's filling in for Mrs. Smithwick, and doing a wonderful job, I might add. Cynthia, please meet my father, Mr. Lawrence Prince."

"Mr. Prince," she murmured as he took her hand in a delicate squeeze.

"Please, call me Lawrence. Otherwise, there are too many Mr. Princes around."

"Is Larry here already?" Richard asked. He turned to Cynthia and said, "That's my older brother."

Lawrence nodded and said, "I believe he and your mother are already sampling the hors d'oeuvres. I thought I would take an early look at what is on the silent auction table."

Clenching her hands together in front of her, Cynthia felt awkward standing with the two heads of Prince Hotels. Her gaze landed on Christine, and even though the event planner had everything well in hand, she murmured her need to go check on things.

As she made her way back into the main hall, she could see that many more guests had arrived. Approaching Christine, who was standing in the back corner, she asked, "Is there anything you need me to do?"

Shaking her head, she said, "Not right now. But, I will have you check with Mr. Prince when we're close to his speech. For now, just go and mingle. Enjoy yourself!"

Christine darted away, leaving Cynthia alone. Sticking to her plan of fading into the background, she walked along the perimeter, finding a quiet place where she could stand.

She had certainly seen enough movies to not be surprised by the elegance of the event. White-shirt-black-pants servers moved silently among the guests, holding their platters of hors d'oeuvres and champagne. She wondered about their jobs, pondering for a moment if that was something she would like to do. *They, like me as a housekeeper, are paid to do a job, and most people ignore our presence.* Seeing one server bobble a tray, barely catching it before it spilled, she shivered and decided she had no desire to try to move effortlessly amongst that crowd.

She watched as many of the men shook their heads slightly, refusing the champagne as they made their way over to the open bar. She did not know a lot about spirits but had no trouble discerning that many of them preferred whiskey over champagne.

The women's gowns were the next thing that caught her attention as they floated by, easily moving on stiletto heels as though they were born with an innate ability to know how to balance on stilts. The lovely eveningwear ran the gamut from the occasional short cocktail dress to the matronly gowns of some of the white-haired women. Most wore gowns that, to a casual observer, might appear similar to hers, only she knew they would have this year's designer labels inside.

Jewelry dangling from ears, necks, and wrists also caught her eye. Her hand reached up to the small diamond studs in her ears, and her lips curved ever so slightly, knowing her parents would be so pleased.

She watched the crowd as it grew to so many people that they began to meld together in her sight. Her place against the wall was no longer as quiet. The loud greetings called out and firm handshakes from the men, all seeming to jockey for position around whomever they determined was the right person to be seen with. The women began to appear as peacocks, giving air kisses to each other as their gazes assessed the other women's gown and jewelry.

She had walked into the room an hour ago feeling like a princess. But knowing it would all be over with by the end of the night, it did not seem so enchanting. The children's story Cinderella popped into her mind, and she wondered what it was like for Cinderella to know that at midnight everything would change back to the way it was. *Did Cinderella feel like she was on borrowed time or was she just happy to enjoy the ball while she could?*

Loud laughter nearby startled her out of her musings, and she looked over, seeing Christine near the other corner of the room, giving a little wave. Excusing herself as she gently pushed her way through the throng, she came to the planner and asked, "Is it time?"

Nodding, Christine said, "Yes. If you would find Mr. Prince and tell him that it's time for him to make his way to the podium. He will be talking for just a few minutes in a welcome speech and making a few comments about the fundraiser."

"No problem. I'll find him right now."

Giving her arm a squeeze, Christine said, "Thank you. You are so much easier to work with than Mrs. Smithwick. She always made me feel like a bumbling girl instead of a professional event planner. I don't suppose you'll be able to stay, will you?"

Shaking her head, she said, "No, I was only hired to fill her shoes as a temp. She comes back in a week, and I'll go back to housekeeping."

If she thought Christine's expression would register shock, she was pleased to see that instead, the other woman just shook her head slightly, and said, "Well, they're lucky to have you."

It took her several moments to find Richard, and when she did, he was engaged in a rather large group all chatting. Moving to where she could catch his eye, she signaled that she needed to speak to him, and he immediately came over.

"The planner wants me to tell you that it's time for you to make your way to the podium," she said.

He thanked her warmly, excused himself from his group, and began walking through the crowd. It was then that she saw Bob, slamming down his drink while glaring her way. Refusing to give him any thought, she moved toward the back of the room where she chose another hidden post, this one close enough that she could see Richard as he spoke.

As soon as the large gathering spied Richard at the podium, the noise quieted. He gave off an air of self-assurance, wearing a casual elegance about him. He began speaking, and it dawned on her that if she was having to speak in front of a group that large, her voice would be quivering. But instead, his voice was clear and sure.

He opened with his welcome, followed by his thanks for the people who had made the event possible, including those who had generously given items to be auctioned as well as mentioning the Richmond Museum of Art and the Prince Hotel employees.

As soon as he mentioned the latter, his gaze seemed to land on her, and he smiled. She had wondered if perhaps there was another job at Prince Hotel that she could be considered for when Mrs. Smithwick came back and felt sure that if there was he would consider her for it.

At the mention of the homeless shelters in the city, her

attention snapped back to his speech. He talked about the work they did, the expenses needed to run the shelters, and how the Prince Hotel was honored to have chosen the homeless shelters as the recipients of this year's fundraisers. "I hope, by the end of the evening, I'll be able to give you an idea of how much your generosity will have raised. So, until then, visit the silent auction room, bid generously, eat, and drink, and dance, and most of all, enjoy yourselves. Thank you." The applause was deafening as he walked off the stage, accepting the handshakes from those around.

"I see you enjoy staying in the background."

Startling, she looked to the side and saw Lawrence Prince standing nearby, a beautiful woman with silver-blonde hair standing next to him.

Blushing at having been caught daydreaming, she said, "Yes, sir. The event is beautiful but not something I'm used to."

The woman chuckled and said, "I've been going to these events for years, and sometimes I feel like I'm not used to them, either."

"Cynthia, I'd like to present my wife, Barbara. This enchanting young woman is filling in for Mrs. Smithwick, working with Richard."

"Oh, how nice to meet you," Barbara said, stepping forward to take Cynthia's hand.

"It's very nice to meet you, too," she said. She felt the woman's warm acceptance and looked to the side to see another man and woman approaching. This man was so similar to Richard in appearance she assumed he must be his brother, Larry. She was proven correct when

Barbara greeted the couple and introduced them as Larry and Linda Prince.

Surrounded by the Prince family, she could not slip away easily but found their conversation to be light and easy, lacking the pretense that oozed from some of the other attendees.

A noisy group was approaching, and she spied Richard, Bob, and several others making their way to them.

"The homeless shelter?" one of the women said, clinging to Richard's arm. "You couldn't find anything more worthy than that?"

"Well, if the homeless are in the shelter, they're not lying about the streets blocking the sidewalks," another man said, his words slurring slightly.

"I agree," another man said. He lifted his drink as though to make a toast and said, "We'll rally the others so that we can keep the rabble off the sidewalks."

Eyes wide, heart pounding, Cynthia glanced over to see Barbara and Lawrence glaring, their lips pinched tightly. If she was not mistaken, they were not happy with the way the conversation was going.

"If they can't get a job, I don't see why we should have to help them find a place to live," another woman said, her Botox lips frozen in a permanent pout.

Anger began to course through Cynthia's veins, but before she had a chance to say anything, Bob stepped up to the group. Looking straight at her, he said, "Even our little temp worker had been in a homeless shelter. I suppose she's glad to see money gets thrown their way."

All eyes turned her way, and her stomach clenched

as her body began to shake. She glanced around at the stunned expressions of some of the people near Richard, then halted when she saw his wide eyes piercing her.

"Cynthia? You lived in a homeless shelter?" he asked.

His voice was more curious than imperious, but at that moment, she did not care. Lifting her chin, she speared Bob with an icy stare and said, "Most of us have no clue that we're so close to losing everything we hold dear. A house that catches fire. A job that gets down-sized. A medical emergency with no insurance. A veteran who served his country but had nothing to come home to. You've categorized who ends up in a homeless shelter without even thinking that it could ever be you or someone you know." Her legs began to quake underneath her long gown, and she wondered if they would continue to hold her up. Swallowing deeply, she said, "I would rather spend my time with honest, hard-working people who were down on their luck than any more time in a room filled with minnows pretending to be whales."

Tears filled her eyes and her chin began to quiver, but she refused to let them see her cry. Turning, she pushed past the crowd, making her way toward the door. Pulling her phone out, she hit Zeke's number, and without giving him a chance to say anything, she cried, "I'm leaving. Can you come to get me?"

"Babe, I'm here. I'm in the front."

She ran to the lobby, her ankles twisting in her ridiculous heeled shoes. Stopping long enough to jerk them off, she tossed them to the side as she pushed open the heavy front door. Grabbing handfuls of her skirt to hold it up, she raced down the concrete steps of the museum toward the man who was just climbing from his truck. The long-haired, bearded, tatted, blue jean and motorcycle boots-wearing man. He looked nothing like the men that had been attending the gala, but everything like the man she respected and loved.

---

## 26

Zeke had no idea what had happened, but hearing Cynthia's tearful voice on the phone calling for him caused him to leap from his truck. By the time his boots hit the sidewalk, he looked up and could see her racing down the steps.

Her beautiful gown was hiked up around her knees, exposing her bare feet. Her long hair was flying behind her, and he barely had time to pray she would not trip.

He ran forward but stopped, seeing that she was still coming. He planted his legs apart and braced as he opened his arms. She slammed into him, and he rocked back a foot as his arms wrapped around her, holding her close.

"Baby, baby, talk to me. What the fuck happened?"

A tear slid down her face, but she simply burrowed deeper against him. The sound of someone calling out had them both jerk their heads around, looking toward the top of the steps.

Richard was standing there, his black tux stark

against the white granite of the building. And in his hands dangled her sparkling shoes.

"Cynthia! I'm sorry!"

Still having no idea what had happened, Prince's apology had Zeke seeing red. He gently set Cynthia away from him and started up the steps, his hands curled into fists.

"No, no," she cried, racing after him and grabbing his arm.

Unheeding, he continued forward until her voice finally penetrated his fog of rage.

"No, Zeke, no, they're not worth it."

He forced his body to slow and turned toward her, cupping her cheeks and bringing her close. "Baby, what happened?"

"Nothing. Honestly, it wasn't anything other than I just found out that they're all fakes. Sparkly and shiny on the outside and just mean on the inside."

His gaze swung back up toward the top of the steps, but she placed her hand on his cheek and turned him back toward her. "Please, take me home," she begged. "I just want to go home with you."

Still not understanding everything that had happened, his heart ached that something occurred that made her desperate to leave. But if he was honest, he was thrilled that she wanted to leave with him.

With one last glare shot toward Richard Prince, he lifted her in his arms and carried her to his truck. Settling her inside, he said, "I'm afraid your chariot ride this time isn't quite as fancy as the one you came in."

She wiped her tears and offered a wobbly grin.

"Believe me, this princess has no desire to go back to the ball."

He leaned over and gave her a kiss, pouring his love into the touch. "Send a message to Miss Ethel," he said. "Tonight, you're coming back to my castle."

Still smiling, she admitted, "There's nowhere else I'd rather be."

---

It was on the drive home that she explained what had happened, and while it seemed that she was calmer in the repeating, it served to incense him more.

Shaking her head, she said, "It wasn't like anyone was saying anything to me directly. Well, except for Bob, but he's just an asshole."

"Babe, it doesn't matter if they were talking about you at all. And it doesn't even matter that they thought they were speaking to others who would have no idea what it's like to be homeless. I agree, Bob was an asshole, but he wasn't the only one."

"No, you're right, he wasn't. Although I left before everything played out."

Turning his head, he looked at her in curiosity and asked, "Played out? What do you mean?" Her nose scrunched, and he thought she was adorable. How she could appear so elegant and cute all at the same time he did not know, but she did.

"I had a chance to meet Richard's father, the elder Mr. Prince, and his mother, brother, and his wife. I only had a few minutes to talk to them, but they seemed...I don't know...real. At least nowhere near the pretense of the others. When the crowd that Richard was with began talking down about the homeless shelters, I saw the expression on his parents' faces, and it wasn't good. I'm almost sure that they would have rebuffed the others." She shrugged, and added, "But I'll never know because I jumped in."

"You know, I called you a princess earlier, but I think that's wrong. I should've called you a warrior." A giggle slipped from her lips, and he loved hearing the sound.

"Well, I could be a warrior princess," she declared.

As they pulled up to his house, he looked over and smiled. Lifting his hand, he cupped her cheek and rubbed his thumb over her petal-soft skin. "My warrior princess. Yeah, I like that."

---

Once inside, Cynthia snuggled closely as Zeke carried her up the stairs to the master suite. Even though they were inside the house, he kept her in his arms until he entered the bathroom, setting her feet on the plush bathroom rug.

"This is perfect," she enthused. "I want to strip out of this dress and take a long hot shower, washing the evening off me."

"Whatever you need, babe," he said.

She turned her back to him and asked, "Can you help me get out of this? There's a hidden zipper in the back."

Now it was his turn to scrunch his face as he asked, "What's a hidden zipper?"

She lifted her long hair and draped it around the front, exposing the back of the dress. Reaching behind her, she found the small tab to the top of the zipper hidden in a seam. "It's just a zipper that's sewn in a way that makes it look like a seam in the dress and not an actual zipper. Just grab this and pull."

As he followed her instructions, she felt the material loosen and began pulling it away from her arms and over her breasts as he lowered the zipper to her ass. She let the material pool to the floor and stepped over the puddle of blue silk. Her hands went to her hair where she unfastened the sparkly barrette, laying it to the side so that she could give it back to Regina.

Without the trappings of the formal evening wear, she already felt lighter. Turning to face him, she caught his blatant stare of unapologetic lust as he cast his gaze from the top of her head down to her toes and back up again, halting on her breasts spilling from her strapless bra.

She lifted her hands to the front clasp and deftly unhooked the bra, letting the material fall to the bathroom floor, her breasts bouncing free. Seeing his gaze staring at her naked body, she asked, "See anything you like?"

"Oh, fuck, babe," he moaned, lifting his hands to cup her breasts, his thumbs circling her nipples.

"That's the idea," she cooed. Glancing over her shoulder, she amended, "But first, I need to take a shower."

He reached behind him, grabbed a handful of his T-shirt, and jerked it over his head, exposing his muscular chest and the light furring of hair that covered it. "A shower sounds like a good idea to me."

Grinning, her eyes widened at the thought of them taking a shower together. Hooking her thumbs into her panties, she slid them down her legs and kicked them to the side. He watched every movement, and she made sure to take her time. He stepped around her, his naked chest brushing against her nipples, and flipped on the water. Her hands went to his belt, and she soon had his jeans undone.

With his boots and socks off, she had no trouble shimmying his jeans and boxers down his thighs. As the clothing landed at his ankles, she dropped to her knees, taking him in her mouth. She slid her moistened lips over the tip and down his shaft. His groan filled the room as her hair filled his hands. She clutched at his ass as she sucked and licked his cock.

Just when she thought he was ready to explode, he pulled out, lifted her up from her armpits, and carried her into the shower. Keeping her hoisted, he pressed her back against the shower tiles, allowing the water spray to hit his back instead of her.

She wrapped her little legs around his waist, and he lowered his head, moving between her breasts, feasting until she cried out with need. He leaned his head back and speared her with his gaze, and she nodded, desperate to feel him deep inside her.

He acquiesced, and with one swift push, he plunged in to the hilt. For a moment, he did not move, and while she felt the overwhelming fullness, she was desperate for friction. Shifting slightly, she begged, "Please, Zeke."

He began pumping, moving her up and down on his shaft, and as she moaned, he captured her sounds as his lips covered hers. Their tongues tangled, eventually settling into the same rhythm as his cock plunging deep inside.

"Close, baby?" he mumbled.

All she could do was nod, and with his pelvis rubbing against her clit, she soon shattered. The vibrations scattered from her core outward, moving through every cell in her body. Just then, he roared, and she opened her eyes to watch him come.

He threw his head back, and she could see the strain in his neck muscles as he powered through his orgasm. He continued to pump until she felt sure there was nothing left. He held her in place as their breaths slowed before he allowed her feet to slide back down. As though he knew they would be weak, he continued to hold her until she was steady.

With her arm still around his neck, she leaned her head back and stared into his face. It was as though every fiber in her body was sated and relaxed. He turned her slightly so that the shower spray sluiced over her body, and together they soaped and rinsed. She then washed the product out of her hair, allowing everything about the evening to swirl down the drain.

After they dried off, he handed her a soft, worn T-shirt. Pulling it over her head, it hung halfway down her thighs. Slipping on her panties, she stood and looked into the bathroom mirror. He came up behind her, wrapped one arm around her waist and the other across her chest, and rested his head on top of her head. "I'm so sorry it ended the way it did."

She felt her smile slip a little as her thoughts moved over the event. "Honestly, it's okay. I only had another week to work in the office before going back to house-keeping anyway. I'll talk to Carlos on Monday and see if I can go back right away."

"Monday?"

"I doubt they still want me in the office, but there's no way I'm going to work for someone that callous," she declared.

"I said you were beautiful earlier," he said, grinning. "That wasn't a lie. You were. But seeing you standing here, in my house, in my shirt, you're the most beautiful thing I've ever seen."

She turned in his arms and allowed her hands to drift up over his shoulders. Lifting on her toes, she kissed him, his tongue plunging in once more as though drinking her in. He finally lifted his head and asked, "Did you get anything to eat earlier?"

Shaking her head, she replied, "No. At first, I was too nervous, and then I was just angry and ran out." Grinning, she asked, "Can we raid your refrigerator?"

"Babe, as far as I'm concerned, it's our refrigerator. And you can have anything you want."

A little later, they sat at the kitchen counter, their plates filled with scrambled eggs, bacon, fried potatoes, and pancakes topped with butter and syrup. Eating more at one time than she could ever remember,

Cynthia laughed. "What is it about eating late at night that makes everything taste so good?"

Just then, Zeke's phone alarm dinged, indicating that it was midnight. Shaking his head, he said, "I was sitting outside waiting for you, just wanting to be close. I knew I wasn't going to need an alarm to tell me when the event was over, but I guess I set it nonetheless."

"Midnight," she said, shaking her head slightly. Looking over, she blushed and said, "Would you believe that when I was in there, I actually thought about Cinderella? Isn't that silly?"

"Oh, baby..."

Shrugging, she said, "Zeke, midnight was always going to come for Cinderella. She even knew that. Her Fairy Godmother even warned her."

Chuckling, he agreed. "I guess you're right."

She looked at him, the thought entering her mind that she had not considered earlier. "Why were you sitting outside? I figured you would have gone to Grimm's."

Brows lowered slightly, he said, "It was Miss Ethel. She suggested that I might want to be close in case you needed me. So, I drove downtown, parked close by, and was just reading on my phone." Holding her gaze, he said, "I have no idea how she might have known that I should be there, but I'm glad I was."

Looking away, nibbling her lip as he went back to his food, she whispered, "Fairy Godmother."

## 27

For the first time, Zeke awoke with the warm body of Cynthia tucked in his arms. Daylight was just peeking through the blinds, and they may have been up past midnight gorging on comfort food, but his morning wood had him raring to go.

Not wanting her to think that was the only reason he wanted her to spend the night with him, he tried to ease his hips backward away from her ass.

"Uh-uh," she mumbled, pressing her hips back against his erection.

"Babe, don't worry about it. There's nothing we need to do—"

"Shut up," she mumbled again, this time her hands sliding into her panties and shimmying them down.

She seemed half-asleep, but he was not about to pass up that invitation. Sliding into her warm sheath, he cupped her breast with one hand and slid his hand down to circle her clit with the other. Soon, they were both coming together, their cries ringing in the morning.

Breakfast this time consisted of cereal and milk and coffee. Looking at her, he asked, "Do you want to move in today?"

Nodding, with a grin playing about her lips, she said, "I'd love to."

It did not take long for them to drive to Miss Ethel's house and pack Cynthia's suitcase. While she was upstairs collecting her clothes and toiletries, Zeke talked to Miss Ethel, filling her in on the previous evening.

Shaking her head, Miss Ethel clucked, "I'm so sorry that happened to Cynthia. I'm afraid ignorant people abound at all levels of society."

They both looked up as Cynthia came down the stairs, and Zeke rushed to pluck the suitcase from her hands. He set her luggage by the front door, then leaned against the door as Cynthia walked over to Miss Ethel.

"I don't know how to thank you for opening up your heart and your home to me," she said, reaching out and taking the older woman's hands in her own.

"Oh, posh, my dear. No thanks are needed. Just take care of yourself, and that's all I'll need to be happy."

With her head tilted to the side, Cynthia hesitated, then asked, "Miss Ethel, how did you know? How did you know that I would need Zeke last night?"

"My dear, to paraphrase the words of Avijeet Das, 'You are a beautiful princess who has chosen him to be the prince in your life. You both deserve the love that is truly beautiful and magical. Love each other with all your sensitivity and tenderness.'"

Grinning, she looked over her shoulder at Zeke smiling back at her. Turning toward Miss Ethel, she bent and kissed her cheek, whispering, "I love you."

Miss Ethel hugged her tightly, then smiled at Zeke over Cynthia's shoulder and said, "And I love you both."

Back at his house, after she hung her clothes in the space provided in his closet and set her toiletries on the double sinks next to his, they declared the rest of the Sunday to be their lazy day. He had considered bringing up the subject of her working for Grimm's but hesitated. Wanting her to relax as much as she could, knowing the next day she was going back to the Prince Hotel to face the unknown, he simply tucked her into his side as they lay on the couch, watching old movies and snacking.

Truthfully, it was the best kind of day for both of them.

When Cynthia's alarm sounded the next morning, she turned it off and snuggled deeper under the covers. Zeke's arm was banded around her waist, his face buried in her neck. Instead of reveling in where she was, she sighed heavily.

He stretched, pulling her tighter against him, and asked, "How bad are you dreading this?"

She shifted onto her back so that she could stare into

his eyes, reaching up to rub her hand over his bearded jaw. "Pretty bad."

"You don't even have to go in, babe. Just give that fucker a call or...hell...send him an email."

Another sigh escaped her lips, and she shook her head. "No, I'm not going to take the coward's way out. I want to see him. I want to see him squirm when I talk to him."

Zeke, still on his side, cocked his elbow and propped his head in his hand, peering down at her. His free hand was still resting across her middle, his fingers sliding under her shoulder blades to pull her close. "I'm not sure someone like him would even squirm."

She pondered his words, then said, "Bob? You're right. I think he's a snake, and he might slither, but there's nothing I could say to make him squirm. But Richard? I don't know. I think he might actually feel bad." She snorted, then added, "At least if his parents have anything to do with it, I think he'll feel bad."

"Are you going to go by and see Carlos?"

She held his gaze and nodded. "He hired some temporary help in housekeeping. I need to see if I can come back a week early."

His fingers pressed into her back, massaging the tense muscles. "Is that what you want to do? Go back to housekeeping?"

She sucked in her lips for a moment, then said, "It's not my dream job, it never was. But it paid the bills, and I like who I worked with. I don't have any formal education or training to do anything else." She shrugged and said, "It's what I know."

He dropped his head back to her shoulder, and they lay for several minutes, quietly letting their thoughts roam as they held each other tightly. Her alarm went off again, and she groaned. "I've got to get up, honey. It's time to face the day."

Leaning over, he kissed her and said, "You shower, and I'll get you breakfast."

Several minutes later, standing in the shower, letting the warm water wash the shampoo from her hair, she thought about going into the Prince Hotel and how today was different than in the past. Today, she was making her own choice. Today, she was standing up for herself. Today, when all was said and done, she was coming back to a man she loved.

With those thoughts in mind, she finished her shower. By the time she had toweled off and dressed, partially drying her hair with the blow dryer and had light makeup on, the scent of coffee and bacon had drifted upstairs. With renewed vigor, she jogged down the stairs, ready to face the day.

When Zeke drove her to the Prince Hotel, he parked on the street just down from the front entrance. She leaned forward and looked at the impressive building through his truck's windshield. The red brick exterior with the Prince Hotel emblem etched in the front glass doors as well as on a large banner hanging on the front of the building. The tall first-floor windows that opened to the lobby and the restaurant, pouring light inside. Leaning forward, her eyes continued to move upward.

She knew floors two through five held the regular rooms, still exclusive by other hotels' standards, and floors six and seven were the executive suites. She thought of her friends, the daytime housekeepers who cleaned the rooms, making sure that each guest who stayed walked into a room that was perfectly ready for them. She thought of the nighttime housekeeping staff that cleaned the restaurant, lobby, and offices.

"Do you want me to go in with you?"

She startled at the question, having been so lost in her musings. Glancing over, she saw Zeke's concerned face staring at her. She offered a little smile and said, "I'll be okay."

He reached over and took her hand, giving it a little squeeze. "I know you'll be fine. But I'd like to be with you, or at least close by."

Nodding slowly, she said, "Yeah, I'd like that. You could wait in the lobby?"

"I'll wait wherever you want me to, babe."

"I think that will be best. I'll stop in to see Carlos first, and then I'll go and speak to Richard."

"What if Carlos can't take you back until next week when you were planning on returning anyway?"

Nibbling on her bottom lip, she said, "Then I guess I've got a week of unpaid vacation."

Leaning even closer, he cupped her cheek and said, "If that happens, I can always use you at Grimm's Two."

Smiling at the thought of spending more time with Zeke, she nodded. "Thanks. I might just have to take you up on that." Closing the distance between them, she offered her lips in a kiss, the familiar electricity moving through her as he took the kiss deeper. As their tongues tangled, she allowed herself to become lost in the feel and touch of him.

He slowly pulled back, regret in his eyes. "If we keep kissing my truck's going to get steamy, and if I get steamy with you, I want to be where I can do everything to you that I want to do."

Laughing, she agreed. "You're right. Anyway, I don't want to put this off any longer." She grabbed her purse, allowed him to assist her down, and they walked up the steps and through the front door of the hotel. He gave her another quick kiss for luck before settling on one of the sofas in the lobby.

She walked down the hall, but when she arrived at Carlos' office, she found the door open but Carlos not inside. She hesitated for a moment, wondering if she should wait, but knew that if he was up on one of the floors it might be a while before he came back to his office.

Sucking in a deep breath of air, she pulled herself up to her full height and walked toward the elevator to the executive offices. Entering the outer office, she glanced around and was struck with the thought that if she had never gone to the event on Saturday night, she would be sitting down at the desk right now, placing her purse in the drawer before getting coffee for Richard and Bob. Rolling her eyes, she knew her position had been point-less; the only interesting part of it was the last week in assisting with the event.

She lay the garment bag with her gown on the desk, not knowing if Richard would be able to return it but knew she no longer wanted the reminder of the gala.

Richard's door was slightly ajar. She knocked softly and peeked in, but it did not appear he was in his office. The sun coming through the windows reflected off of something sparkly on his desk, and she stepped forward, stunned to see her shoes from Saturday night. Moving toward his desk, she stared at the beautiful shoes. The blue straps crisscrossed from the toes up to the ankle, encrusted with rhinestones. When the saleslady has presented them to her, she could not imagine a prettier shoe to wear with her gown. Now, they simply represented a night she would like to forget.

A voice came from Bob's office, and she turned, wondering if Richard was with him. She preferred to talk to Richard alone, but was determined to not let Bob intimidate her. Walking across the plush carpet of Richard's office, she moved to the door that connected with Bob's office.

The door was closed, but as she waited before knocking to see if she heard Richard's voice, she could tell Bob's one-sided conversation indicated he was on the phone.

"I told you I got the money. You can't back out on me now. I'm telling you the maid did not see the note and no one knows the money was for us. We stick to the same schedule that we've been doing, and everything will be fine."

Her body locked in place, not understanding Bob's side of the conversation other than she was the only maid who had seen a note with money. *It was for him?* Her heart began to pound, but her feet did not move.

Instead, she leaned slightly closer to the door to see if she could hear more.

"I know, I talked to him. He doesn't want to get rid of her," Bob said.

"Tell him that's not what we agreed on," Richard added in.

Outside the office door, Cynthia startled, hearing Richard's voice. *So, he is in there? He knows? Richard knows that Bob was supposed to get the money?* Unable to process what they were saying fast enough for it to make any sense, she pressed her fingers against her lips to keep from making a sound, continuing to listen.

"Richard, shut the fuck up," Bob said, his voice whispering. "I'm dealing with this." After a few seconds' pause, Bob said, "Yeah, I'm here. Just checking to make sure everything's okay. Yeah, yeah, no change. Leave the money the same way. Our Head of Housekeeping has been informed to keep the schedule from now on. Nobody will get to the money until I have a chance to retrieve it."

A gasp left her lips as she realized whatever they were discussing, it had to do with the money she discovered left in the room safe...and Carlos was involved. Fear settled deep inside of her quickly, and she hurried back through Richard's door into the outer office, hoping to remain out of sight. She glanced at the garment bag on the desk, but before she could retrieve it, the knob on Bob's door began to turn. The desire to flee took over, and she turned and ran.

## 28

Cynthia raced out of the office, glad that she was wearing sneakers and not heels as she careened around the doorframe and down the hall toward the elevators.

She did not hear footsteps behind her but raced on her tiptoes to the end of the hall. Afraid to wait on the elevator, she jerked her head around to ascertain that no one was behind her and spied the sign for the stairs. Heaving on the door to open it, she slipped through then hesitated just long enough to make sure it did not slam closed behind her, hoping to keep her presence a secret.

Heartbeat pounding, she rushed down the stairs, her feet stumbling as she pulled her phone from her purse. Calling Zeke, she barely waited for him to answer before she said, "I'm in the stairwell. I'm coming down. I don't want them to know I heard."

His voice, instantly on alert, barked, "What are you talking about? Babe, where are you?"

"I'm in the stairwell past the offices that are beyond the lobby. I'm coming down."

"I'm heading to you right now," he said, and she breathed a sigh of relief as she rounded the first level.

"I didn't see anyone in the office, but I heard Bob talking about the money that was left here. I think he's got something going on. I don't know what," she said, her words tumbling out in a rush.

"Babe, don't worry about that now. Just keep coming down the stairs, and I'm coming for you. But stay on the line."

Her feet skidded off one of the steps, and she threw her hands out to grab onto the railing to keep from landing on her face. The phone clattered to the concrete floor, and as she pulled herself back up to a standing position she grabbed it and shoved it into her purse.

Legs shaking and knees wobbling, she glanced upward to see if she could hear anyone coming from above. Between the heaving breaths and the blood roaring in her veins, she was uncertain what she was hearing. The sound of a door opened from above and Bob's voice called out.

"She must be on the stairs!"

Racing down another half-flight, she heard a door open from below, thankful that Zeke had found the stairway. Racing around the next landing, she came face-to-face with Carlos as he was running up.

"Oh—" The words halted in her throat as she glanced down, seeing a gun in Carlos' hand. Gasping, she whirled but was unable to take more than two steps before his hand reached out and clamped onto hers.

"No!" she cried, pulling on her arm but unable to get away from him. He let go of her for only a few seconds while he pulled open the door leading to the fourth floor. Once more, before she was able to take a step away, his hand clamped onto her upper arm, and he dragged her to a room and through the door.

Giving her a push, her hands began to windmill, but with the bed directly behind her, she only plopped onto the soft mattress. Scrambling backward, she tried to get away from him, but her eyes remained firmly on the gun in his hand.

The sound of heavy footsteps pounding down the hall caused her heart to stutter. Uncertain if Bob or Richard were coming after her, she stared wide-eyed toward the door. A few seconds later, the door crashed inward, slamming against the wall. Zeke raced through, his gaze raking past Carlos and landing on her.

"He's got a gun!" she screamed.

"Let her go, you fucker," Zeke ordered, his voice deep with fury and his fists clenching and unclenching at his side.

"Quiet, you two," Carlos said, sticking his hand in his pocket.

He pulled out something and held it up for Zeke, but she was unable to see what was in his hand. She watched as Zeke's eyes stared at the object before his brows lowered, and he rumbled, "What the fuck? Federal agent?"

Carlos lowered his gun and swung his hand around, flashing her a badge. Feeling the breath rush out of her lungs, her body sagged. Before she had a chance to speak, Zeke bypassed Carlos, rushing to her.

Pulling her into his arms, he held her tightly, saying, "I've got you, babe. I've got you. Don't know what the fuck is going on, but I've got you."

She looked up as Zeke turned his head around, pinning Carlos with a hard stare. Twisting her head, she asked, "Carlos?"

"I'm sorry to manhandle you, Cynthia, but I had to get you out of the stairs and out of sight. We've had Bob Shelton and Richard Prince under surveillance for over six months. They've been using this hotel to launder money, and the raid is happening right now. You coming in early today meant you were about to stumble into the middle of a takedown."

Before she had a chance to ask any questions, Carlos began talking into his radio. Listening to him continue to coordinate with whoever was on the other end of the signal, she looked up at Zeke and said, "I heard them. They didn't know I was there, so I rushed out." His arms tightened around her, and she added, "Thank God you were here. You came for me."

With his lips pressed against her forehead, he mumbled against her skin, "I'll always come for you. You're safe...you're safe now."

She startled and said, "The note. The note with the money. That must've been for Bob or Richard."

Carlos jerked his head around and said, "You found a note?"

Nodding, she admitted, "Yes. But Bob said he would take care of everything so I didn't mention it."

His face hard as stone, Carlos turned to them and ordered, "Stay here. I don't want you going anywhere else. Stay here, and when all is safe, I'll come back and get you."

They watched as Carlos left and the door closed shut behind him. Zeke and Cynthia stared at each other for a moment, neither speaking.

"I guess I won't be asking him if I'll be back in housekeeping," she deadpanned, a nervous giggle slipping out.

Zeke scrubbed his hand over his face, settling on the edge of the bed with her tucked close into his embrace. "Cynthia, this might be the wrong time, but I wanted to ask you if you'd consider coming to work at Grimm's for me and Zander as a manager."

Eyes wide, she said, "Are you serious?"

Chuckling, he replied, "Absolutely, babe. I just didn't want to say anything while you had so much going on here. I know it might not be your dream job, but I'd feel a lot better if you were working with us."

"I'd love to be a part of Grimm's," she said, her hands going to either side of his face, pulling him in for a kiss. She breathed him in as though he were the very oxygen she needed to live.

After taking the kiss wet and wild, he pulled back, saying, "I can't believe we're in a nice hotel room, and I can't take this kiss all the way."

Laughing, she said, "Then maybe we'll need to come back sometime as guests. I know exactly which rooms are the best."

"Hell, if the owner and his right-hand man have

been laundering money, who knows what the fuck is going to happen to this hotel."

Thoughts tangling, she shook her head slowly, saying, "I haven't even had time to process what might happen to the hotel. There are so many good people who work here, I hope it doesn't go under."

"I guess it depends on how far up the rot goes. If it's just this hotel, then Prince Hotels International can step in and take it over."

It was not long before Carlos strolled back into the room, his face showing much more relief than what they had seen earlier. "Cynthia, we're going to need to get your statement. Once we have that, you're free to go."

Standing on shaky legs, she was glad Zeke kept his arm around her as they followed the agent out of the room. Uncertain of where they were going, she was surprised when they moved to the elevator and went up to the executive floor.

As she entered the office behind Carlos, it was now crowded with FBI agents. They were walking out with computers, laptops, and boxing up files. Looking around, Carlos motioned for them to follow him, and they walked into the empty conference room, followed by another agent. They did not object to Zeke staying with her, for which she was glad. Her life had turned upside down, and he was the one constant that she held on to.

The dining room in Miss Ethel's house was filled to capacity, although she always said there was room for one more. Zeke had called Zander to let him know why he was not coming in that day, and that started a flurry of phone calls between all the brothers, their women, and Miss Ethel.

Finishing her story, Cynthia said, "I don't think they really needed my statement because they'd had had their eyes on Bob and Richard for a while. But since I had seen the note on the money, had been the one to find the money and turn it over to Bob, and then over-heard their conversation this morning, I think Carlos just needed to make sure there was nothing else I knew."

"So, the day you found the money, Bob was supposed to get to it first?" Zander asked.

"Carlos didn't tell us much, but that's my assumption. Somebody would leave money in the hotel safe, and Bob would get to it, obviously not going through the proper channels."

"And you messed up that chain when you found it first," Regina surmised.

Jumping in, Cael added, "They must've had a fit when that money had to go through security instead of straight into his pocket."

"Maybe I'm just dense," Rosalie began, "but didn't they think it was a risk having you working right there?"

Shrugging, she said, "I know Bob didn't want me working up there, but Richard seemed to want me around—"

"Because he wanted in your..." Zeke began, then stopped as he glanced over toward Miss Ethel. "Uh...he thought you were pretty."

She rolled her eyes, then said, "I just don't understand it. From all indications, the hotel was doing well. He had looks, wealth, and from the women I saw at the event, he certainly wasn't lacking for female companionship. His parents seemed really nice. I just can't understand why he would risk all that."

"Who knows what lies in a man's heart," Miss Ethel said, gathering everyone's attention to her. "Wealth does not bring goodness..."

"Socrates!" came the shout from the men, almost in unison. The gathering laughed, the heaviness of their conversation lightening for a moment.

Miss Ethel smiled, saying, "A pauper may do great deeds with a kind heart, but a *prince* with wealth is capable of evil."

Zeke's brows lowered as he glanced at his brothers. Turning to Miss Ethel, he asked, "Who wrote that?"

Continuing to smile as she stood, Miss Ethel said, "No one. I just made it up." She walked back into the kitchen to the laughter of her family.

## 29

TWO WEEKS LATER

Cynthia stood at the steps leading to the front of the Prince Hotel, holding tightly to Zeke's hand. She looked up at the large building, so familiar, and yet having only been gone for two weeks, it seemed like another part of her life.

"You okay, babe?" he asked, tugging gently on her hand so that she faced him, his gaze searching her face.

She sucked in her lips and nodded, then said, "This just feels weird. I don't really know what to expect."

"Well, let's go see. Standing out here won't give you any answers."

She nodded her agreement, and they walked up the front steps and through the glass doors into the lobby. She had received a call from Lawrence Prince who asked to speak with her. Setting up an appointment, she was here to see what he wanted.

For the past two weeks she had worked at Grimm's, learning everything she could about taking stock, ordering supplies, and managing employee schedules.

Zander and Zeke planned on her managing Grimm's Two. She discovered she loved the camaraderie with the staff, and her organizational skills were perfect for the job.

As a housekeeper, she had worn a uniform. As an assistant, she had worn skirts and blouses. As a bar manager, she loved wearing jeans, T-shirts, and her favorite sneakers. Now, getting ready to meet with the head of Prince International Hotels, she wore slacks and a blouse along with low-heeled pumps.

As she walked into the outer office, she was met by an older woman sitting in the desk she used to occupy. The woman smiled and introduced herself as Mrs. Smithwick before she knocked on Richard's—now Lawrence's—door.

"I'll wait right here," Zeke said as Cynthia was ushered inside. She sent a smile over her shoulder toward him and followed Mrs. Smithwick in.

Lawrence, looking very much like she remembered from the fundraising event, only in a suit instead of a tux, stood from behind the desk and came to greet her. "Ms. Ellison, I'm glad you were able to come in today." He waved his hand toward the sofa and said, "Please, let's have a seat." As he approached, she could see that there were deeper creases in the lines in his face and darker circles underneath his eyes that were no longer bright.

She sat, crossing her ankles with her hands clasped in her lap. Licking her dry lips, she said, "Mr. Prince, please, call me Cynthia. And I'm so very sorry for what your family is going through." She halted as she watched pain slash across his face. Her words felt so inadequate, but there did not seem to be a way to have a Hallmark moment when all she could think of was, *I'm sorry your son was laundering money and now will go to prison.*

"My son..." he began, then looked away for a moment and sighed. "My son had been given everything and yet made such poor decisions. Bob was a wholly unscrupulous man, and my son was weak." His eyes jumped to hers, and he hurried to add, "That's not making excuses for my son. It's just hard for a father to admit that their son is weak and easily led down the path that he was taught was wrong."

Her heart ached for the anguish she saw on Lawrence's face and heard in his voice. This time, her words were filled with more sincere sympathy. "I truly, truly am so sorry."

He looked away, sucked in a deep breath, and nodded. He straightened, sitting up taller, seeming to draw upon some inner resolve. "I appreciate your sympathy, Cynthia. Barbara and I, as well as our elder son Larry, were stunned to find out that Richard was involved in illegal activity. And that the activity was taking place here at the Prince Hotel compounded our anguish."

She nodded and remained quiet, deciding to let him take charge since he was the one who had asked her to visit.

"For now, I have come in to make sure everything continues to run at the Prince Hotel, not wanting our guests or employees to feel the change. We are bringing this hotel under the International Corporation that

Larry and I both run, so the transition should be smooth. I will have one of our experienced managers come in to run the hotel once I'm assured that everything is in order."

She continued to nod politely, still wondering why her presence has been requested.

He held her gaze and said, "I want you to know that my wife and I enjoyed meeting you at the fundraiser. We were unhappy at the comments about the homeless shelter that were being made and mortified that they seemed to be echoed by our own son. Your comments and defense of the homeless struck us deeply. We realized, more than anyone in that group, you were a person of integrity. I know that you have great experience as a housekeeper here at the Prince Hotel, and obviously, we will need a new Head of Housekeeping. I'd like you to consider taking that position if you're interested."

Blinking, she repeated, "Head of Housekeeping?" She now knew that Carlos had been working undercover, and, of course, someone would have to be hired.

"It would be a salaried position, with full benefits including health and retirement, and certainly room for growth," he said, dangling enticements in front of her.

The basement of the Prince Hotel had been her employment home for years, and there was a time, not too long ago, that she would have loved to have had a position of importance and status there. She closed her eyes for a moment and thought about the man who was just outside the office waiting for her. A man who gave her a home when she was homeless. A man who gave her a job when she was jobless. A man who gave her his love.

She opened her eyes and smiled at Lawrence and said, "I'm honored that you are considering me for this position. But I now have another job that means a great deal to me, so I have to decline your generous offer."

They stood, and he reached over to clasp her hand warmly as he said goodbye. "I wish you the very best of luck, Cynthia. Whoever has you now, they have a true jewel."

She turned to leave, then, as a thought struck her, turned back to him. "Mr. Prince, I have no idea if you'll even consider this. But there's a woman who's been working in housekeeping here for many years. She's smart, hard-working, and very dedicated to Prince Hotel. If you're looking for a new Head of House-keeping and would like to offer the position to someone from the inside, please, consider Lucy Bonez."

He smiled as he inclined his head and repeated, "Lucy Bonez. Thank you for the recommendation, Cynthia. I would like to hire from the inside. I'll arrange for an interview today."

With that, she smiled her goodbye and headed to the outer office, her gaze landing on Zeke. He immediately moved toward her, his gaze assessing as it swept over her. As they walked down the hall, he asked, "Are you all right?"

As they stepped onto the elevator, she said, "He wanted to offer me the position that Carlos had, Head of Housekeeping. Salary with full benefits."

Zeke startled, then said, "Congratulations, babe. You'll be amazing at whatever you do."

Smiling, she leaned her back against the elevator wall, tugging on his hands so that he was leaning toward her. Lifting her hands to clasp behind his neck, she said, "I'm glad you think so. Of course, I turned him down because I have a new job as manager of Grimm's Two."

She watched as a smile curved his lips just before they came crashing down on hers. She lost herself in the feel and taste and emotion swirling all about. It was not until the doors opened on the lobby floor that they pulled apart. Linking fingers, they hurried through the lobby and down the front steps.

After he assisted her into his truck, she peered up at the Prince Hotel as Zeke rounded the hood. When he climbed into the driver's seat, he leaned over and kissed her soundly before they pulled into the traffic, heading back home. She leaned back into the seat, her heart light, full in the knowledge that fairytales can come true.

## TWO MONTHS LATER

Zeke stood at the bottom of the stairs and called, "Babe? Are you about ready?"

"Coming!"

He sipped coffee from his travel mug, holding another one in his other hand. It took a moment, but Cynthia appeared at the top of the stairs. As always, she was beautiful. Dressed in a Kelly green long-sleeved T-shirt, jeans, and a pair of kickass boots, he watched her hips sway as she came down the stairs. Her hair was down, unadorned but flowing around her shoulders. Her makeup was simple, showcasing her blue eyes which seemed to shine even more when they landed on the coffee in his hand.

"Oh, just what I need!"

As she reached for it, he held it above her head and said, "Pay the toll."

She stood on her toes and kissed him. He expected hard and fast, but as usual, Cynthia surprised him. She slid her tongue over his lips, and as soon as he opened, she plunged her tongue inside his mouth. He gave her that play for a few seconds before he angled his head and took over the kiss. A moment later, they broke apart, his cock pressing against his zipper and her wide eyes staring up at him.

"Damn, woman. If I knew that was the kind of toll you'd pay, we would have had more than just shower sex this morning."

She laughed as she reached for the coffee, which he handed to her. Her kiss-swollen lips were curved in a smile, and her laughter rang in his ears, a sight and sound he knew he could never get enough of.

Two months had passed since she had joined the team at Grimm's, and last week they had had the grand opening for Grimm's Two. Other than a few minor hiccups that occur with the opening of any business, it had been wildly successful. The servers were all pleasant, efficient, and well-trained. The bartenders were entertaining, knew their drinks, and kept an eye on the patrons. Roscoe had worked with the bouncers who kept an eye on the entire bar, including being available to walk females to their car. Hell, even grumpy Zander had to smile at the way Grimm's Two opened.

Of course, Zander and Rosalie were there for opening night, but it had been exciting to see Rafe and Eleanor, Cael and Regina, Jaxon and Morgan, Jayden and Ruby, and Asher and Penny. Even Cas had brought Miss Ethel by earlier in the afternoon on the day they opened so that she would have a chance to see the place. Cynthia had greeted her warmly, and the bartender had made a grand showing of presenting her with a glass of sparkling wine.

Cynthia had blossomed with the responsibilities, quick to learn a new business while using her skills to make the position her own. She and Zeke worked together and lived together, easily sliding into a routine, one that he could never have imagined being so good.

They soon arrived at their destination and hurried inside. Making their way to the kitchen, they smiled at the shelter residents helping out as they quickly went to work. Zeke began scrambling dozens of eggs and frying sausage patties as Cynthia slid trays of bread into the oven to toast.

Several of the residents worked in the kitchen with them, and he watched as Cynthia chatted amongst them. Once everyone was served, they gathered their plates of food and moved to one of the tables, sitting with a young mother, her two children, and a couple of male residents.

Cynthia quickly made friends with the little girl, helping her eat her breakfast and giving the mom a chance to focus on her youngest child. He chatted with the two men, finding out that they were both veterans. One of them had a job, but it had just started, and he had not saved up enough money for a down payment on an apartment but hoped to do so soon. The other one was looking for a job.

When the first one finished his breakfast and said goodbye so that he could go to work, Zeke slid over a seat and continued his conversation with the other man. Miss Ethel always said he was a good judge of character, and he believed it was true. He had a good feeling about this man, and by the end of their conversation had offered him an interview at Grimm's Two.

The man stood, grateful tears in his eyes, and shook Zeke's hand. As the man walked out of the dining hall, Zeke looked over to see Cynthia hugging the little girl. A strange feeling moved over him, one where he could see her hugging a child in the future...their child. Smiling, he wrapped his arm around her and kissed her forehead as they walked back into the kitchen to oversee the cleanup.

"I heard you offer Thomas an interview at Grimm's," Cynthia said, smiling.

"I let him know that he would not just be interviewed by me but by you also since you were the manager."

Laughing, she said, "Honey, if you've already decided you want him, you're the boss. That's fine with me."

Shaking his head, he said, "I think he would be good, but he needs the experience of a job interview. I'm not trying to make him jump through too many hoops, but we both need to make the decision."

As they walked hand in hand back into the lobby, the director, Lori, popped her head out of her office, and said, "Cynthia, I'm glad I caught you. Can I talk to you in my office?" Her eyes cut over to Zeke, and she added, "You can come, too, Zeke."

They changed directions and headed into her small office. An older woman was standing inside, and Zeke startled when Cynthia said, "Mrs. Prince?"

Cynthia remembered Richard's mother, elegant and beautiful at the fundraiser, a woman seemingly in charge of all that was around her. She also remembered seeing her face pinched in irritation at some of the comments being made. The woman standing in front of them now was casually dressed in slacks and a blouse. Her only jewelry was silver hoop earrings and her wedding rings. Barbara moved toward her, a smile on her face and her hands extended in greeting.

Taking her hands in her own, Cynthia gave them a squeeze and said, "It's so nice to see you again." She turned toward Zeke, and said, "This is my boyfriend, Zeke Kemp. Zeke, I'd like you to meet Barbara Prince."

Zeke stepped forward and took Barbara's hand in his own, greeting her warmly. His eyes jumped back to Cynthia's, and she gave a little shake of her head, indicating she had no idea why they were there.

Lori had squeezed an extra chair into her small office and said, "Please, let's sit down." Once settled, Lori said, "Barbara has come to me with an idea, and she'd like to have your input, Cynthia."

Completely baffled, she reached over and held Zeke's hand while turning her attention to Barbara.

Barbara sat, her hands clasped in her lap, her ankles crossed, and smiled. Cynthia could see that there was pain etched into the smile lines at the corner of her eyes and knew that Barbara's life had been somewhat tumultuous since Richard's arrest. Giving the woman her full attention, she cocked her head slightly to the side, meeting her smile with one of her own.

"I want you to know that both Lawrence and I as well as Larry and his wife were extremely upset with the callous remarks made at the fundraiser about homelessness and the shelter. I was ready to shut down that line of disgusting comments when you spoke up. Your words were right on point and heartfelt which made them so much more poignant than anything I could've said. In the last few months, I have searched my heart as a businesswoman and a mother, to see where I went wrong--"

Leaning forward, Cynthia placed her hand on Barbara's and gave a squeeze, saying, "You didn't go wrong. Richard is responsible for his behavior, not you."

Inclining her head slightly, Barbara said, "That is what everyone tells me, but I think as a mother, we always tend to search ourselves for the fault when our children…even adult children… make poor choices. But that's not why I'm here. I'm here because I have a proposal for you."

Cynthia's eyes widened, and she glanced toward Lori, who was smiling widely.

"Not only did the fundraiser raise over twenty-five thousand dollars for the city's homeless shelters, but my family feels strongly that we would like to do more to showcase the plight of the homeless. Your words about most people only being one crisis or trauma away from being homeless struck us as well as your comments about the number of military veterans who are now homeless. Prince International Hotels are pledging continued financial support of the homeless shelters in the cities where we have properties. But we also want to do what we can to educate others. I would very much like you to have a position on my committee on homelessness."

Cynthia's mouth opened, then she snapped it shut quickly, giving her head a little shake as Barbara's words sunk in.

Barbara quickly added, "I know you have a new job. This would be an added position on my committee. A volunteer status only and would not require much of your time. But instead of having a group of wealthy people sitting around talking about a subject they have no clue about, I would like the committee to be made up of people who truly understand the problem and what is needed. I can think of no better person to start my committee with than you."

Stammering, she said, "I...I don't know what to say."

Lori, still smiling, said, "As Barbara and I have talked over the last few weeks, I let her know about Zeke and Asher and the work they do here."

Barbara, now smiling toward Zeke, said, "I have the contact information for your brother, Asher, but my invitation to assist us in knowing the needs of the homeless extends to you as well."

Cynthia's head swung around toward Zeke, their eyes meeting and understanding passing between them. Turning back, she said, "I would be honored to be part of your committee."

Zeke squeezed her hand and added, "I, too, would be

honored. I certainly can't speak for my brother, Asher, but I have a feeling he would be thrilled."

With a nod of her head, Barbara stood, and the others quickly followed. "Thank you so much for your consideration," she said. "I'll let you know when the committee will have their first meeting." She walked to the door, then halted with her hand on the doorframe and looked back over her shoulder toward Cynthia. "I'm sorry that my son never met a woman like you years ago. He could've used that kind of good influence." With that, she turned and walked out the door, followed by Lori.

Turning, Cynthia smiled up at Zeke. Wrapping her arms around his neck, she loved the feel of him pulling her in for a hug. Rising on her toes, she offered a sweet kiss which he accepted. As her heels lowered back to the floor, she said, "I found you, Zeke. I found my own prince."

---

"So, do you think they'll like it?" Cas asked.

Miss Ethel looked at her youngest and shook her head in mock surprise. "Like it? Oh, my dear, Cas, they will be ecstatic!" He had just proposed crafting solid wood, handmade beds for Zander's daughter and Rafe's son. "They will love the beds but will cherish your talent and hard work."

He blushed slightly and ducked his head. Of all her boys, Cas was the one who preferred solitude, something she had readily offered him when he was growing up. Having finished their visit, she walked him to the door, her hand lightly holding on to his arm.

He hesitated, and she waited patiently to see what else was on his mind. He finally turned and said, "All my brothers have found someone special. I'm glad for them."

She nodded but remained quiet.

"I wonder...well..." His gaze drifted out the front door to the house across the street. Giving his head a little shake, he turned his eyes back to her and smiled. "I should be going. I've got some beds to create."

He bent and kissed her cheek, and she held him tightly, patting his back. "Good things are coming, Cas," she said. He stared as though he was waiting to see if she had more to say, but she just smiled.

She watched as he walked to his truck, stopped, and looked across the street again before climbing into the driver's seat. Staring for a long moment, she observed as he tossed a wave her way and drove down the street. Her gaze moved to the house opposite hers, and she smiled to herself. "Yes, good things are coming."

Closing the door, she moved back to her living room and sat in her comfortable chair. Picking up her knitting needles, she began working on the new booties she was making.

## 3 1

### TWO YEARS LATER

The hospital staff was used to the scene in the labor and delivery waiting room. So much so they were recognizing Miss Ethel and the large gathering of family. Each time one of her sons was expecting a baby, the entire entourage came for support.

This time, it was Cynthia in labor with Zeke at her side. The waiting room held Miss Ethel, all of his brothers, and their women. Most of the couples were holding their own children, each being very familiar with the setting.

Inside the delivery room, Zeke grabbed a towel to wipe his own brow after having carefully dabbed the perspiration off Cynthia. He knew from his brothers' experiences that all deliveries are different, each baby deciding when they wanted to appear. Of course, knowing that fact and living it were two different things. Cynthia's pregnancy had been easy, little morning sickness or swelling. But she had now been in labor for almost twenty hours, and he was uncertain how much more either of them could take.

When the doctor finally declared that she could push, he held her hand tightly and looked down at her exhausted face and wondered if she would have the energy to comply. But digging deep, she leaned forward with his help and pushed.

"Almost there," the doctor said, smiling up at them. "Another push."

Cynthia gripped Zeke's hand fiercely and said, "I don't know if I can."

Moving so that his face was directly in front of hers, he said, "Babe, you're amazing and I've got nothing but faith in you. Together we can do anything."

He watched as she gave a quick nod, tightened her hold, and leaned forward, pushing once more. Looking at the mirror, they both watched as their son came into the world. As the nurses and doctor efficiently handled the immediate needs of the infant, their son was soon placed on her chest.

As though she had not been struggling for almost a full day, Cynthia cooed and smiled, snuggling the baby as she kissed his head. Zeke's legs began to shake, and he was grateful for the chair next to the bed, slumping into it as he kept one hand on his son's back and the other on her. Tears streamed down his face as he stared at the miracle in front of him.

Thirty minutes later, with Cynthia cleaned and dressed in a fresh hospital gown, her blonde hair brushed and pulled back with a ribbon and their son swaddled in her arms, Zeke welcomed his family into the room. Within a moment, the room was filled to bursting, hugs and smiles and kisses all around.

Miss Ethel made her way to the bed, bending to kiss Cynthia's forehead before touching her lips to the sleeping baby. Standing, she moved to Zeke who welcomed her with open arms. "You have a beautiful son, Ezekiel. Tell us what you and Cynthia have decided to name him."

He looked at Cynthia, and they shared a smile before he turned to the gathering and said, "We are pleased to introduce you to Owen Kemp."

As everyone called out more congratulations, Miss Ethel reached up and patted Zeke's cheek. "So, my strong champion has named his son appropriately. Warrior champion."

Chuckling, he knew that she would understand the significance. "I'll teach him to be the protector of others by protecting him myself. He will not learn the lessons my father taught but everything that I learned from you instead."

A day later, the family met Zeke and Cynthia at their house, the women making sure the refrigerator was full of food and the nursery full of diapers. Cas presented them with a hand-crafted, solid oak crib that he had made in his workshop. The craftsmanship was magnificent, and as they peered closer at the carvings on the head, they could see a princess and prince riding a horse.

Everyone gathered around, their praise for Cas effusive. He smiled his thanks, then deflected everyone's attention back to Owen. The gathering soon began saying their goodbyes, wanting to leave the young family to their privacy.

Finally closing the door, Zeke walked over to their sofa where Cynthia sat, opening her shirt for Owen to nurse. Gently sitting next to her, he wrapped his arm around his beautiful wife and watched as his son filled his belly. He was sure that he had never seen a more perfect sight.

Don't miss the next Heroes at Heart
For all of Miss Ethel's boys:
Heroes at Heart (Military Romance)
Zander
Rafe
Cael
Jaxon
Jayden
Asher
Zeke
Cas

## ALSO BY MARYANN JORDAN

Don't miss other Maryann Jordan books!

Lots more Baytown stories to enjoy and more to come!

Baytown Boys (small town, military romantic suspense)

Coming Home

Just One More Chance

Clues of the Heart

Finding Peace

Picking Up the Pieces

Sunset Flames

Waiting for Sunrise

Hear My Heart

Guarding Your Heart

Sweet Rose

Our Time

Count On Me

For all of Miss Ethel's boys:

Heroes at Heart (Military Romance)

Zander

Rafe

Cael

Jaxon

Jayden

Asher

Zeke

Cas


Lighthouse Security Investigations

Mace

Rank

Walker

Drew

Blake

Tate (August 2020)


Hope City (romantic suspense series co-developed

with Kris Michaels

Hope City Duet (Brock / Sean)

Carter

Brody by Kris Michaels

Kyle

Ryker by Kris Michaels


Saints Protection & Investigations

(an elite group, assigned to the cases no one else wants…or
can solve)

Serial Love

Healing Love

Revealing Love

Seeing Love

Honor Love

Sacrifice Love

Protecting Love

Remember Love

Discover Love

Surviving Love

Celebrating Love

Follow the exciting spin-off series:

Alvarez Security (military romantic suspense)

Gabe

Tony

Vinny

Jobe

SEALs

Thin Ice (Sleeper SEAL)

SEAL Together (Silver SEAL)

Letters From Home (military romance)

Class of Love

Freedom of Love

Bond of Love

The Love's Series (detectives)

Love's Taming

Love's Tempting

Love's Trusting

The Fairfield Series (small town detectives)

Emma's Home

Laurie's Time

Carol's Image

Fireworks Over Fairfield

Please take the time to leave a review of this book. Feel free to contact me, especially if you enjoyed my book. I love to hear from readers!

Facebook

Email

Website

I am an avid reader of romance novels, often joking that I cut my teeth on the historical romances. I have been reading and reviewing for years. In 2013, I finally gave into the characters in my head, screaming for their story to be told. From these musings, my first novel, Emma's Home, The Fairfield Series was born.

I was a high school counselor having worked in education for thirty years. I live in Virginia, having also lived in four states and two foreign countries. I have been married to a wonderfully patient man for thirty-five years. When writing, my dog or one of my four cats can generally be found in the same room if not on my lap.

Please take the time to leave a review of this book. Feel free to contact me, especially if you enjoyed my book. I love to hear from readers!

Facebook
Email
Website

Made in the USA
Coppell, TX
28 February 2022

74193682R00187